"Anyone who's been a mother or had one
will welcome the arrival of this entertaining new sleuth."
—Gillian Roberts, author of the Amanda Pepper series

NECESSITY IS THE MOTHER OF INVENTION . . .

From my front window, I watched the PI squish into his
compact car. Where would he go next? Maybe he could
lead me to George.

I contemplated following Galigani.

Yeah, right. With a newborn? Like I'd ever be able to
get out of the house in time.

I heard Laurie's wake-up call. I went to my bedroom
and picked her up from the bassinet. Cold. Wet. Hungry.

A mother's job is never done. I changed her, swaddled
her tight, then settled down on our sofa to nurse her. I
absently looked out the front window again. Galigani's
gray Honda was still there. What was he doing hovering
outside my house?

Was I being staked out?

Outraged, I gathered Laurie up and ran down my front
steps. This guy was getting paid two hundred bucks an
hour to sit in his stupid Honda outside my house, while
I nursed my baby! His job didn't seem that tough. Ask
questions, drive around some, and charge a lot of money. I
could do that, couldn't I?

"Deftly plotted with a winning protagonist and a glorious
San Francisco setting, *Bundle of Trouble* is a page-
turning read . . . Highly recommended."
—Sheldon Siegel, *New York Times* best selling author of
Judgment Day

"You'll love keeping up with this amazing mother and
sleuth in the fun, fast-paced *Bundle of Trouble*."
—Margaret Grace, author of the Miniature Mysteries

Bundle of
TROUBLE

Diana
Orgain

BERKLEY PRIME CRIME, NEW YORK

THE BERKLEY PUBLISHING GROUP
Published by the Penguin Group
Penguin Group (USA) Inc.
375 Hudson Street, New York, New York 10014, USA

Penguin Group (Canada), 90 Eglinton Avenue East, Suite 700, Toronto, Ontario M4P 2Y3, Canada
(a division of Pearson Penguin Canada Inc.)
Penguin Books Ltd., 80 Strand, London WC2R 0RL, England
Penguin Group Ireland, 25 St. Stephen's Green, Dublin 2, Ireland (a division of Penguin Books Ltd.)
Penguin Group (Australia), 250 Camberwell Road, Camberwell, Victoria 3124, Australia
(a division of Pearson Australia Group Pty. Ltd.)
Penguin Books India Pvt. Ltd., 11 Community Centre, Panchsheel Park, New Delhi—110 017, India
Penguin Group (NZ), 67 Apollo Drive, Rosedale, North Shore 0632, New Zealand
(a division of Pearson New Zealand Ltd.)
Penguin Books (South Africa) (Pty.) Ltd., 24 Sturdee Avenue, Rosebank, Johannesburg 2196,
South Africa

Penguin Books Ltd., Registered Offices: 80 Strand, London WC2R 0RL, England

BUNDLE OF TROUBLE

A Berkley Prime Crime Book / published by arrangement with the author

PRINTING HISTORY
Berkley Prime Crime mass-market edition / August 2009

Copyright © 2009 by Diana Orgain.
Cover illustration by Fernando Juarez.
Cover design by Annette Fiore Defex.
Interior text design by Kristin del Rosario.

ISBN: 978-0-425-22924-8

BERKLEY® PRIME CRIME
Berkley Prime Crime Books are published by The Berkley Publishing Group,
a division of Penguin Group (USA) Inc.,
375 Hudson Street, New York, New York 10014.
BERKLEY® PRIME CRIME and the PRIME CRIME logo are trademarks of Penguin Group (USA) Inc.

PRINTED IN THE UNITED STATES OF AMERICA

10   9   8   7   6   5   4   3   2   1

This book is dedicated to
Tom, Carmen, Tommy, Jr.,
and Robert, who complete me.

ACKNOWLEDGMENTS

I'm most grateful to my loving and supportive husband, Tom Orgain. He is my right-hand man, always ready to provide me with the precise words for my prose, help with babysitting, or just plain make me laugh. Without him this book simply would not have been possible.

Thanks to my dear friend Seana Patankar for her endless faith and optimism. I also appreciate the many writers, friends, and family who offered feedback and encouragement—especially my mother, Maria Carmen Noa.

Special thanks to my critique group: Bette and J. J. Lamb, Margaret Lucke, Shelly Singer, Nicola Trwst, Mary Walker, and Judith Yamamoto.

Finally, thanks to my wonderful editor, Michelle Vega, and to Lucienne Diver, agent extraordinaire.

CHAPTER ONE

Labor

The phone rang, interrupting the last seconds of the 49ers game.

"Damn," Jim said. "Final play. Who'd be calling now?"

"Don't know," I said from my propped position on the couch.

I was on doctor's orders for bed rest. My pregnancy had progressed with practically no hang-ups, except for the carpal tunnel and swollen feet, until one week before my due date when my blood pressure skyrocketed. Now, I was only allowed to be upright for a few minutes every couple of hours to accommodate the unavoidable mad dash to the bathroom.

"Everyone I know is watching the game. It's gotta be for you," Jim said, stretching his long legs onto the ottoman.

I struggled to lean forward and grab the cordless phone.

"Probably your mom," he continued.

I nodded. Mom was checking in quite often now that

the baby was two days overdue. An entire five minutes had passed since our last conversation.

"Hello?"

A husky male voice said, "This is Nick Dowling . . ."

Ugh, a telemarketer.

". . . from the San Francisco medical examiner's office."

I sat to attention. Jim glanced at me, frowning. He mouthed, "Who is it?" from across the room.

"Is this the Connolly residence?"

"Yes," I said.

"Are you a relative of George Connolly?"

"He's my brother-in-law."

"Can you tell me the last time you saw him?"

My breath caught. "The last time we saw George?"

Jim stood at the mention of his brother's name.

"Is he a transient, ma'am?" Dowling asked.

I felt the baby kick.

"Hold on a sec." I held out the phone to Jim. "It's the San Francisco medical examiner. He's asking about George."

Jim froze, let out a slight groan, then crossed to me and took the phone. "This is Jim Connolly."

The baby kicked again. I switched positions. Standing at this point in the pregnancy was uncomfortable, but so was sitting or lying down for that matter. I got up and hobbled over to Jim, put my hands on his back and leaned in as close as my belly would allow, trying to overhear.

Why was the medical examiner calling about George?

"I don't know where George is. I haven't seen him for a few months." Jim listened in silence. After a moment he said, "What was your name again? Uh-huh . . . What number are you at?" He scratched something on a scrap of paper then said, "I'll have to get back to you." He hung up and shoved the paper into his pocket.

"What did he say?" I asked.

Jim hugged me, his six-foot-two frame making me feel momentarily safe. "Nothing, honey."

"What do you mean, nothing?"

"Don't worry about it," he whispered into my hair.

I pulled away from Jim's embrace and looked into his face. "What's going on with George?"

Jim shrugged his shoulders, and then turned to stare blankly at the TV. "We lost the game."

"Jim, tell me what the medical examiner said."

He grimaced, pinching the bridge of his nose. "A body was found in the bay. It's badly decomposed and unidentifiable."

Panic rose in my chest. "What does that have to do with George?"

"They found his bags on the pier near where the body was recovered. They went through his stuff and got our number off an old cell phone bill. They want to know if George has any scars or anything on his body so they can . . ." His shoulders slumped. He shook his head and covered his face with his hands.

I waited for him to continue, the gravity of the situation sinking in. I felt a strong tightening in my abdomen. A Braxton Hicks?

Instead of speaking, Jim stood there, staring at our blank living room wall, which I'd been meaning to decorate since we'd moved in three years ago. He clenched his left hand, an expression somewhere between anger and astonishment on his face. He turned and made his way to the kitchen.

I followed. "Does he?"

Jim opened the refrigerator door and fished out a can of beer from the bottom shelf. "Does he what?" He tapped the side of the can, a gesture I had come to recognize as an itch to open it.

"Have any scars or . . ." I couldn't finish the sentence. A strange sensation struck me, as though the baby had flip-flopped. "Uh, Jim, I'm not sure about this, but I may have just had a contraction. A real one."

I cupped my hands around the bottom of my belly. We both stared at it, expecting it to tell us something. Suddenly I felt a little pop from inside. Liquid trickled down my leg.

"I think my water just broke."

Jim expertly navigated the San Francisco streets as we made our way to California Pacific Hospital. Even as the contractions grew stronger, I couldn't stop thinking about George.

Jim's parents had died when he was starting college. George, his only brother, had merely been fourteen, still in high school. Their Uncle Roger had taken George in. George had lived rent-free for many years, too many years, never caring to get a job or make a living.

Jim and I often wondered if so much coddling had incapacitated George to the point that he couldn't, or wouldn't, stand on his own two feet. He was thirty-three now and always had an excuse for not holding a job. Apparently, everyone was out to get him, take advantage of him, "screw" him somehow. At least that's the story we'd heard countless times.

The only thing George had going for him was his incredible charm. Although he was a total loser, you'd never know it to talk to him. He could converse with the best of them, disarming everyone with his piercing green eyes.

Uncle Roger had finally evicted George six months ago. There had been an unpleasant incident. Roger had been vague about it, only telling us that the sheriff had to physically remove George from his house. As far as we knew, George had been staying with friends since then.

I glanced at Jim. His face was unreadable, the excitement of the pending birth diluted by the phone call we had received.

I touched Jim's leg. "Just because his bags were found at the pier doesn't mean it's him."

Jim nodded.

"I mean, what did the guy say? The body was badly decomposed, right? How long would bags sit on a pier in San Francisco? Overnight?"

"Hard to say," he muttered.

I rubbed his leg trying to reassure him. "I can't believe any bag would last more than a couple days, max, before a transient, a kid, or someone else would swipe it."

Jim shrugged and looked grim.

A transient? Why had the medical examiner asked that? George had always lived on the fringe, but homeless?

Please God, don't let the baby be born on the same day we get bad news about George.

Bad news—what an understatement. How could this happen? I closed my eyes and said a quick prayer for George, Jim, and our baby.

I dug my to-do list out from the bottom of the hospital bag.

To Do (When Labor Starts):

1. Call Mom.

2. Remember to breathe.

3. Practice yoga.

4. Time contractions.

5. Think happy thoughts.

6. Relax.

7. Call Mom.

Oh, shoot! I'd forgotten to call Mom. I found my cell phone and pressed speed dial. No answer.

Hmmm? Nine P.M., where could she be?

I left a message on her machine and hung up.

I looked over the rest of the list and snorted. What kind of idealist had written this? Think happy thoughts? Remember to breathe?

I took a deep breath. My abdomen tightened, as though a vise were squeezing my belly. Was this only the *beginning* of labor? My jaw clenched as I doubled over. Jim glanced sideways at me.

He reached out for my hand. "Hang in there, honey, we're almost at the hospital."

The vise loosened and I felt almost normal for a moment.

I squeezed Jim's hand. My husband, my best friend, and my rock. I had visualized this moment in my mind over and over. No matter what variation I gave it in my head, never in a million years could I have imagined the medical examiner calling us right before my going into labor and telling us what? That George was dead?

Before I could process the thought, another contraction overtook me, an undulating and rolling tightening, causing me to grip both my belly and Jim's hand.

When my best friend, Paula, had given birth, she was surrounded mostly by women. Me, her mother, her sister, and of course, her husband, David. All the women were supportive and whispered words of encouragement while David huddled in the corner of the room, watching TV. When Paula told him she needed him, he'd put the TV on *mute*.

When I'd recounted the story for Jim, he'd laughed and said, "Oh, honey, David can be kind of a dunce. He doesn't know what to do."

Another vise grip brought me back to the present. Could I do this without drugs? I held my breath. Urgh! *Remember to breathe*.

I crumpled the to-do list in my hand.

Bring on the drugs.

• CHAPTER TWO •

Delivery

After checking into the hospital and spending several hours in "observation," we were finally moved to our own labor and delivery room.

"When can I get the epidural?" I asked the nurse escorting us.

"I'll call the anesthesiologist now," she said, leaving the room.

Jim plopped himself onto the recliner in the corner and picked up the remote control.

"Hey, I'm having contractions here . . . they're starting to get strong. Aren't you supposed to be breathing with me?"

"Right," he nodded, flipping through the channels. "He he he, ha ha ha," he said in an unconvincing rendition of Lamaze breathing.

"Jim!"

"Hmmm?"

"I need your help now."

His eyebrows furrowed. "No TV?"

"Get me the epi . . . oooh."

He pressed the *mute* button. I sighed and gave in to the contractions.

Another hour passed before the anesthesiologist walked in. I was horrified to see that he looked all of about seventeen.

"Sorry to make you wait," he said. "There was an emergency C-section."

"I'm just glad you're here now," Jim said.

The anesthesiologist laughed. "How are we doing?"

"She's doing great, really great," Jim said.

I would have told him to shut up, but that would have taken more energy than I had. Was this teeny bopper qualified to put a fifteen-inch needle in my spine? What *exactly* could go wrong with the epidural? I was about to chicken out when the nurse rushed in.

"Oh, here you are," she said to the anesthesiologist. "Let's go, before she's too far along."

Before I could back out, my torso and legs were blissfully numb.

The nurse placed a metal contraption, resembling a suction cup, on my belly and studied a monitor. "Do you feel anything?"

"Nope."

"Good, because that was a big contraction."

I smiled. "I didn't feel a thing."

The anesthesiologist nodded as he left the room. The nurse advised us to get some rest. Jim returned to the recliner and put the volume back up on the TV. I glanced at the clock: 3 A.M. already. Where was my mother?

My thoughts drifted back to George. What had his bags been doing on the pier? An image of a swollen corpse with a John Doe tag on its foot crept into my mind. I shook my head trying to dissociate the image from

George and willed myself to think sweet, pink, baby thoughts.

I scratched my thigh to double-check the effectiveness of the epidural.

During my pregnancy, I had heard dozens of horror stories about infants with umbilical cords wrapped around their tiny necks, only to have the doctor push the infant's head back into the birth canal and perform an emergency C-section. In most of the stories the poor mother had to go through the C-section without any anesthesia. At least I'd already had the epidural.

At 7 A.M., the door to the room opened and my mother appeared, dressed in jeans and sneakers, with binoculars around her neck.

"How you doing?" she asked cheerfully. Without waiting for a reply, she reached up and put two hands on Jim's shoulders pulling him down to her five-foot-two level to kiss his cheeks. After which she handed him her purse and said, "I'm here now, Jim. You can sleep."

Jim smiled, clutched the purse, and happily retreated to his cot. Mom had adopted Jim long ago, even before we were married; it was a relationship Jim treasured since he had lost his own parents so many years earlier.

Just seeing Mom relaxed me. She placed her freezing hands on my face and kissed my cheeks. "Are you running a fever?"

"No. Your hands are cold. Where have you been? You look like a tourist," I joked.

"What do you mean?"

I indicated the binoculars.

"Well, I want pictures of my first grandchild!"

From Jim's corner came a snorted laugh, the kind that comes out through your nose when you're trying to suppress it. I laughed freely.

"What?" Mother demanded.

"They're binoculars," Jim said.

Mother glanced down at her chest.

"Oh, dear! I meant to grab the camera."

Jim relaxed, lying back on the cot.

Mom stroked my hair, then leaned over and kissed my forehead.

"You're frowning," she said.

"I'm worried about the baby. I'm worried about George." I looked over at Jim. His eyes filled with tears.

"George?" Mom turned to look at Jim. Jim covered his face with his hands.

Mom clucked. "Let's start with the baby. Why are you worried?"

I shook my head and took a deep breath. "Don't know. Nervous, maybe."

Mom patted my hand. "Well, that's normal. Everything is going to be fine. When did your labor start?"

"Around nine last night. Didn't you get our messages? Jim must have called at least three times. Where were you?"

Mom settled herself in the chair next to my bed. "I was at Sylvia's. She had a dinner party. There was a lady there who wanted to take home some leftover crackers. Can you imagine? They had sat out all night on an hors d'oeuvres plate. And she wanted to take them home!"

Mom knew me too well. She was making small talk, trying to distract me from thinking thoughts full of doom and gloom. It was working. I was actually laughing.

I peered over at Jim. His eyes were closed, a grimace on his face. He wasn't listening to Mom. He was stressed out. Mom followed my gaze.

"Now, what's happened with George?"

Jim flinched. "Let's not go there, Mom. We got a phone call, right, Kate? Just a call—"

I clutched Mom's hand. "Not just a call! It was a call from the medical examiner. They found a body in the bay and George's bags on the pier."

Mom eyes turned into saucers and she gasped.

"We don't really know anything yet," Jim said. "Let's not get all melodramatic."

Mom and I exchanged looks. "Everything will be fine, you'll see." She gave my hand a squeeze, then released it and folded her hands into her lap.

An awkward silence descended over us. Just then the nurse slipped into the room. "Don't mind me," she said. "I want to see how far along we are."

Jim watched the nurse, his brow creased in concern. I tried to remain calm, my attention returning to the beeping monitor reporting the baby's heart rate.

"Oh, goodness, the baby's practically here," the nurse announced.

I sat up a little. Mom clapped her hands in childish delight and Jim crossed the room to stand next to me.

"I'll call your doctor," the nurse said, turning to leave.

Mom started to follow her. "I'll be right back. I just need to feed my parking meter."

The nurse spun around and stared at Mom. "Don't leave now. You may miss the birth."

"The baby's coming that fast?" Mom asked.

"I hope I can get the doctor here in time," the nurse said, rushing out.

"I hope I don't get a ticket," Mom said.

I laughed. "Why didn't you park in the hospital parking lot?"

Mom shrugged. "There was a spot in front." She hurried across the room to the window, straining to get a peek at her car.

Jim tried to hide the smile that played on his lips. He leaned in close to me and whispered, "Here I am worried about you, the baby, and my brother the screwup, while I could be worrying about really important stuff like getting a parking ticket."

I giggled. "Or who took home stale crackers from a party."

Our eyes locked. Jim's face broke into a huge smile. "I love you, Kate."

Mom came away from the window. "No ticket yet, that I can *see*."

Dr. Greene, my ob-gyn, popped into the room, her brown hair held in place with two tortoiseshell clips. She walked straight to my side, looking confident in her blue scrubs. She smiled into my face. "How are you doing, Kate?"

"Okay, I guess. I don't feel a thing."

She smiled wider. "That's the beauty of modern medicine. Just push when I tell you."

After about twelve minutes of pushing, Dr. Greene said the words I'll never forget in all my life: "Kate, reach down and grab your baby."

What? She wanted me to pull the baby out?

Startled by her words, I instinctively reached down.

There she was. I grasped my baby girl and pulled her to my chest.

I clutched her to me with a desperation I had never felt before, trying to press her right into my heart. Everyone else in the room seemed to fade into the background. My little angel, my little love.

She was the most beautiful thing in the world. Her round, pretty face was punctuated with a button nose, and strawberry blond hair graced the top of her head. Dark blue eyes peered at me, examining me with the wisdom of an old soul.

I realized Jim was crying. He reached down and enveloped the baby and me in his arms and I forgave him for muting the TV.

Out of the corner of my eye, I saw Mom pull a hankie from her purse and wipe a tear. "Don't worry, darling, I've already memorized her face. No one's switching her on us."

CHAPTER THREE

Recovery/Discovery

We were moved to a bright recovery room with a view of Saint Ignatius Church. Jim slouched in a corner of the room on a hospital cot.

Mom had left for the day, ticketless. It was only 5 P.M., but felt much later.

I held my sleeping pumpernickel in my arms. I was told that newborns mainly sleep the first week. It's difficult to wake them even to nurse. Right now sleep sounded great. Jim and I were exhausted.

"I wish I had space in this stupid hospital bed for you," I said, raising the bed slightly, then lowering it again.

Who could ever get comfortable in one of these?

"Don't worry, honey, I'm fine," Jim grumbled from the corner cot.

"I miss you way over there."

He stood, stretched, and hobbled over to me, his legs cramped from a long night of worry and catnapping on a bad cot. "Let me hold her awhile."

I handed the baby to him. He settled himself against

the windowsill and admired her. "Hope for the next generation."

I knew, of course, that his remark was connected to George. But I didn't have the energy to think about that. "I need to sleep awhile, honey . . ."

I was already drifting off when I felt the covers being tucked against my chin. "Take care of Laurie," I mumbled.

"Is that her name?"

"If you like it," I said, drifting to sleep.

"I do. Get some rest. I promise to take good care of Laurie."

I slept a fitful hour, dreaming that I was swimming in the bay. In the dream, I became entangled with a dead body that seemed to pull me under. As I freed myself from the corpse to swim toward the surface, my ankle caught in the strap of a bag. The sound of cries pierced the water. Suddenly, the water was full of bags and corpses. A shrill cry startled me awake.

I gasped for air as I awoke. Jim was standing over me with the baby in his arms. "Are you all right?"

I nodded, dumbfounded.

"Sorry, honey, I didn't mean to wake you. She's crying and I don't know what to do." Jim handed me the baby.

"I think she's hungry, or wet, or both." I placed her near my breast. Instead of latching on, she only cried louder, howling into my face. Jim laughed but I felt like crying, too.

"Maybe we should call the nurse," I said.

Before we could do anything, a tall, slender African-American nurse glided into the room. Her name tag read GISELLE.

"What is it now? Little baby girl giving her parents a

hard time? Hush now, they don't know what they're doing, girl." She rewrapped Laurie's blanket around her.

In an instant the crying stopped. Laurie gratefully
curled into Giselle. Jim and I stared at her.

"Did anyone teach you how to swaddle?" she asked.

"I thought she was swaddled," Jim replied.

"Not tight enough. Babies like to be wrapped tight, like
a little burrito, or they feel like they're falling." She
handed Laurie to Jim and turned to me. "How's Mama?"
she asked, expertly taking my blood pressure and tem-
perature.

"Now that you mention a burrito, hungry."

Giselle smiled. "Dinner's coming up. What about pain
medication?"

"Yes, please," Jim said.

When dinner was served, I handed Laurie off to Giselle.
Laurie would spend the night in the nursery down the hall.
Giselle would bring her in whenever she needed to nurse,
which felt like every couple of minutes but at the same
time too long in between. I missed Laurie terribly when
she was out of the room, but felt exhausted when she was
brought in.

After gobbling down the hospital dinner of cardboard
sliced ham and runny applesauce, I eagerly turned to chat
with Jim. He was sacked out on the cot in the corner.

I shifted to the edge of the bed to make my way to the
restroom.

Wait a minute.

I didn't need to pee. What a miracle, to go from running to the restroom every five minutes to not needing to
go for an *entire* night. I sat in silence.

Finally, I reached for a pen and paper and scratched out
a to-do list.

To Do (When I Get Home):

1. Get better at breastfeeding.

2. Lose weight.

3. Take a gazillion pictures of Laurie.

4. Call work and let them know about Laurie and plan a return date—yuk!

5. George? Where is he?

Was he dead? What could have happened? I thought about suicide. Certainly if he had become homeless, it seemed possible. Why hadn't he come to Jim and me if his only option was the streets?

What about an accident? Could George have *fallen* into the bay and drowned?

The medical examiner had said the body was badly decomposed. How long would it have to be underwater to decay? Had it been caught on something that kept it submerged? Seaweed?

My mind flashed on the Mafia movies and bodies being held down with concrete.

What if he had been murdered?

"Jim," I called. He lay motionless on the cot, in a deep, exhausted sleep. "Jim," I called again.

He sat up, startled. "What is it, honey? Something wrong?"

"I can't sleep. I'm thinking about George. What if it's him, dead in the bay? What if he was murdered?"

"Murdered? My God, Kate! I mean, he's probably not hanging out with the cream of the crop, but . . ." He paused, letting out a sigh. "We don't know anything yet. The medical examiner asked if George had any identifiers on his body, you know . . . to help them . . . George has a pin in his ankle and he's also had his appendix out."

My heart stopped.

We could have known if it was George twenty-four hours ago!

In my calmest voice, I asked, "Why didn't you tell the medical examiner that?"

Jim shrugged. "Part of me is always trying to protect him. What if the guy who called wasn't even from the medical examiner's office? What if it was someone who's just trying to find out where George is? Like someone he owes money to or something like that."

I held out my hand for Jim. He got up and crossed the room, sitting on the bed. "Honey," I said. "That makes no sense. If it was someone George owes money to, why would they ask about his scars?"

Jim shrugged, then pinched the bridge of his nose. "All my life everyone has tried to help George. Growing up, my mom told me to take care of him. Your best friend for life, she always said. I did my best, but nothing was ever good enough for him. He always demanded more, giving nothing in return and managing to poison everything and everyone around him." His face contorted in anger, then turned to sadness. "I didn't want the joy of Laurie's birth clouded over by news about George." After a moment, he said, "I took down the guy's phone number. I'll call him when we're home, make sure I'm really reaching the medical examiner's office."

We sat in silence for a moment. I put my arms around him and pressed my cheek against his. I understood his desire to postpone bad news.

As the sun came up, the room began to glow. I glanced at the clock and realized Laurie was due back at any minute.

"Sorry I woke you," I said.

He stroked my hair. "Try not to worry about George. I'm doing it enough for the both of us. You focus on Laurie and on recovering."

* * *

The day nurse wheeled in our little bundle, wrapped in a pink and blue striped swaddling blanket with a pink cap on her head. She looked like a tiny cherub with rosy cheeks. I noticed a scratch on her face. Laurie's itty-bitty nails were extremely long. The nurse explained that hospital staff refused to trim them "because of the liability."

How ridiculous was that? A qualified nursing professional wouldn't trim those microscopic things. I'm supposed to?

How could I trust myself not to cut off a finger? Where was Giselle? And who was this day nurse who didn't even have the decency to help us trim the little talons?

Laurie swung her hands frightfully close to her bright blue eyes. Jim and I decided filing them seemed a much safer option.

As I manicured Laurie, Jim called our family and friends announcing the birth of our daughter. When Jim dialed his Uncle Roger, I found myself holding my breath.

"Uncle Roger? It's Jim . . . we had the baby . . . yeah . . . beautiful baby girl . . . six pounds, five ounces . . . Laurie. Katie's doing great."

Jim listened as Roger spoke. I continued to eavesdrop, but couldn't make out much from Roger's end.

I mouthed to Jim, "Ask him about George."

Jim waved me away, then turned his back to me.

I checked Laurie's diaper. Her diapers were so tiny, Jim and I laughed every time we had to change one. She was dry.

I wondered if the nurse had changed her. In the baby preparation class, they told us we would now become "waste watchers." Laurie needed to have as many wet diapers per day as she was days old. Two days old, two wet diapers. At least until the mother's milk came in. Right now she was surviving solely on colostrum, the premilk.

How would it feel to have milk come in? Were you

supposed to feel anything? So far, I'd noticed nothing. What if it didn't come in? What then? How would I know anyhow? And even if it did come in, would it be enough?

Earlier this morning the day nurse had stood over our bed and observed me breastfeeding. She frowned as she wrote down on my chart: "Breastfeeding: mother—poor, baby—poor."

How could she write that?

I'm an overachiever by nature, but the nurse's remark about me didn't bother me as much as the remark about Laurie. How could she say Laurie was "poor" at anything? I felt an immediate instinct to defend my little one. Forget that nurse. We would show her. We were going to become breastfeeding wonders.

When did Giselle's shift start?

Jim hung up the phone, the sound interrupting my thoughts. "Uncle Roger hasn't heard from the medical examiner's office."

"Oh? I didn't hear you ask him."

"I didn't. But he didn't say anything about it, so I know they didn't call him."

"Why didn't you just *ask* him?"

"Why bother him? Hasn't Roger been through enough?"

I felt my stomach tighten. "Aren't you worried?"

Laurie answered with a wail as though she sensed her father's distress.

Avoiding my question, Jim teased, "Go ahead and try that breastfeeding thing again. I hear you two are *poor* at it."

•CHAPTER FOUR•

The First Sleepy Week

Morning came soon enough. The hospital personnel checked out our car seat. Laurie and I were given a clean bill of health and released.

Panic.

There wouldn't be any specialized nursing staff at home. What if Laurie developed a fever? Or wasn't getting enough milk? How many wet diapers was she supposed to have?

Who was going to answer all my questions? I suddenly missed Nurse Giselle terribly.

Jim studied my face as he rocked Laurie back and forth. "We'll be fine, honey."

"At least I'm not considered a breastfeeding risk anymore."

He laughed. The night before, I'd had a special session with a lactation consultant, and afterward they changed my chart from "poor" to "fair." Laurie, on the other hand, had been upgraded to "good," which made me very proud.

I slipped on my maternity jeans and grumbled at the

fact that they still fit. I was hoping they would be so big that they might even slide off. No such luck.

I started to pack, jamming more items into the bag that was already full. With a little patience and some struggle, I managed to zip it closed.

I glanced up at Jim. "I brought extra stuff hoping I would be able to wear regular clothes out. But packed maternity stuff, too, just in case."

He smiled. "You look lovely, Mommy. Now let's get out of here."

After a few newborn photos of Laurie and hugs with hospital staff, we scrambled into the car. Laurie felt extremely far away from me all the way in the backseat. I rode home twisted around in the front seat, watching her as though she were a fragile egg ready to crack over the slightest bump in the road.

Mostly we rode in silence. Exhaustion and excitement danced inside me.

Jim had only been able to take a week off from work. I had six short weeks of maternity leave from the large architectural firm where I was an office manager.

Now, more than ever, I wondered how I would be able to return to work. Jim and I both needed to work. We lived in one of the most expensive cities in the United States. But how could I leave my peanut for forty-plus hours a week?

Out of the corner of my eye, I spotted a homeless guy. My heart stopped. His red hair vaguely resembled Jim's. His face was covered with a scraggly beard.

I whispered, "Is that George?"

Jim nearly careened off the road, trying to get a good look.

It wasn't George.

The dirty, decrepit-looking homeless guy *wasn't* George. I didn't know whether to be relieved or not.

* * *

Jim called the medical examiner, but was unable to reach anyone. He got Nick Dowling's voice mail and, at my prodding, left a detailed message about George's various scars.

The week went by with no return call.

Home seemed different now. Everything was special. Laurie's first home, her first dining room and living room. Her own bedroom, decorated in pink and mint green. Although I kept her bassinet in my room, so she spent her first sleepy week right beside Jim and me.

Unfortunately, she was sleepy only during the daytime hours and kept Jim and me, well really mostly me, up all night.

I was panicky about everything. Was she getting enough to eat? Why wouldn't she sleep at night? Was it good for her to sleep *all* day? Would she scratch her eyes out with the little nails that grew immediately after I filed them? And most of all, was she still breathing?

Mom was over every single day to take care of "her girls." On the day Jim returned to work, I tried desperately to get a little rest. I was barely awake when Mom arrived around 10 A.M., my arms and back achy from holding Laurie all night.

Mom eyed me up and down. I had on pink flannel pajamas with black French poodles and glow-in-the-dark Eiffel towers. I had worn the same pajamas all week.

"Kate, you look exhausted."

Tears streamed down my face, landing directly on my fluffy blue slippers. "I know."

"It's nothing to cry about," Mom said, alarmed. "Give me the baby and go get some sleep."

"It's not that," I whimpered.

"What it is then?"

"I love her so much."

"I know, dear."

I clutched Laurie. "What if I do something wrong?"

"You're not going to do anything wrong, honey. You're going to be a great mom. You are a great mom."

Mom hugged Laurie and me.

I felt better. The logical part of my mind knew that hormones were responsible for these tears, but that didn't seem to make it any easier.

"Mom, do you love me as much as I love Laurie?"

"Yes."

Tears welled again in my eyes. "I never knew."

"I know." She stroked my hair. "Go to bed. I'll watch Laurie."

I moved to the bedroom feeling a little giddy over the thought of sleep. My head hit the pillow fast, and although I expected to be asleep immediately, I lay awake. I listened to the sounds in the house. I could hear my mother in the kitchen, doing dishes.

"Mom," I called. "You're supposed to be watching Laurie!"

"I am watching her."

"You're doing dishes," I called from my room.

"She's asleep."

"You have to *watch* her. Make sure she's breathing."

"Of course she's breathing."

"I can't sleep unless I know you're watching her."

Mother peeked through the bedroom door. "Okay, Katie, I'll watch Laurie every minute. Just rest, for God's sake. You're turning a little nutty." She shut the door tightly behind her.

I tried to will myself to sleep. I couldn't have been more exhausted, and yet sleep eluded me.

The phone rang. I picked it up.

"Mrs. Connolly? This is Nick Dowling from the medical examiner's office."

My blood surged to my toes, leaving me light-headed. "Yes?"

"Is Mr. Connolly available?"

"No. He's at work. Did you get our message? About George's scars."

"Yes, ma'am, I sure did. I'm sorry I didn't call you back sooner. The victim's family had to be notified. Now I can confirm that the body we recovered was definitely not George Connolly."

Air rushed back into my lungs. "Thank God!"

Not George! Not George!

"Will someone be able to pick up Mr. Connolly's bags? We don't need them any longer and we haven't been able to reach him."

Maybe a little excursion was what I needed. Nothing too strenuous, just something to get my mind off milk and diapers.

"I can get them."

After I hung up with Dowling, I immediately dialed Jim's work number. I got his voice mail and left a message with the good news. The body was most definitely *not* George. What a relief. I felt as if a heavy weight had been lifted from my heart. George and I had never been close, and Jim and George's relationship was tenuous at best, but an untimely death would have been staggering.

I made my way to the living room and peeked in on Mom and Laurie. The baby was still sound asleep in her bassinet. "I'm going to make coffee. Want some?"

Mom barely looked up from her knitting. She was making something out of hideous green yarn. "I thought you were going to get some rest?"

"I can't sleep. I talked to the medical examiner. The body they recovered was *not* George."

Mom's head jerked up and she peered at me over her reading glasses. "Thank goodness. Jim will be very relieved to hear that." She lowered her gaze to her knitting, and almost on automatic pilot her hands continued their work.

"What are you knitting?"

"Booties for Laurie."

Great.

"Green?"

She glanced up at me. "Well, she has so much pink already. Are you allowed to have coffee when you're breast-feeding?"

"A little. Will you watch Laurie, Mom? I need to shower and get dressed."

"I *am* watching Laurie, dear. Are you going somewhere?"

"I'm going to get George's bags from the medical examiner's office. They can't locate him."

Mom tsked. "What do you suppose his bags were doing on that pier?"

I shrugged. "I don't know."

"I could go for you," she offered.

"I'd like to get some fresh air."

"Don't overdo it. You're up and around much sooner than I was after I had your brother, Andrew."

Mom prattled on about her childbirth experience as I prepared for my first solo outing since Laurie's birth.

I trudged up the steps to the medical examiner's office and asked the receptionist, a girl with bleached blond hair pulled taut into a ponytail making her look no older than seventeen, if I could speak with Nick Dowling. I braced myself against the reception counter, out of breath and feeling a little light-headed from my walk. I had finally parked about three city blocks away at a thirty-minute meter. The receptionist gave me a sympathetic smile, dazzling me with teeth that must have been as bleached as her hair and indicated the waiting area. I sat, exhausted, as she went to get Dowling,

My jeans were straining at the seams. I had gambled on wearing a pair of nonmaternity jeans. No elastic waistband! I reasoned that the pair I had selected were stretch jeans and should fit fine. However, they were too binding, making me feel more bloated than ever. When was I supposed to get my figure back?

I glanced down at my protruding tummy, then worried that milk might leak through my blouse. I realized I hadn't thought of Laurie in a few minutes, and my mind flashed on her little face. I felt ridiculous in the waiting room.

What was I doing here?

I should be home with Laurie.

I remembered when Jim and I first met and fell in love, five years ago. I would think about him night and day, and when I caught myself thinking of anything other than him, I was surprised by the feeling of guilt that flickered through me. Now, I felt the same way about Laurie.

Before I could turn around and leave, the door opened and in walked a tall, bearded man.

"Mrs. Connolly, I'm Nick Dowling," he said, extending his hand.

His face was kind, with bright blue eyes that peered at me through dark lashes. I shook his hand.

"Follow me," he said.

For an instant I hesitated, thinking he was going to bring me back into the morgue. I didn't have the stomach to see any cadavers. Instead, he led me to his office.

A huge desk covered with scattered papers dominated the room. A phone, hidden under a stack of papers, rang. He ignored it as he crossed the office toward a box in the corner.

"Can you tell me who the body was?" I asked.

He scratched his head. "It was in the papers. Didn't you read about it?"

"I just had a baby. I haven't been doing a lot of reading lately."

"Congratulations! This business must have come at an

inopportune time. I'm glad it wasn't your brother-in-law," he said, his kind eyes shining. "Fellow by the name of Brad Avery. We were able to positively identify the body using dental records." He opened the box and pulled out two duffel bags and a sleeping bag.

Was it true, then? Was he homeless? Where was he sleeping now?

Dowling helped me load the duffel bags one on each shoulder and then handed me the smelly sleeping bag.

I returned to the lobby, looking for the receptionist, hoping she might be able to help me carry George's things. No receptionist in sight, just an elegantly dressed woman waiting at the desk. She glanced up at me lugging George's bags.

I froze. It was Michelle Dupree, an old friend from high school, who had also been my rival in theater. I hadn't seen her in ages.

She was dressed in gray gabardine pants with a button-down, pinstriped blouse. For as long as I had known her, she had always been fashionable, even in high school. We went to an all-girls private high school where we had to wear uniforms. Somehow, Michelle always looked better than the rest of us in them. She would wear the navy sweater around her neck, like Jackie O, or she would wear red shoes, which would have looked just plain silly on anyone else, but on her managed to be striking.

I glanced down at her feet. Some things don't change. She wore bright purple suede boots. They looked fabulous. Me? Squeezed into jeans and tennis shoes, lugging George's stinky stuff. Figures, I'd run into the fashion queen.

"Michelle Dupree?" I asked.

"Katie Donovan?" She matched my astonished tone. Then she grabbed me by the back of the neck and pulled me to her. George's bags shuffled to the floor. She squeezed me a little too tightly, almost knocking the wind out of me.

"It's Connolly now." I hugged her back for a second, then tried to extract myself from her viselike grip.

"Right. Of course. You would be married, of course." Michelle smiled somewhat sadly and released me. "With a ton of kids, I'm sure."

"Actually, only one. She's all of eight days old."

Before Michelle could react, we were interrupted by the receptionist. "Thank you for waiting, Mrs. Avery. I need your signature here." She handed Michelle paperwork to sign.

My breath caught. Mrs. Avery? Michelle signed, then handed the forms back to the receptionist who said, "I'll be right back with your copies."

Michelle put her hand to her temple and stared out the windows for a long moment. She took a deep breath. "I found out that . . . my husband . . ." Her mouth twitched. "They recovered his body in the bay." She covered her eyes with her hands and sobbed.

"Oh, Michelle!" I put my arms around her. "How awful, awful, awful."

"I came here so that they can release his remains to me. Can you imagine, Kate? He was only thirty-five." Michelle wiped at her eyes with her fingertips.

I tsked. "So young."

It could have been George.

It could have been any number of people I knew. I felt a sadness pull at me.

She gripped me, whispering, "Brad was murdered, Kate. He was shot and his body was discarded into the bay." Her eyes darted back and forth across the lobby. "The police aren't telling me much. I suppose they always suspect the wife but . . ."

The receptionist returned. Michelle became silent, composed herself, then took the forms from the girl.

"Let me help you with your things," Michelle said, grabbing one of George's bags and heading toward the door.

From her tone, I understood she wanted to speak to me in private, and hey, I needed help with the bags, so how could I refuse?

We walked in silence toward my car. The wind had picked up, and despite the fact we were enjoying Indian summer, the best time of year in San Francisco, it was starting to get chilly.

I tried to process what Michelle had said. Her husband had been murdered? What were George's things doing on that pier? Was he connected to the Averys?

At my car, Michelle dumped George's bag into the trunk. One bag caught on the trunk latch, toppling over. A few T-shirts spilled out onto the street. Michelle and I bent to pick them up.

I had to lean on the car in order to get up. Maybe leaving the house hadn't been such a good idea. I felt like I'd been hit by a bus.

"What were you doing at the medical examiner's office?" she asked.

I stuffed the T-shirts into the bag.

What could I say? If Michelle was a suspect in her husband's murder, wouldn't George be a suspect also?

I slammed my trunk shut. "My brother-in-law's bags were found on the pier where—"

"Brad was found. Yes, the police mentioned something about that," she said, trying to keep her hair from flying into her face. "They think it's totally unrelated and I'd like to keep it that way."

"What?"

"The cops think it's unrelated because George's bags were found last week and Brad's been missing since June." She handed me a silver bracelet. "Here, this fell, too."

Too tired to open the trunk again, I stuffed it into my pocket. "Do you know George? Did Brad?"

Michelle hesitated and looked around. The receptionist

from the medical examiner's office walked toward us, then past us, presumably on her way to lunch since it was almost noon. I needed to get back and feed Laurie, not to mention myself.

My stomach growled. I placed a hand over it, trying to suppress it. "Do you know where George is? Is he all right?"

Michelle's eyes lingered on the receptionist as she clicked away from us in her fake Jimmy Choos.

She put a hand on my forearm and pulled me close to her. "Listen, Kate, will you come to my place tomorrow?" Her face looked drawn and she seemed tired. What did my face look like with all of the two hours' sleep I'd gotten since Laurie was born?

"I'd love to talk to you . . . catch up and stuff . . . well, and I'd like to talk to you"—Michelle looked up and down the block again—"about Brad."

I nodded. "I'll bring Laurie over so you can meet her."

Michelle's face brightened. "Would you? Oh, Kate." She grabbed me again in another bear hug. "Oh! That would mean so much. Come over, what? Around noon? I'll have lunch ready for us."

We exchanged addresses and phone numbers and I climbed into my car, trying to make a getaway before she squeezed me again. I didn't make it. She leaned in through the car window and placed her skinny arms around my neck. "See you tomorrow!"

CHAPTER FIVE

The Second Week—Bonding

I sped home. I missed Laurie so much, it hurt. I parked my car and transferred George's bags from the trunk to a shelf in the garage. They seemed too heavy to lug upstairs. Or was I too weak? Either way, I'd ask Jim to bring them up when he got home.

I hobbled up the stairs, clinging to the banister. The ligaments in my pelvis felt sore and tight. This was normal for me when I started up my running routine after having a long break, but a three-block walk was hardly the equivalent of a three-mile run, right? Maybe an outing so soon after having a baby hadn't been such a good idea.

Once upstairs, I barely looked at Mom. I scooped Laurie from the bassinet. "Did she miss me?"

Mom laughed. "No. She didn't even wake up."

Mom made her way toward the kitchen. I limped after her and saw pots boiling on the stove.

"I made us lunch." She handed me a plate with a ham and provolone cheese sandwich, my favorite. The table was set with a pitcher of homemade iced tea.

"Thanks, Mom. What's on the stove?"

"Your dinner."

I smiled. Mom winked and put two tablets of Motrin in my hand, then poured me a glass of tea. Nothing like a mommy. I gazed down at Laurie, in her new bright green booties, and eagerly swallowed the pills.

After Mom left, I nursed Laurie and tried to rest. I thought about bringing George's bags up from the garage, but that would mean, of course, getting up and going downstairs. I shifted my position on the couch; Laurie snuggled close to me.

I'd get them in a minute . . .

I looked at Laurie dozing in my arms. I stared and stared at her, her perfect little round face, rosy cheeks, and tiny chin. When I glanced at the clock, I was shocked to see that an hour had gone by. I nestled her closer and closed my eyes.

I woke to a ringing phone.

Oh my God! I had fallen asleep next to Laurie on the couch! I could have rolled over and squished her. And I hadn't actually checked to see if she was breathing in—how long?

What time was it?

I put my hand to her tummy; it rose up and down.

I grabbed the cordless and Jim's voice filled the line. "Definitely *not* George Connolly! What a relief!"

"You obviously got my message."

"Yes. Thank God! Listen, honey, a client called last minute, wants to do dinner and drinks, is that okay with you? This is a big account for me. I should go."

I yawned. "No problem. I'll just be hanging out here enjoying my new favorite pastime."

"What's that?"

"Staring at my beautiful daughter."

The next morning I fed Laurie and got dressed, two activities that are mind-numbingly simple but took over an hour.

How could one little infant be so much work? It took almost forty minutes to feed her. Oh, well, I could take comfort in the fact that we were getting better. We were twenty minutes faster than last week.

Before heading to Michelle's, I reviewed my to-do list.

To Do:

1. Get better at breastfeeding.

2. Lose weight.

3. ✓ ~~Take a gazillion pictures of Laurie~~.

4. Call work and let them know about Laurie and plan a return date—yuk!

5. George? Where is he? What's happened to him? Check out his bags today, see what I can find.

6. Visit Michelle.

7. Return well-wishers' phone calls (Paula, Andrew, etc.).

8. Make dinner.

I parked outside the Averys' refurbished Victorian house on Noe Street. It was dark green with white trim and there were delicate potted yellow flowers on each step. I couldn't wait to get a peek inside.

I hopped out of the car with a little too much gusto. My body immediately complained. I fished for the Motrin in my purse.

I pulled a screaming Laurie out of the car. Well, not entirely screaming. Newborns are funny that way. They try to scream, but only a pitiful little cry comes out.

Poor thing. Can't even cry properly yet.

I hiked up the front walk toward the Avery home, rang the bell, and rocked Laurie back and forth, hoping she would quiet down before Michelle answered.

The door swung open, revealing Michelle clad in a silk dress and stockinged feet. Laurie wailed at the top of her little lungs.

Michelle ushered me into her living room. "Come in, come in." She peered over the blanket at Laurie. "Oh! She's too cute! What can I get you? I have a wonderful chardonnay."

I settled onto the sofa. "I'd love to, but I can't. I'm breastfeeding. I'll have some water."

Michelle was eagerly cooing at Laurie, ignoring me. "She's beautiful, absolutely beautiful. She looks nothing like you."

I laughed. "Thanks."

"Oh my God, I didn't mean that. You're beautiful, you know that, Katie. I just meant . . . well, she's so fair, so blond, so delicate."

"Don't worry, I know what you meant," I said, self-consciously running my hand through my dark curls. Had I even brushed my hair today?

Michelle extracted herself from Laurie and disappeared down the hall. I glanced at myself in the mirror above her fireplace. I relaxed. My locks were in place. Somehow, I'd managed to whip a comb through my hair. And Jim's red flannel shirt, the only thing I could find that I fit into, actually added some color to my face. I may not have been dressed as stylishly as Michelle, but at least I was keeping up with general hygiene and good grooming.

On her mantel I noticed photos of Michelle and a man I assumed was Brad. There was a picture of them swimming with a dolphin, one of them on their wedding day, and another standing next to Michelle's mother, who was in a wheelchair.

Michelle reappeared, carrying a tray with mineral water and a newly opened bottle of wine.

"I thought you moved to L.A. Trying to make a go of the acting thing after making off with my award," I joked.

"Are you still sore about that?" Michelle laughed, then became serious. "I came back to San Francisco when I found out my mom was sick. She died of cancer last year."

"I'm sorry."

Michelle nodded. "How's your mom?"

"Great. Crazy about Laurie."

"I'll bet." Michelle took a sip of wine.

"What's up with your sister?" I asked.

Michelle grimaced. Either the wine was bitter or I'd asked the wrong question.

"Oh, we're on-again, off-again. She was no help with my mother, as you can imagine, and even though I've called her a bunch of times since . . . since Brad . . ." Michelle studied her nails a moment, then shrugged. "I called her last night to tell her you were coming over for lunch. I thought she might want to join us . . . Well, she's probably busy, is all."

Michelle's half sister, KelliAnn, had gone to school with us for only a short time. Despite Michelle's parents' long-term marriage, her father had had an affair and the by-product was KelliAnn.

Michelle and I looked at each other in awkward silence. "Do you want to see the house?" she asked.

"Sure."

Her home was beautifully restored. Wooden, built-in buffets in the dining room and built-in bookshelves gave the house a classic feel, while wainscoting and hardwood floors warmed it up.

The bedrooms were smaller than the other rooms, in keeping with the tradition of the era in which it was built. Entertaining was important, large sitting rooms and family rooms dominated the houses, leaving only a small area for sleeping quarters with no closet space. The master bath had vintage purple tile and lilac paint.

"I couldn't bring myself to knock out that tile, it's so wild," Michelle said.

I laughed. "It suits you."

Michelle face warmed with a smile. "Thank you." She sighed. "Brad hated it."

Silence fell between us. Finally I said, "Did you restore the house yourself?"

"It's my hobby. When we bought it two years ago, it was in shambles."

We ended our tour back in the living room, where Laurie had finally settled down and was now content in her car seat. Michelle gazed at Laurie. "Brad wanted kids, but . . ." She picked up her wine and swirled it in the glass. "Not with me."

"What do you mean?"

"The last time I saw Brad, he told me he was leaving me . . . that he was in love with someone else. This might be a terrible thing to say, Kate, but I didn't mind all that much. He was unhappy. I knew that. Unhappy with me, with our marriage, with our life in general, I suppose. So, when he said he was leaving, I accepted it."

She wrapped a strand of her long hair around two fingers. "I thought he'd left me. Then this police officer comes over last week, tells me they'd matched the dental records and that Brad was . . ." She covered her face with her hands.

What do you say in situations like this?

I patted her back. "I'm so sorry, Michelle."

"I told the officer that Brad left me on June fifteenth and I hadn't seen him since. I told him . . . about Brad's affair. The officer kind of insinuated that . . . well, he made me feel like he was accusing me or something. Can you imagine? Like, I was so upset about Brad leaving me and the affair and all, that I could have shot him and dumped him in the bay. Isn't that ridiculous?" She refilled her wineglass. "I told them to go look into the other woman." She rubbed at her eyes. "They said, you won't believe this, that maybe there was no other woman."

"Do you know who she is?" I asked.

"How would *I* know!"

Oops. Wrong question again.

I shrugged. "I thought maybe he told you. On the night he was leaving, he could have told you."

"He didn't. Sorry. I didn't mean to snap at you. I'm not myself. I'm edgy . . . I'm—"

"You don't have to explain."

Michelle put down her glass and cradled her forehead. "I have to find out what happened to Brad. They think it's likely he died the same day he left me, because of the condition of his body."

"Do you have any idea what could have happened?"

She shook her head, looking overwhelmed. "No. I don't. I was with George Connolly that night."

My heart stopped. "Do you know how I can reach him?"

Michelle polished off her wine, then sighed. "He works at our restaurant. Well, I guess it's my restaurant now, now that Brad's . . . George was here that night. The night Brad left me." She closed her eyes. "The night Brad was killed."

"What was George doing *here*?"

"He drops off the deposits from the restaurant." She paused to refill her glass. "Only don't tell anybody I told you so."

"Why not?"

"Well, it's just that . . . see, if George's bags were found on the pier where Brad was recovered . . . well, it's really too coincidental to be a coincidence, isn't it?"

"You think George killed Brad?"

"No. I was with George, so I know he didn't. He couldn't have. But, well, what would the police think if I told them that? They'd think that George and I killed Brad together. I mean, if George is my alibi and he looks guilty, then it doesn't look good for me, does it? So, I lied."

She took another sip of wine, which turned into a kind of a guzzle, then refilled her glass with the last of the wine. Where was the food? Hadn't she promised me lunch? Was a bottle of wine lunch for her?

"What did you tell them?" I asked, wondering if I had any crackers in Laurie's diaper bag.

"That I was home alone after Brad left. That I didn't know George Connolly."

"Michelle, how can you expect the police to think you don't know him if he works for you?"

"He works under the table, you know, for cash, so he's not on any employee list or payroll or anything." She finished off the wine, then wiped her mouth with the back of her hand, smearing her pink lipstick.

"Where can I find George?"

"He should be at the restaurant, El Paraiso, on Market Street. Kate, why did they call *you* about the bags? I mean, what was in them?"

"They couldn't find George."

Michelle nodded. "He likes keeping a low profile, which is good. Was there anything, you know, special in his bags?"

Like what?

"I haven't opened them."

Michelle looked disappointed.

What was she looking for?

We stared awkwardly at each other. Finally Michelle said, "I'm scared, Kate. What if . . . whoever killed Brad . . . what if I'm next?"

CHAPTER SIX

The Second Week—
Umbilical Cord Emancipation

I left Michelle's house and packed Laurie into the car. When I pulled out from the parking spot, my trunk flew open.

I reparked the car and jumped out to slam the trunk shut. It ricocheted back in my face. I examined the lock.

Jimmied.

Someone had broken into my car. A wave of desperation came over me, filling me with the urge to cry.

How ridiculous is that? I'm going to cry over a car? No! I'm just tired, not to mention all the hormones raging through my body. This is nothing to cry about.

I looked into the trunk. My overdue library books were still there and so was my leather jacket. Nothing seemed to be missing. Still, I couldn't shake the feeling that I had been violated.

Someone had rummaged through my stuff. My car. My library books. My jacket.

* * *

I pulled into our garage. When I got out of the car, my pelvic bones ached from so much activity. Jim sat on our steps sorting through George's bags.

"How's my little lima bean?"

"Not good. Someone broke into my car."

"What? Where?" Jim stood and came over to me.

"In front of Michelle's."

"Who?"

"Michelle Dupree, who is now Michelle Avery. My friend from high school. Do you remember her?"

Jim unstrapped Laurie from her car seat. "Not really."

"You met her at the ten-year reunion."

"Oh! Vaguely." A corner of Jim's mouth twitched up. "Is she the one who won the drama award that should have—"

"Been mine? Yeah."

Jim smiled.

"It *should* have been mine. What are you smirking at?" I demanded.

"You got the popularity award, or whatever it was called. Popularity? Personality?"

"I wanted the drama award. I earned it. They only gave it to her because of their stupid philosophy about spreading out the awards, so that no one student would dominate."

Jim's smirk turned into a laugh. "They thought they could stop you from dominating?"

"If you weren't holding Laurie right now, I'd punch you."

"Have a baby, lose a sense of humor?" Jim teased.

I covered my face with my hands. "I'm tired. It was her husband. The guy they found in the bay. Brad Avery."

Jim's face darkened, his playful mood vanishing. "That's awful." He rubbed my back with his free hand. "I'm so sorry, honey. Where's Michelle live?"

"Noe Valley. Not a bad neighborhood. I had to tie my trunk down so it would stay shut."

"Anything missing?"

"Not that I can tell. My jacket's still there. They didn't even have the decency to take the library books and return them."

He laughed and kissed my neck. "I'm glad nothing happened to you or Laurie." He handed the baby to me. "I'll take your car in for repair tomorrow on my way to the office and drop your books off for you, too."

"That's why I love you so much." I pointed to George's bags. "Anything interesting?"

"Nope. Clothes and crap. You know, toothbrush, a toilet kit, jeans, T-shirts. Looks like he was living out of these bags, Kate. No wonder the medical examiner asked if he was a transient. I found the cell phone bill. I called the number. No longer in service. What a shock." He squeezed his eyes shut and shook his head. "My brother, a fucking bum. My parents are probably spinning in their graves."

I pressed my head against his chest. "Michelle said he works at El Paraiso." I pulled back and looked at Jim.

A glimmer of hope flashed on his face. "She knows him?"

"Yup. Says they were together the night Brad was killed."

Jim moaned and shook his head. "I knew nothing good was going to come from any of this."

I hardly slept that night. Well, better said, Laurie hardly slept. We were up nursing, rocking, and singing. As soon as daylight started to peek through the window, Laurie conked out. I slipped into bed next to Jim as the alarm went off.

He turned to me. "Are you just getting to bed now?"

"Mmmhmm."

"I'll take the night shift tonight," he said.

I nodded off, wondering how he would take the night shift without breasts.

At 9 A.M., after a three-hour nap, Laurie awoke hungry. I nursed her, then rose to change her diaper. Her umbilical stump had come off. I examined her new belly button. Beautiful. My little girl was beautiful.

Images of her at fifteen years old, with her belly button pierced, flashed through my mind. My baby was growing up so fast.

I clutched her to me. "Take your time, will you?"

I laid her on my bed, then ransacked Jim's closet in search of anything that fit, settling on a blue plaid shirt that hung over my now too-large maternity pants. I stuffed my feet into my favorite pair of black strappy sandals. The shoes were so tight, they cut off the circulation to my toes.

How depressing.

I kicked off the stupid sandals and shoved on a pair of stretched-out Keds. Would my old shoes ever fit again?

Laurie patiently gazed into space. I took advantage of her good mood and sat for a moment to compose my to-do list.

To Do:

1. Lose weight (What? I'm still the same weight after having given birth two weeks ago. Aren't the pounds supposed to melt right off when you breastfeed?)

2. Call work and let them know about Laurie and plan a return date—yuk! (Send the office an e-mail with photos of Laurie. That way I don't have to talk to anyone right now about my return

date. Don't even want to think about heading back to Corporate Hell and leaving Laurie.)

3. Find George—El Paraiso—drop off his bags.

4. What happened to Brad???

5. Grocery shop. (Right now would only be able to make Cheerios for dinner!)

6. Laundry. (How does the addition of one six-pound baby create so much laundry?)

7. E-mail Paula—tell her about Michelle Avery.

I found parking relatively close to El Paraiso, with the only hitch being a one-hour maximum on the meter.

Oh, shoot! George's bags! With all the preparation required to get Laurie out of the house, I had forgotten his bags.

I had become extremely forgetful during my pregnancy, locking myself out of my car three times and even getting into the car or on the bus and not remembering where I was going. I had been hoping I would get my memory back, along with my figure, shortly after giving birth.

Was that another pipe dream?

I adjusted the rearview mirror and spied on Laurie through the Elmo mirror pinned to the backseat. "You're supposed to help Mommy remember things."

She kicked her legs in glee, flashing her sporty green booties. They were ridiculously bright, but at least they stayed on her feet. Newborns' feet are so tiny and slender that socks usually just slip right off.

"Well, we're parked now. And I don't know about you, but I'm definitely hungry. Uncle George can pick up his bags later."

I pushed Laurie's stroller into the trendy restaurant. Red walls were a backdrop to etchings framed in hardwood. Leather booths were filled by the San Francisco downtown lunchtime crowd. Everyone was dressed in corporate garb. The men in their suits and the women in tight-fitting skirts and impossibly high heels.

I immediately felt out of place, but the one thing I was learning fast was that no one looked at me anymore. Every time I stepped out of the house with Laurie, all eyes were on her.

A hostess with a stud through her nose and another in her eyebrow stared at Laurie, then squinted at me. "Should she even be out?"

I squinted back. "Should you have that thing through your nose?"

She flipped her hair at me. "Follow me."

Once seated, I pulled Laurie's stroller as close to me as possible, trying not to block the aisle.

What a hassle, dining in a non-kid-friendly place. I read the menu.

Peruvian Marinated Skewers of Beef Heart in a Tangy Aji Panca Sauce, Grilled Adobo Rubbed Pork Loins, Sweet Potato Purée, Pisco Marinated Dried Fruit Chutney, and Traditional Peruvian Cold Potato Torte Layered with Sliced Avocado.

It was worth the hassle.

What would I order? I couldn't decide. Breastfeeding works up an enormous appetite, so I decided not to decide and ordered both the marinated skewers and the cold potato torte. My mouth watered as I watched the waiter serve a couple seated near me.

The waiter twirled around. He was tall and lean with a dancer's build.

"My name is José. I'll be your waiter today."

José raised an eyebrow at my double order, then asked, "Is someone joining you?"

"No. I'm eating for two."

José's face flushed.

Well, I sort of was anyway.

José spun on his heel, but before he could get away, I asked, "Is George Connolly working today?"

José turned back to me, his brow furrowed. "George?" He quickly glanced over his shoulder. "Sorry, I don't know anybody named George."

While waiting for my lunch, I mulled over José's answer. Did George really work here? Why would Michelle lie to me about that? It made no sense. Maybe José was being secretive because George was working "under the table"?

The business lunch crowd started to thin. Everyone was returning to their human filing cabinets, as Jim and I called our offices. Cubicle after cubicle that files you away from each other and the world.

My stomach churned as I thought about my inevitable return to my own office.

Ordering office supplies, doing payroll, and shuffling paper were the absolute last things on earth I wanted to do right now. How could I leave my little apricot? I needed to earn a living, that much was true. We wouldn't be able to afford our mortgage on Jim's salary alone. But wasn't there something I could do while I was with Laurie?

Work from home!

Doing what? There was a gal from my office who hadn't returned after her maternity leave. Monica. She'd started her own business making and selling children's jewelry.

Could someone really make a living selling jewelry? I dismissed it from my mind. Monica had always been craftsy, and the baubles she'd brought into the office had everyone raving. I, on the other hand, didn't have the slightest clue about glue guns and glitter.

José served my lunch, which I wolfed down. The beef

dish would have been too spicy for me on its own, but the potato torte and avocado mellowed out the spices.

Would the spices affect Laurie later? I hoped not.

I studied the staff. When he wasn't waiting on me, José was busy hitting on the hostess. She snubbed him, just like she had me.

Where was the manager? I could ask him about George.

By the time my bill rolled around, I felt satiated and sleepy. I fought the weight of my eyelids and the impulse to run out and check on the parking meter. Instead, I asked José to direct me to the manager.

His face creased with concern. "Was everything all right?"

I smiled. "Yes."

He seemed unconvinced. "May I tell him your name?"

"Kate Connolly."

His eyes widened, then his face flushed again. "One minute."

I watched as he hurried through swinging doors. Why was he so flustered?

I pulled Laurie out of her stroller. Still sleeping? I gently rubbed her face. She twitched her feet. Good. Still breathing.

After several minutes, José reappeared, followed by a disarmingly handsome man. He was about five-foot-ten, with black hair. His eyes were so blue I wondered if he was wearing colored contacts. He was sharply dressed in slacks and a blue button-down shirt, accented by a burgundy tie. The only thing that contradicted his elegant style was a five o'clock shadow. Which, while some consider in fashion, has always struck me as unkempt.

Maybe he had a rough night?

He sauntered over to me and casually rested both hands on the table. "Rich Hanlen. May I help you, Ma'am?"

Ma'am, was it? I sighed. I guess when you have a baby, no one calls you "Miss" anymore.

"Is George Connolly working today?"

He straightened, folding his arms across his chest. "George? I don't believe—"

"Michelle Avery told me he worked here."

He scratched the stubble on his chin, then glanced around the restaurant. "Why don't you come back to my office?"

I bundled Laurie into her stroller, not bothering with any of the straps as the manager was already through the restaurant and at the kitchen door. I maneuvered the stroller toward him, the front wheel catching on a chair and further delaying me. Out of the corner of my eye, I saw Rich take a deep breath. I struggled to free the wheel.

Why did I feel rushed? Couldn't he wait a second for a woman with a baby?

I caught up to him then followed him through the kitchen doors and down a narrow hallway to a dark, cramped room. To call the space an office was a joke. My human filing cabinet cubicle was larger than this.

"Is this your baby?" he asked.

"Yeah," I answered.

Why else would I be lugging an infant around?

Up close, the colored lenses made his eyes seem like they were floating. Eerie.

He reached out to touch Laurie. "She's tiny."

I moved her stroller before his hand could reach her cheek. His eyes locked on mine. We stared at each other for a moment, sizing each other up.

No way was Mr. Creepy touching my baby.

He shifted subtly, understanding. Don't mess with baby cub when Mama Lion's around.

"How old is she?"

"Almost two weeks."

He looked me up and down. "You look pretty good for a chick that just popped out a baby."

What happened to "ma'am"? Maybe it hadn't been

such a good idea to follow this guy into a dark room.
Suddenly, it was difficult to breathe.

He circled around behind me. "So, you know Michelle?"

Was he checking out my ass?

I shifted, forcing him to face me. He smirked.

"I know Michelle." I said, "You know George?"

He nodded, clearly enjoying himself.

I imagined him asking the female staff "to his office,"
then copping a feel.

Hoping to intimidate him a little, I pulled a notebook
from the diaper bag that was now serving double-duty as
my purse.

Oops. No pen.

I eyed the pencil cup on his desk.

If I leaned in to grab one, I'd give him a shot of my
milk-engorged cleavage. I flipped opened my notebook
and hoped he wouldn't notice that I wasn't actually writing anything down.

In my most official voice I said, "I need to reach George.
Can you tell me when he's scheduled to come in?"

He leered. "I haven't seen him in a while. I don't know
what Michelle told you, but he's not on any schedule or
anything."

"What does he do here?"

"This and that."

Why all the secrecy about George?

"How long have you been managing the restaurant?"

He scratched at his newly forming beard. "'Bout three
months."

"Around June?" I asked, for clarification.

"That's right."

"June fifteenth or sixteenth, would you say?"

"What are you getting at?"

"You started managing the restaurant after Brad's . . .
disappearance? I take it you knew Brad Avery."

He shrugged his shoulders. "Sure. Yeah. 'Course I knew Brad. He and I were good buddies."

"Didn't you think it was odd, his vanishing like that?"

He moved toward the desk and sat on the edge, forcing me to step back. I bumped into the wall behind me and jarred Laurie's stroller. She wailed and kicked, protesting being awakened.

I jiggled the stroller to soothe her and pressed backward as far away from Mr. Sleazy as I could. I felt the coolness of the wall through Jim's shirt. I resisted the urge to shiver.

He licked his lips and smiled a crooked little smile. "You a cop?"

"No."

He squinted. "What's with all the questions, then?"

"I just think that you'd have wondered when suddenly your boss, your *good buddy*, didn't show up."

He crossed his arms over his chest. "Michelle told me they'd had a fight, that he was leaving her. When he didn't come to work, it was obvious that he'd left her. So she and Mrs. A asked me to run things for her."

"Mrs. A?"

"Brad's mother. She's part owner," he clarified.

"Michelle told me Brad was having an affair."

"Don't know nothing 'bout that."

Didn't he? Mr. Rico Suave here, with the jet black hair and colored contacts. Mr. Leery. Mr. Good Buddy of the deceased.

"Do you know who might?" I pressed.

He unfolded his arms and stood up, leaning in a little too close to me. "Might what?"

"Never mind," I mumbled. It was none of my business anyway.

I closed my notebook and bent over to shove it into the diaper bag. The notebook caught on a little rag doll I'd packed for Laurie. I had to do a quick rearrange and cram everything in. When I straightened, my heart jumped into my throat.

He had Laurie in his arms.

He gazed down at her. "She's really beautiful. Fragile, huh?"

"Yes," I whispered, swallowing the lump in my throat.

"I love babies," he said.

Why hadn't I strapped her in!

I forced myself to breathe.

And think.

I reached past him and pulled the office door open. Light flooded into the room, causing Laurie to stir and wail again.

"Here," he said, handing Laurie back to me.

Such relief washed over me that my knees felt weak. I snatched Laurie from him, barely able to contain myself. I pushed her stroller into the hallway muttering, "Jerk."

The office door clicked closed behind me. But not soon enough that I didn't hear his snicker.

Laurie wailed again and I stopped short of the swinging kitchen doors to soothe her. She kicked her feet up at me. One foot with Mom's booty on, the other bare.

I did a quick check underneath her, then down the hallway. No booty.

Probably left behind in the office.

Forget it. No way was I going back in there for a stupid booty.

Mom will kill me.

Maybe I could knock and not go inside. I pulled Laurie's stroller backward down the hallway toward his office. I heard his voice through the door. ". . . asking a bunch of questions 'bout Brad."

There was silence. I froze.

Then he said, "No way. Why would I tell her 'bout the fight?"

He paused again. I held my breath.

Then I heard him say, "Haven't seen George since last week, but he'll be here tomorrow for the delivery."

I abandoned the booty and wheeled the stroller out of the restaurant. I hustled toward Jim's car hoping to dodge a parking ticket. Shattered glass littered the street. The driver's side window was broken.

Not again.

I swallowed the panic building in my chest. I glanced up and down the street. Empty.

Thank God. What would I have done anyway? Beat the burglar with my diaper bag?

I dialed Jim. Voice mail. I dialed Michelle. Voice mail. Why was no one around when you needed them?

A vehicle pulled in front of Jim's car. A stocky balding man stepped out. He noted the glass on the street, then moved toward me. He reached into his pocket and produced a badge reading INSPECTOR PATRICK MCNEARNY. "Miss, I'm with SFPD. This your car?"

Ah. Miss *again!*

"Yeah."

"Anything taken?"

"No. I . . . uh . . . I haven't checked."

I glanced over my shoulder into Jim's car. Everything seemed to be in order. I leaned over the driver's seat and pulled open the glove box. Papers were crumpled, as if someone had rummaged through it.

"It looks like someone went through this," I said.

The officer nodded.

"My address is on the registration," I said.

"They were probably looking for money. I'll write a report for you. The best I can tell you is to file an insurance claim." He pulled out a notebook. "Your name?"

"Kate Connolly."

He raised his eyebrows. "Connolly?" He frowned, flipped through his book, and read an old entry.

My heart tightened. Could this officer be looking for George?

The officer scribbled something. "Is this car registered to you?"

"My husband, actually. My car . . ." I took a breath. "My car's in the shop."

I didn't have the guts to tell him my car had been broken into outside of Michelle's house. What if George was behind this? Was he looking for his bags? Would he really break into my car and Jim's?

Was I getting paranoid?

Could it be a coincidence? I'd lived in San Francisco my entire life and had never had my car broken into. Now twice in two days?

The officer copied information off the registration. "Like I said, I suggest you file an insurance claim." He handed the registration back to me, his eyes narrowing.

"Meter's expired."

I watched in silence as he crossed the street and pulled open the door to El Paraiso.

• CHAPTER SEVEN •

The Second Week—
Crying for Assistance

I awoke, still groggy, to Laurie's hunger cries at 3 A.M. I leaned over the bassinet and picked her up. She was soaked all the way through her little jammies.

I poked Jim. "You're the night shift, remember?"

"Yeah," he murmured.

"She's wet. She needs a full costume change."

No answer.

"Jim! Wake up."

"Mmmhmm."

Laurie wailed. I put her right next to his ear. No movement.

"How can you sleep through this?"

Men!

I walked down the dark hall, to her nursery, bumping into the walls as I went. Somehow it seemed easier to get out of bed and change Laurie myself than try to get Jim up.

I switched on the light, rousing Laurie and me into wakefulness. She continued to complain throughout the entire diaper and pajama routine.

I was so exhausted I buttoned her pajamas wrong and had to undo everything, then redo it. I vowed to buy only pajamas with zippers in the future.

I made my way back to our bedroom, now fully awake, thinking about our cars getting broken into. Could George have done it? I couldn't imagine George breaking into our cars; besides, how would he even know we had his bags? If not George, then who?

I recalled the mundane items in the bags. Why would anyone want them? Had I missed something?

I collapsed into the rocker with Laurie, trying to soothe her into quiet mode.

Michelle hadn't returned my call. Maybe I should go over there tomorrow. After all, what else did I have to do all day?

Sleep?

Ha.

I filled the time the best way I could and dialed the only person I could think of that would be up at this ungodly hour, my girlfriend, Paula, in France. Paula and her husband, David, had relocated several months ago. David worked for a top consulting firm. In order to move up in his career, he'd been "asked" to take an assignment in France and relocate his family.

I jiggled Laurie in my arms and listened to the phone ring. With no sleep, I felt incapable of doing the math on the time difference. I figured it must be sometime in the afternoon. Her voice mail kicked on and I left a sluggish, incoherent message.

I logged on to the computer and e-mailed her.

Tried to call you. Lots to tell, but its 4am here and even though I can't sleep because Laurie is awake I

can't really type with her in my arms either. Thinking of you. Call or email when you get the chance.
   XOXOXOX.

I finally successfully placed Laurie in her bassinet and crawled back into bed as the alarm went off at 6 A.M. Every earlier attempt had been fouled by Laurie's startle reflex; as soon as I set her down, her little arms would shoot straight up as though she were falling.

Jim jarred awake. "Were you up all night?"

"Practically."

He rubbed my back. "Oh, honey, why didn't you wake me?"

"I tried."

"You did?"

My eyelids felt like sandpaper, and my arms and back were sore from rocking Laurie. "Yeah."

He stroked my hair. "If she wakes up again tonight, get me up."

If she wakes up again?

"Nite-nite," I whispered, falling into a fitful sleep.

The phone woke Laurie and me. I glanced around, surprised to see that Jim had already left for the office. The clock glowed 9 A.M. No wonder. Had I really slept three hours straight? I felt much better. What a difference a little sleep made.

I grabbed the ringing phone.

"Where have you been? I called and called yesterday."

"Hi, Mom."

"What have you done with my granddaughter? I need to see her before she doesn't recognize me. And I finished her knit cap."

Uh-oh.

"Green?"

"No. I ran out of that yarn. Orange."

I laughed. "Come over. I need to run a couple errands."

After yesterday's ordeal with Mr. Creepy and the cars being broken into, I didn't want Laurie in tow. Just in case.

I made my daily list while waiting for Mom.

To Do:

1. Find George.

2. Ask Michelle if she told George I have his bags.

3. Learn how to use hideous breast pump.

4. Catch up on z's.

5. Restart diet.

6. ✓ ~~E-mail Paula~~.

7. Send out birth announcements.

8. Make birth announcements.

I dug in my closet, searching for something to wear. Fortunately, my bones weren't as achy as the day before and some of my pregnancy bloat was starting to disappear. I tried on a pair of nonmaternity slacks. They actually fit.

Except for the waist.

I found a flowing silk blouse that I could leave untucked to hide the fact that the button was held in place with a rubber band. Hey, progress was progress, and I'd do anything not to have to wear maternity pants.

What did they say about pregnancy weight: nine months

up, nine months down? I sighed at my reflection in the mirror and hurriedly put on lipstick.

I left Laurie with Mom cooing over her and made my way to Michelle's.

I parked in front of the house and found myself checking the street for anyone hanging around. No shady characters or car thieves, but since I hadn't seen anyone before, I didn't exactly feel secure.

I rang Michelle's doorbell.

No answer.

I rang the bell again, puttering around a bit, waiting. There was no chipping paint to pick at, so I traced the outlines of the numbers of her address. About fifteen times.

I dug out my cell phone and dialed her. It rang and rang; finally her voice mail clicked on.

Hmm. Maybe she went somewhere? To get groceries? Buy herself more wine?

When I turned to leave, I saw the day's newspaper was still on the stairs. I peered through the tiny window, made of brick glass, on her front door. It was meant to let light in but keep Peeping Toms out. I couldn't see a thing inside.

An uneasy feeling was building inside me. I decided to check around the house and see if I could find any accessible windows. I fought the paranoia flaring up.

It's probably nothing, Kate.

I peeked into the mail slot at the garage. A gold hardtop Mercedes was visible. I went around to the side of the house and tried to reach the dining room's stained glass windows, but they were too high.

A heavy planter box was nearby. I dragged it about a foot so I could climb onto it and look through the window. Even on my tiptoes I wasn't tall enough.

I retreated to the front of the house and spotted several thick phone books on the curb. When was the phone company going to stop printing those? With everyone searching the yellow pages online, I couldn't imagine a need for them much longer. But thankfully they hadn't stopped yet as they might just give me the boost I needed.

I grabbed the books and placed them on top of the planter box then climbed up holding on to the old window trim, praying it wouldn't give. I was able to pull myself high enough to peer through the window into the dining room.

Michelle was sprawled across the floor.

I rapped sharply on the window. She didn't move. I swallowed the fear in my throat and rapped again.

Nothing.

Maybe she's fainted. Maybe she's passed out drunk.

I started to climb off the phone books and lost my footing. I fell off the planter box, tearing my slacks on a protruding nail.

I sat dumbfounded on the cement, the back of my right thigh throbbing from the fall.

Michelle!

I picked myself up and hobbled to the front of the house and up the steps again. Leaning on the doorbell, I willed Michelle to get up and answer the door.

In a last-ditch effort, I tried the knob. It turned in my hand. Pushing it open, I called, "Michelle! Michelle!"

I ran to her and turned her over.

Her body was limp. She was pale as a ghost, her black hair strewn across her face. I brushed it away with my hand. "Michelle? Oh Michelle, please don't be dead," I whispered even though I knew she was.

Oddly, she had a peaceful expression. There was a small cut on her temple where blood had trickled. I imagined her collapsing and cutting her head against the coffee table.

I looked around the room and noticed two wineglasses on her coffee table. She'd had company. My God, what could have happened?

I dialed 9-1-1 from Michelle's phone.

After I reported Michelle dead, the operator said, "I'm sending someone now. Did you try CPR?"

"Oh my God. I don't think . . ."

The operator instructed me to feel for a pulse.

I knelt next to Michelle and took her hand in mine, placing two fingers over her wrist. I confirmed the lack of a pulse.

"Ma'am, the police will be there shortly. Please don't touch anything in the house," the operator instructed. "Stay on the line."

I remained kneeling next to Michelle, helplessly holding her hand and feeling a heaviness in my gut.

Someone had killed Michelle. My high school friend. Someone had *killed* her, had murdered her husband. Someone had broken into my cars.

I squeezed my eyes shut, not wanting to think his name. It popped into my head anyway.

George? Charming, flaky, pain-in-the-ass George.

Please, no. Please, don't be behind this.

CHAPTER EIGHT

The Second Week—
Seeing is Believing

I waited in stunned silence until I heard sirens down the street. I told the 9-1-1 operator that the paramedics had arrived.

"All right, ma'am. Please wait for the police. They'll be there shortly to take your statement."

My statement?

I opened the door for the paramedics. They tried to re-suscitate Michelle. They couldn't. Soon the police arrived, headed by Inspector McNearny, the same cop who'd helped me with Jim's car the day before. He came into the house and barely looked at Michelle. Instead, he looked straight at me, cocking his head to the side. "Well, well, well, who do we have here? Mrs. Connolly, is it?" He jutted his chin at me a bit, challenging me. "Kind of a surprise to find you here. How's your car? File that insurance claim yet?"

What was he accusing me of? Insurance fraud? Something worse?

"No. I didn't. Not yet." I could feel his gaze. I supposed he was waiting for an explanation. "I came over to see my friend, Michelle."

McNearny nodded at me, then at his partner. "Jones, this is Ms. Connolly."

Jones was younger than McNearny, with kind eyes and short dark hair that was gelled back. He smiled sympathetically at me.

McNearny gestured toward the wineglasses. "Did you have wine with her?"

"No. No! I just got here. She didn't answer the door. I tried her phone and left a message. I saw her through the window . . . on the floor. I . . . the door was open. I thought maybe she passed out."

Inspector McNearny squinted at me, then pulled a small notebook from his breast pocket. "You looked through the window? What window?"

I pointed to the dining room stained glass window. McNearny walked into the dining room and peeked out. "It's high."

"I know. I had to move the planter box and climb up."

McNearny scratched his chin, still looking out the window. "You moved it?"

I nodded. Jones looked around the living room. "How did you gain access to the house?"

"The front door was open," I repeated.

"I don't get it. Why look through the window?" Jones asked.

"Well, I rang the bell. She didn't answer. I didn't think to try the door. Who leaves their door unlocked in San Francisco? So, I wanted to peek through a window."

"Why?" McNearny countered. "Why didn't you leave? Maybe she wasn't home."

"But she was home. Sort of . . ."

"Do you normally climb planter boxes to look through people's windows when they don't answer the door?" McNearny asked.

"No. I just . . . her husband—"

"Was murdered. Yes." McNearny nodded.

"I was worried about her."

"Why?" Jones asked.

I shrugged uselessly. "The last time I saw her, she told me she was scared."

"Scared of what?" McNearny scowled.

I stared at him. "Scared that whoever killed her husband would come after her."

"Ah," McNearny said, tapping his pencil on his notebook. "And did she tell you who that was?"

I took a deep breath. "No."

A uniformed officer bent over Michelle, measuring something. I averted my eyes, pressing on them to keep from crying.

McNearny walked over to Michelle's body and studied her for a moment. "You found her like this?"

"Yeah. No. I mean, she was facedown. I turned her over."

"Can you tell us what you've touched?" Jones asked.

"The phone, the door, Michelle." I spun around, taking inventory of the room. "I think that's it."

"What happened to your pants?" McNearny asked.

I felt the back of my pants. They were torn around my hamstring. "I tore them when I fell off the planter," I said, rubbing at the bruise I was sure was forming on the backside of my leg.

McNearny grunted, making no effort to conceal his skepticism. He scribbled something into his notebook, then indicated a pair of prescription glasses on the coffee table. "What about those glasses over there? Are they yours?"

"No."

"Are they Michelle's?" Jones asked.

My stomach churned. "I don't know."

McNearny made a note, then looked up at me. "I thought she was your friend."

"She *was* my friend. I just hadn't seen her for a long time. I don't know if she wore glasses."

The front door squeaked open and Nick Dowling, the medical examiner, poked his head through. "Got a call." His eyes landed on Michelle. "I see I'm in the right place," he said, nodding at McNearny and Jones.

McNearny and Jones nodded back. I tried my best to look inconspicuous.

Dowling spotted me. "Mrs. Connolly! Didn't think I'd see you so soon."

McNearny's and Jones's heads spun toward me so fast I was afraid they'd break their necks. I smiled despite gritted teeth and raised my eyebrows in acknowledgment to Dowling.

McNearny, Jones, and Dowling all exchanged glances, then McNearny barked, "Downtown!"

Jones crossed to me, while McNearny and Dowling huddled over Michelle.

"Mrs. Connolly, I know how upsetting all this can be," Jones said. "Finding your friend and all. Maybe it's best if you come downtown with me to the station. We'll be more comfortable and I'll be able to take your official statement."

I froze.

Downtown?

"I . . . I have a newborn," I stuttered. "I have to get home and feed her."

Suddenly I felt nauseated. What had I gotten myself into?

Jones was expertly maneuvering me toward the front door. "A newborn? Really? I got a nine-month-old. Aren't they great?"

McNearny instructed another officer to start dusting for fingerprints.

Jones pulled open the front door. The fresh air relieved

my nausea, a bit. We walked in silence down the front steps.

Once on the curb, Jones gestured to a car parked nearby. "This your car?"

I shook my head and pointed to my Chevy Cavalier parked down the street.

"You want to follow me downtown?" he asked. "Or you want to ride with me?"

"I can drive myself?"

"Sure, no problem. You're going voluntarily, right?"

Was I?

From the relative safety of my car, which I was happy to see had not been broken into again, I dialed home and instructed Mom to give Laurie a formula bottle.

The only good thing about my initially being rated "poor" at breastfeeding in the hospital was that, upon hearing this, Mom had immediately run out and bought formula. When I caught her smuggling it into my pantry, she had mumbled, "Just in case."

Which I took to mean: "Just in case you're too lame to get the hang of what every mother has been doing naturally since the beginning of time."

Outwardly I was a little offended; inwardly I was relieved. Just in case I *was* too lame, there was no reason for Laurie to starve. Besides, you never know when you're going to stumble across a dead friend and need your mom to feed the baby.

At the station, I was escorted by Jones to a small room with a mirror, a table, and a few chairs. On the table was a box of tissues, a couple of notepads, and a small recorder. Jones sat across from me and hooked a microphone into the recorder.

"Do I need a lawyer?" I asked nervously.

Jones smiled. "For what?"

I shrugged.

"Mrs. Connolly, you are not under arrest. I just want to get a statement from you. You want coffee or something?"

"No."

"Water? Soda?"

"Water would be nice."

Jones continued fussing with the recorder. A female officer appeared in the doorway with my water. I glanced from her to the mirror. Two-way mirror? Who else was watching me?

"I need a few things from my desk, okay?" Jones said, "Drink the water. Relax. I'll be back in a minute." He left me alone in the room.

I drank my water and waited and waited. My breasts were starting to burn. I glanced at my watch. It was feeding time. I doubled-checked myself in the two-way mirror. Thankfully my breasts hadn't leaked through my blouse; otherwise, I'd have given whoever it was on the other end quite a show.

At least half an hour passed before Jones returned empty-handed. Empty-handed but with McNearny by his side. He'd been buying time for McNearny to return.

Both officers seated themselves across from me, Jones smiling, McNearny scowling.

Jones leaned forward and said the date and time into the microphone. He mentioned all our names then looked up at me. "Mrs. Connolly, can you tell us the last time you saw Michelle Avery?"

"The day before yesterday."

"Where was that?" Jones asked.

"At her house. She'd invited me for lunch."

"Tell us about it," Jones said.

I shrugged. "She was very upset. She was drinking. She drank a bottle of wine while I was there."

"Was that unusual for her?" Jones asked.

"I don't know. I thought so. A whole bottle? But, you know, you're right, I hadn't seen her in a long time. I have no idea what her drinking habits were."

McNearny cleared his throat. "So, she was a drunk."

"I'm not saying that. I don't really know. I just know she was upset . . ."

Jones leaned in close to me. "So upset, you think maybe she could have killed herself?"

Before I could answer, McNearny said, "You got her suicide note in your purse or anything?"

"What?" I practically yelled. The anger that bubbled up inside me turned to tears. I plucked a tissue from the box on the table and wiped at my eyes. Jones bowed his head, giving me a moment to compose myself. McNearny simply watched me.

I blew my nose and crumbled the tissue in my hand. The adrenaline from finding Michelle dead had left my system and now all I felt was sadness, disbelief, and bone-deep weariness.

I sighed. "I really don't think she killed herself."

"Earlier, you said Mrs. Avery thought whoever killed her husband might come after her," Jones said. "Did she give you any indication, any at all, about who she thought that was? Take your time."

I shook my head.

"You said you hadn't seen her in long time?" McNearny asked. "When was the previous time?"

"I hadn't seen her until . . ."

How much should I say? Surely the medical examiner had told McNearny I'd retrieved George's things.

They waited for me to answer, exchanging looks. Finally Jones prompted gently, "Until when?"

"Monday," I said.

"I see." Jones made a note.

There was a deafening silence in the room as they both consulted their respective notebooks. I licked my lips. I was parched again. Couldn't they get me more water?

"Where did you see her?" McNearny asked.

Didn't he already know the answer?

"I saw her at the medical examiner's office."

"Ah, yes. Mrs. Avery would have had to sign release papers," McNearny said. "What were *you* doing there?"

If he didn't already know, he could find out. Why mess with me like this? I sat back in my chair, crossed my feet, then uncrossed them.

Honesty would be best.

I fidgeted with my empty water cup, finally depositing the crumpled tissue inside it. "I was picking up my brother-in-law's bags."

Inspector McNearny flipped through his notebook. "Ah, brother-in-law. Would that be George Connolly?"

Jim had been right. Nothing good would come from meddling in George's business. "Yes," I mumbled.

"Interesting. Very interesting. Mrs. Avery said she didn't know George Connolly." He tapped his fingers on his notebook. "Do you know why she would say that?"

I felt a protective surge for George, Jim's brother, Laurie's uncle. Not to mention I was getting tired of McNearny's attitude. "What makes you think they knew each other?" I challenged.

"Well, if he was your brother-in-law and you and she were friends . . ."

"I went to high school with Michelle. Before Monday, we hadn't seen each other since . . ." When had been the last time I'd seen Michelle? "I don't even remember when. Probably our reunion a few years back. It was a coincidence seeing her at the medical examiner's office."

McNearny frowned. "Was it?"

I nodded emphatically. "Um-hum."

McNearny sucked some air between his teeth, sort of

tsking at my response. "Now see? That's where I have a problem."

The weariness in my bones was slowly turning to dread.

Why not tell them everything I know?

But then, what did I know, really? Michelle had said George was with her the night Brad died. Therefore, George couldn't have killed Brad. He couldn't have, right?

Unless, Michelle and George were in on it together. Or he killed Brad after leaving Michelle. Who killed Michelle? Dread was overcoming me.

No! George is not a killer!

"I don't believe in coincidences, Mrs. Connolly," McNearny said.

Of course, neither did I. Normally anyway, but in this case I really *really* needed to believe. I blurted, "Sometimes things happen for no reason at all. An accident, a fluke, chance."

"I had to release those bags to your family, because I couldn't prove there was any connection to Mr. Avery. He was last seen on June fifteenth and the medical examiner places his death in June. George Connolly's bags were found on September nineteenth on the same pier where Mr. Avery was recovered. Months apart. Is there a connection?" McNearny opened his hands toward me in question. "Mrs. Avery tells me she doesn't know a George Connolly. So technically, I can't prove a thing. But this"—he patted his broad stomach—"isn't technical. My gut says there is a connection between the Connollys and the Averys."

"I already told you I went to high school with Michelle."

He breathed more air in through his teeth and grimaced. "Something more recent. Something that involves your brother-in-law."

"I haven't seen George in a long time. When I see him, I'll ask him for you."

"One more thing, Mrs. Connolly. When your car was broken into yesterday, the location was curiously close to El Paraiso, the restaurant owned by the Averys."

"Yep."

"What were you doing there exactly?"

"What everyone does at restaurants, eat."

"Kind of strange, isn't it? You don't see your *friend* for a long time, then all of sudden you're frequenting her restaurant?" McNearny asked.

"Is there a law against that?"

"I'm just trying to understand why you were there. Were you meeting her there?"

"Nope. Just eating. Alone. Well, with my daughter actually, whom I've got to get home to."

McNearny and Jones exchanged glances. Jones said, "Thank you, Mrs. Connolly. We appreciate your time. If we need anything else, we'll contact you."

I stood. Jones stood with me. McNearny remained seated, his arms folded across his chest. I made my way toward the door. I glanced over my shoulder; McNearny was still watching me.

Let him watch.

Where was the condolence? I'd found a friend dead and he'd shown no sympathy. All he wanted to do was try and pin the murder on George. Close the case, narrow his workload.

And yet, the dread turned to nausea. Maybe McNearny was right. George had to be connected somehow.

When I arrived home, Laurie was screaming in Mom's arms.

"She won't take the formula."

I wrinkled my nose at the yellowish bottle Mom was putting in Laurie's face. "I don't blame her."

"You used to love the stuff."

Obviously, my daughter had a more discriminating palate.

I collapsed onto the couch and nursed Laurie. I don't know who was more relieved, me as the burning sensation dissipated from my breasts, Laurie at being fed, or Mom at the peace and quiet.

We sat in silence. I finished nursing Laurie, then rubbed her back, expecting a little burp. Instead, she threw up all over my silk blouse.

I broke down crying, my bravado from facing Inspector McNearny evaporated.

Mom took Laurie from me and placed her in the bassinet, then put her arms around me. "Oh, honey, don't cry," she said, stroking my hair. "It's just the hormones."

I recounted my afternoon for Mom. She listened, her mouth agape.

She rubbed my back. "That's horrible. Just awful, honey. What a shock!" I let her cluck over me, taking comfort in her support.

My head was throbbing, my legs ached, and I had baby spit-up all over my blouse. Not to mention finding Michelle dead and being interrogated by the police.

Not a good day.

I rose from the couch. I needed to change and take some pain medication, at the very least. "Will you come over tomorrow?" I asked Mom.

She hesitated. "There's something I haven't told you as well."

I sat back down on the couch and held my head. Had Mom's car been broken into, too? Or worse, had someone tried to break into the house while I was gone?

"I'm seeing someone," Mom said.

Mom dating?

My parents had been divorced for nearly fifteen years. Mother had said over and over again that she was through with men, that she lived only to have grandchildren.

"What? Who?" I stuttered.

"A very nice man. His name is Hank."

My body surged with a strange combination of happiness and . . . what? Fear? Jealousy? Was I going to have to share my babysitting mother? How selfish of me. I pushed the thought from my mind and hugged her. "And why didn't you tell me this earlier?"

Mom shrugged sheepishly. "I wasn't sure there was anything to tell."

I smiled. "How did you meet?"

"Well," Mom said hesitantly, "I put myself on Match-dot-Com."

Mom using the Internet?

"What?" I sputtered.

"Match-dot-Com, darling. It's a dating service. Online."

"I know what it is. I just . . . I didn't know . . . that you were . . . That's great, Mom. Really great."

"My profile was up for about a week." Mom made herself comfortable on the couch. "I saw his profile. I already knew he worked at the pharmacy down the street, but that's all I knew about him. I didn't know if he was married or anything. When I saw him online, I thought, 'Well, I'll be. He's single!' So I winked at him. They have a little thing on the computer where you can 'wink' at someone. It sends them e-mail from you."

I sat there, stunned. Jim and I had bought Mom a laptop for Christmas last year. Jim had shown her how to get online. I thought she used it only to read the newspaper.

"So, I winked at Hank," Mom continued, "and he winked at me. We e-mailed for a while. Then we thought,

'Well, this is plain silly, we're both in the same neighborhood.' So he invited me out for a cocktail."

I stared at her. "Mom, you don't drink."

"Well, once in a while . . . there's nothing wrong with that," she said defensively.

I laughed, realizing Mom was at it again, telling me a crazy story to take my mind off my problems. "I'm not judging you, Mom. Tell me more."

"I would but you look terrible, Kate. Exhausted."

"Not to mention I have spit-up on my blouse. Let me go change. I'll be right back."

Mom insisted on leaving so I could get some rest, but promised to fill me in on more Hank details later.

Laurie and I were sprawled on the floor, looking at a farm animals picture book. Mostly, I was looking at the book; Laurie was drooling.

"The cow says moo, moo," I ad-libbed.

I heard the key in the front door and scrambled to my feet. I pulled the door open and grabbed Jim around the neck, squeezed him, and inhaled his scent. "Oh, honey, I'm so glad you're home safe."

"What's wrong?"

"I found Michelle dead this morning."

"Oh my God! Why didn't you call me!"

"I knew you had that big presentation today and I didn't want you to worry."

I recounted the experience for him. When I told him I went into Michelle's house, his eyes popped out of his skull as if he were on the verge of a heart attack.

"What if the killer was still in there?"

"I didn't think of that. She was lying on the floor. What if she wasn't dead?"

"You should have waited for the police or the paramed-

ics or whatever. In your car. With the motor running."
He pulled me closer. "I'm glad you're all right, honey.
Promise me you won't go around breaking into people's
houses, especially if there could be a murderer hiding
out."

"I didn't break in. The door was open."

He clutched me tighter. "And you can always call me,
no matter what meeting I'm in." His voice cracked.

I realized he was crying.

"Nothing's going to happen to me," I soothed, running
my fingers through his hair.

"We need you, honey. Laurie and I need you."

"Except I might collapse from exhaustion and/or star-
vation."

Jim smiled, his face brightening a bit.

"Want to call El Paraiso, get delivery?" I asked.

Jim squinted at me. "Yeah. Call. I'll open you some
wine."

"I'm not supposed to drink."

He rose. "Exceptional circumstances call for exceptional measures. One glass won't hurt you, or Laurie."

Jim headed to the kitchen. My mouth began to water as
I thought of a nice dinner and wine.

Wine?

Someone had drunk wine with Michelle. Her killer had
to be someone she knew, since there was no sign of forced
entry. She let someone in, had wine with whoever it was,
and then that person had let themselves out, leaving the door
open for me.

I pictured George going over to Michelle's and sipping
chardonnay with her.

Wait a minute.

George preferred beer, like Jim. He'd probably consider white wine a "girlie" drink.

Could a woman have killed Michelle?

Brad's affair! The other woman?

Why would Brad's lover kill Michelle? If Brad wasn't dead, then her motive would make sense. But with Brad gone, why kill Michelle?

I called after Jim, "Hey, Jim? Does George drink wine?"

Jim returned, a beer in one hand and a glass of merlot in the other. "I guess he does."

"White wine?"

"Probably. I mean, I'm sure it's not his favorite, but I imagine he'd drink it."

There went that theory.

I dialed El Paraiso. "I'd like to order some food for delivery."

The hostess promptly informed me that they *didn't* deliver.

I looked up at Jim's expectant face. "They don't deliver."

"I thought George was supposed to be the delivery guy?" He sighed. "What, did he quit already? Get fired?"

"She said they've never delivered."

Jim's face clouded, his mouth twisting with concern. "Why would Michelle tell you he worked there if he didn't?"

• CHAPTER NINE •

The Third Week—Digging In

I awoke in a state of panic, drenched in sweat. I'd read that the body rids itself of extra fluids from pregnancy by sweating. What I didn't know was if the sweating was from a postpartum symptom or from the frantic dream I'd just had about Michelle.

In the dream I'd been able to revive her. I'd asked her over and over again who had killed her. She'd clung to me, mute.

I glanced at the clock. Five A.M. Laurie and I had both finally drifted to sleep around midnight. Had she really slept five hours?

Was she alive? Panicked, I leaned over the bassinet and frantically put my hand on her tummy.

Her stomach rose slowly and evenly.

I studied her for a moment, her arms raised above her head, a gesture of pure abandonment.

Wait. Five A.M.? She was still asleep? I couldn't believe it.

At the hospital they had instructed me to wake her for her night feeding if she slept through it.

Give me a break. Hadn't they ever heard the adage "Never wake a sleeping baby"? No way was I going to do it. Forget it. If she slept through her feeding, she must not be hungry.

I lay back on my pillow. The sheets crunched as if made of potato chips. I held my breath. Laurie was still out.

I shook Jim. "Laurie's been asleep for five hours!"

"Great," he mumbled.

"Honey, she's been asleep for *five hours*," I repeated.

"You go to sleep, too."

I suppose new moms need to learn how to sleep through the night also.

Closing my eyes, I tried to clear my mind. Visions of Michelle popped into my head again, crowding out all other thoughts. I tried to think about something else. Laurie. Yes. I'd think of Laurie. Sweet Laurie. Innocence. Pure life.

Suddenly my breasts started to leak, soaking my nightgown. Great. Way to go, Kate.

Hold out on the baby and you leak anyway. I may as well feed her, right? Either that or lie here wet and have nightmares.

The breast pump was in the corner of the bedroom. I could get up and learn to use that. I'd need to start stocking up on milk to cover Laurie during the hours I'd be at the office.

The office? Ugh. How much longer on my maternity leave? Three weeks.

Three weeks. Twenty-one days. Five hundred and four hours. Wait. It was already 5 A.M. So that meant four hundred ninety-nine hours.

I closed my eyes. How depressing.

Wasn't there a way to stay home with Laurie? I mulled

over the question, drifting off to sleep, forgetting to feed Laurie, use the pump, or stress over Michelle and George.

It was 9 A.M. Jim had left for the office hours ago. Laurie and I lay in bed, nursing. It seemed like we'd been nursing all morning. Making up for lost nutrition throughout the night.

I felt even more drained now than I had at 5 A.M. We were about to doze off when the doorbell rang. Laurie nodded off. I groaned. I put her into the bassinet and grabbed a robe. Who could it be at this time of day?

I stumbled to the front door and peered out the peephole. All I could see was a broad chest in a blue button shirt. Definitely not UPS.

"Who is it?"

"Investigator Galigani. Is Kate Connolly in?"

The police? What now? Shouldn't he flash his badge at me or something? Was I getting overly paranoid?

"Where's your badge?"

"I'm not with the police. I'm a private investigator."

"Who hired you?"

He bent down to look through the peephole. I saw one green eye peering at me. I involuntarily pulled away.

"Mrs. Avery," he said into the peephole.

"Mrs. Avery is dead," I said.

The eye shifted. "Gloria Avery is dead?"

Who was Gloria?

I placed the chain lock on the door and opened it two inches.

Investigator Galigani was tall, dark, and *not* handsome. He had a huge black mustache on a very round face. He frowned at the chain, which only succeeded in making him look mean and angry.

"I don't know who Gloria is," I said. "I meant Michelle Avery is dead."

"Ah." His face softened a bit. "Are you Kate?"

I nodded.

"May I come in, ma'am?"

There was the "ma'am" again. I glanced down at my pale green terrycloth robe. No! Why did I have to get interrogated again? Especially looking like this.

"I've got a newborn. I'm really tired—"

"It'll only take a minute."

"How do I *know* that you are who you say you are?"

The ends of his mustache turned up. "Here's my card."

What did that prove? I let his card hang between his fingers. He wiggled it at me. I took it.

"Would you like to call Mrs. Avery?" he asked. "She'll verify that she's hired me."

"Do you have a photo ID?"

His face broke apart with laughter. Mustache going one way, bottom lip the other way.

I tried not to be offended. "What good would it do if she says she hired 'Galigani' when all I have to prove that you're Galigani is a business card?"

"You're right. Here you go." He opened his wallet and shoved his driver's license at me. "This, too." He dug into the wallet and pulled out a worn private investigator license from the State of California issued to Albert Galigani.

"What's her number?"

His face registered surprise. "You're actually going to call her?"

"I'm a new mom, my car's been broken into twice, my brother-in-law is missing, and I found my friend dead yesterday. I can't let a stranger into my house. What if you try to kill me?"

"If I was going to kill you, I could have done it through the crack in the door. But please, by all means, call Mrs. Avery."

He was right. He could have already killed me.

I shut the door in his face. He rang the bell again. I ignored him, got out the phonebook.

Ah! Here was an instance where actually using the phonebook would be faster than an online lookup. Okay, so maybe the books were still good for something.

I found two numbers under Avery, Michelle's and another one. I dialed the second one.

The doorbell rang again. Let him wait.

I got voice mail. Of course. No one answers their phone anymore. I left a message. Why couldn't anything be easy? The bell rang yet again. I opened the door with the chain in place.

"Stop ringing the bell. You're going to wake my baby."

He looked contrite. "Sorry. Did you reach her?"

I rolled my eyes. "No. You're going to have to come back after I hear from her."

Now it was his turn to roll his eyes, tilting his head back in a huge dramatic gesture. "Listen, lady," he said on an exhale. "I got a job to do. People are unsafe, like you said yourself. Your friend ended up dead. If someone killed her, it sure as hell wasn't me. I'm one of the good guys." He opened his hands in an imploring gesture. "I'm trying to get to the bottom of this."

I chewed on my lower lip. I believed him. I'd believed him from the start. But the logical part of my brain told me I couldn't just let strangers into my house.

When had I become fraidycat Kate?

"Don't ring the bell again," I warned. I shut the door. I dialed the number on Galigani's card marked MOBILE.

I watched him through the peephole. He stood on my doorstep and waited, ignoring his ringing cell phone.

"Pick it up, it's me," I said, through the door.

He laughed and dug his phone out of a hip pocket. "Hello?"

"What do you want to know?"

"I just need a little info. You knew Brad Avery?"

"No. Just Michelle."

He pulled a little notebook from his pocket; scraps of paper flew out of the back. I watched him pick up the slips of paper from my doorstep, bunch them up, and shove them into his pocket. "Michelle, huh? The second wife."

There was a first? Was that Gloria?

"You found her dead?" he continued.

"How do you know that?"

The ends of his mustache went up. He looked toward the peephole. "It's my job to know. Are you going to open the door?"

He was right. This was ridiculous. I hung up and opened the door.

I motioned him inside. He stepped forward cautiously, eyeing me up and down.

He visibly relaxed. "You know, I'm probably more frightened than you. You know who I am and what I'm doing here. I never know who I'm talking to. For all I know, you could be the murderer."

I opened my mouth to defend myself, but he raised his hand in protest. "I know! I know! You're going to say you're not. Everyone says that. I don't think you are anyway. The guilty ones are never paranoid. They want you to march right in and start asking questions. They like to think they're so smart they can fool you. Hell, sometimes they do."

I gestured toward the sofa, then shoved a pillow and a blanket to the side to make room for him. "Do you want coffee or anything?"

He shook his head and sat. "How did you know Michelle?"

"We went to high school together."

I recounted for him the details of my finding Michelle dead. I left every single George reference out.

He tapped his notebook and squinted at me. "Why do I get the feeling you're hiding something, Mrs. Connolly?"

I shrugged. If he wanted to know anything about George, let him ask me directly.

"Do you know anything about Michelle's investments?"

I frowned. "Investments?"

What exactly was he getting at?

"I understand she and Brad owned a restaurant."

I pressed my lips together to remind to myself to keep my trap shut about George. "Yup, that's about what I know, too."

"Ever been there before?"

"I ate lunch there day before yesterday. My car got broken into in front. I don't think I'll be going back."

He scratched at his mustache. "You mentioned that earlier. Second time, huh?"

What had I said earlier?

"Something about your brother-in-law missing," he continued.

Big-mouth Kate. "That's right," was the best I could muster. I closed my eyes, willing myself to focus. How much did this guy know or need to know?

Could he help us locate George?

"What do you charge?" I wondered out loud.

He squinted at me. "You want your husband followed or something?"

I looked down at my robe. "Do I look that bad?"

His face flushed. "Uh . . . sorry . . . that's the most common thing people want to hire me for. Two hundred dollars an hour."

I gagged. Obviously, I was in the wrong profession.

"You need help locating your brother-in-law?"

I stared at him.

Yes. The answer was yes. Yet I muttered, "Ummm . . . not sure . . ."

Galigani nodded. "You mind telling me where you were on June fifteenth?"

Was he serious? I studied his face. He studied me back.

"I honestly can't remember. I could look it up on my calendar."

"Please," he said, not taking his eyes off me.

"All right," I mumbled as I made my way toward my bedroom, where I kept my appointment calendar.

I grabbed the calendar and peeked in on Laurie. She was as still as a statue. I stood over her, waiting for any kind of movement.

Her foot twitched, followed by some shadow boxing. She settled down after a moment, still asleep.

I heard Galigani shuffling in the living room and quickly made my way back. I paged to June. "Ah yes!" I said. "June fifteenth. I knew it sounded familiar. Our friend Paula's little boy, Danny, turned two. They had a party for him."

"You went to the party?" Galigani asked.

"Of course."

"Was your husband with you?"

My breath caught. I felt as though Galigani had hit me in the stomach with a baseball bat. "Jim and I were at the party all day. Together. Plenty of people saw us."

What I didn't tell Galigani was that Jim had left the party early. He had come down with a terrible sinus headache, which he gets at least once every summer when the pollen count is at its highest in San Francisco. Although Jim didn't like leaving me unescorted, I had insisted he go home, but there was no reason for Galigani to know that.

"Hmmm," Galigani murmured as he scratched his mustache. "Can I see that?" He gestured to my appointment book.

"Sure." I handed Galigani my book, trying to act nonchalant. "I've even got the invite somewhere." I reached over his hands and flipped to the back of my planner. Sure enough, Paula's invite with a picture of a smiling Danny peeked out under the flap. I pulled out the invite. "It says noon to four, but we ended up staying longer. The party probably lasted until about six or seven, then people starting leaving, we stayed. Paula's a close friend. We ordered Thai, watched a movie, and just sort of hung out. Her little boy went to sleep early, exhausted from the excitement of the party, the toys, the people. He kept banging a drum that he got—"

"Yeah, yeah, I know how two-year-old boys can be."

"We probably left around eleven or so." I was using the euphemistic "we" as in the yet unborn Laurie and me. Not a lie, exactly.

Omission. Okay, maybe a white lie.

His mustache twisted to the side, then he nodded. "Your alibi appears iron tight. Mind if I take down your friend's address and number?"

With Paula in France, even if Galigani went to her place, he wouldn't find her home. That would buy me a little time to get to her before he did.

I handed him the invite. "No problem. But why? I mean, Jim and I didn't even know Brad Avery."

He jotted the address down. "I understand, ma'am. There are just a few things I need to check out. Your husband's at work today?"

I felt acid churn in my stomach. "Yes."

"And where's that, ma'am?"

"Fortena and Associates, downtown. He's an ad executive."

Galigani nodded, making his way toward the front door, "Thanks for your time."

I stopped him with a question, "What about yesterday?"

"Excuse me?"

"Don't you want to know where Jim and I were yesterday, you know, when Michelle was killed?"

"I'm only being paid to investigate Mr. Avery's murder."

"Don't you think they're connected?"

He waved his hands around, palms up. "Maybe, but I'm only being *paid* to investigate Mr. Avery's murder," he repeated.

CHAPTER TEN

The Third Week—Reaching Out

From my front window, I watched Galigani squish into his compact car. Where would he go next? To interrogate Jim, or try and find my girlfriend Paula? Maybe he could lead me to George.

Stupid George. I couldn't wait to find him, so I could wring his neck!

I contemplated following Galigani.

Yeah, right.

With a newborn? Like I'd ever be able to get out of the house in time.

I heard Laurie's wake-up call. I went to my bedroom and picked her up from the bassinet.

Cold. Wet. Hungry.

A mother's job is never done. I changed her, swaddled her tight, then settled down on our sofa to nurse her. Even though thirty minutes had passed since Galigani had left, I couldn't shake the odd feeling of violation I'd had during his questioning. I absently looked out the front window again. Galigani's gray Honda was still there. What was he doing hovering outside my house?

Was I being staked out?

Outraged, I gathered Laurie up and ran down my front steps. This guy was getting paid two hundred bucks an hour to sit in his stupid Honda outside my house, while I nursed my baby!

Had I nursed Laurie anywhere near the front window?

As I approached his car, I couldn't resist looking back at my house. The sofa was in plain view. Talk about feeling violated.

By the time I rapped on his window, I was fuming. "What do you think you're doing?"

He rolled down his window. "My car won't start. I called road side service."

Just then a tow truck turned the corner. Galigani jumped out of his Honda and greeted the driver.

I slunk back into the house.

Stupid Kate, jumping to conclusions. Where was that going to lead?

Wait a minute. Galigani was still outside. If I hurried and got dressed, maybe I could follow him after all.

I pulled on jeans and a sweatshirt and glanced out the front window. He was jabbering with the tow truck driver. With Laurie in my arms, I raced downstairs to the garage and packed her into her car seat.

I rolled the car out of the garage and waved to Galigani as I turned the corner.

I parked at the end of the next block, comfortably tucked in between a pickup and a UPS van. From this vantage point I could follow him in whichever direction he drove.

I waited. Galigani's Honda passed me. I pulled out behind him, hoping to keep a discreet distance.

Galigani led me to an apartment house in the Haight district. I watched from my car as he rang a bell and waited.

A curtain moved on the third floor. Someone peeked out the window. Galigani didn't notice, just continued to wait without being let in.

I counted the windows. Six from the right. Probably each apartment had two street windows. So that would make it the third apartment from the right. Third floor, third apartment. Easy to remember.

Galigani rang the doorbell again. After a moment, he turned to leave.

He squeezed back into his car. The car sputtered and died.

Shoot!

I couldn't wait around for another visit from road side service. By the time they'd arrive, I'd have to feed Laurie again.

The Honda turned over again and the engine revved up. Galigani pulled out of his space. The chase was on.

I followed him to Pier 23. The pier where George's bags had been found. Where poor Brad had been pulled from the water. I watched as Galigani paced back and forth and took notes. He stopped a couple of passersby and talked for a while. His job didn't seem that tough. Ask questions, drive around some, and charge a lot of money. I could do that, couldn't I?

I puttered around the kitchen, getting dinner ready. Mom had left a homemade lasagna and a box wrapped in comics from the Sunday paper on my front porch. The box had a note attached.

Must have missed you. Here's a little something I couldn't resist for Laurie. Not the lasagna—that's for you. I put plenty of vegetables in it. Are you getting enough greens? Hope you are feeling better today. Call me—must see my granddaughter soon. Mom.

Thank God for Mom. I was pressed for time and the lasagna was a Godsend. I placed it into the oven and put the gift for Laurie in front of her. She eyed the paper and drooled.

"Grandma got you this. Want to open it?"

Laurie reached out and batted the present.

"I'll help you." I ripped open the paper. It was a colorful jack-in-the-box. It popped up with no warning. Laurie howled.

I grabbed the cordless phone and dialed Mom. "Hi, it's me."

"Darling! Where have you been?"

"Here and there. Thanks for the lasagna."

Mom chuckled. "I thought you might like that. Did Laurie like her little surprise?"

"It scared the bejeezes out of her."

"Oh, no! Well, maybe she's still too little. You used to love yours."

I had had a jack-in-the-box? What happens to your memory? Is it the pregnancy? Postpregnancy? Or just plain hitting thirty?

"How are you feeling?" Mom asked.

"All right. Tired. Can you come over tomorrow and watch Laurie?"

"Sure. Where are you going?"

I hesitated. Better not to share my real plans with her, she'd only worry. "Oh, nowhere in particular, maybe do a little shopping. Can you be here around noon?"

Jim called to say he would be home late. I took advantage of the extra time to bathe Laurie.

I set the little green tub into our kitchen sink and ran lukewarm water into it, then laid out all the essentials: a pink hooded terry towel, a yellow ducky washcloth, and special baby body and hair wash.

Undressing Laurie, I gently placed her in the tub. She curled her lips in protest, but as the warm water poured over her she cooed happily.

I put a small drop of the baby wash on the ducky washcloth and rubbed her tiny toes.

"You have tic-tac toes," I said, squeezing each of them between my fingers.

Laurie gave me what looked like a smile.

The doctor said I wouldn't get any real smiles until about six weeks, that any resemblance to a smile was simply Laurie practicing the use of her facial muscles.

Hmmm!

What did that doctor know anyway? This was really a smile. My little jelly bean was a genius.

I tickled her toes again. "This little piggy went to market."

Laurie blinked up at me. Suddenly, I noticed she had grown beautiful black eyelashes. She was so fair that her eyebrows were barely visible. The same had been true about her eyelashes, until today.

"When did you get those gorgeous long black lashes?"

Laurie flapped a response, then turned her head and examined the side of the tub. I finished bathing her, then laid out her towel and gingerly picked her up. I patted her dry as I made my way into the nursery.

The nursery window was open. I rushed to close it. I didn't want Laurie to catch a cold.

Wait.

When had I opened the window? Had I opened it?

Oh, how I wish I had a memory. Any memory at all would be good. My mind was a sieve.

Maybe Jim had opened it before leaving for work. Had it been open all day? My stomach lurched as I glanced around the room. Nothing looked displaced.

A loud beeping sounded throughout the house. The smoke detector. I had forgotten the lasagna in the oven.

I ran toward the kitchen with a howling Laurie in my arms.

"Shh, it's okay, pinochle," I soothed, staring at the oven.

How do you get a burning lasagna out of the oven with an infant in your arms?

I returned to the nursery to put Laurie down, then remembered the window. What if a stranger was in the house? After all, our cars had been broken into. My address was out there in someone's hands. The logical part of my brain was telling me to calm down, but I looked around for a weapon anyway.

Then I heard the footsteps.

Someone was in the house!

Suppressing the scream rising in my throat, I grabbed the cordless and raced with Laurie into the only hiding place I could think of. The closet.

I concealed us as best I could behind some clothes. My heart was racing. I said a prayer as I dialed 9-1-1. The smoke alarm was still ringing.

The operator said, "What is the nature of your emergency?"

"Someone's broken into my house. Please send the police. Hurry, I have a baby!"

Suddenly, the smoke detector stopped. I hung up. I didn't want to give away our hiding place.

Could 9-1-1 trace my call? Could they get my address?

I pressed Laurie to me, trying to keep her quiet. Thankfully, she seemed lulled by the darkness of the closet and her proximity to my wildly beating heart.

I heard the door to nursery creak open.

Dear God. What could I do?

I nestled Laurie onto a fallen jacket on the floor. She seemed content enough to stay quiet. I straightened. If the intruder opened the door, I wanted to be ready.

Ready for what?

The fight of my life.

I clenched my fists and prepared myself. I heard footsteps circle the nursery, then exit.

Air rushed back into lungs. Could it be that the intruder would simply leave?

I heard the footsteps retreat down the hall, then return. This time Laurie betrayed me, letting out an enormous wail.

The door to the closet swung open.

I yelled out my best self-defense karate scream—"Hiyaah!"—while kicking and punching with blind fury. The heel of my foot caught the intruder square in the groin, doubling him over.

Uh-oh!

The intruder was Jim.

He fell to his knees, glaring at me in disbelief. "Kate? What's going on?"

Relief rushed over me. "Darling! Jim! Oh, I'm so sorry! I thought you were . . . I thought . . . the window . . ." I embraced him, tears burning my eyes.

"Where's Laurie?"

I rushed back into the closet and picked her up.

Jim got to his feet. "What are you doing in the closet with the baby?" He scooped her out of my arms. "And why are you screaming at me and kicking me in the—"

"The window was open. I burned the lasagna. The alarm went off. I heard footsteps. You said you were going to be late."

Tears spilled down my cheeks, exhaustion overcoming me. I collapsed into the rocker by Laurie's crib and sobbed.

Jim put Laurie into her baby swing and knelt down beside me. He took me into his arms.

We heard sirens screaming down the block.

"Oh. And I called 9-1-1," I whimpered.

"Let me get this straight. Did you say you *burned* the lasagna?" he said through a smile.

After reporting the false alarm to the police officers on our doorstep, we ate the burned lasagna in silence.

I filled Jim in on Galigani's visit, finally asking, "You remember June fifteenth?"

"No. Should I? It's not our anniversary or anything, right?"

"We were at Paula's party."

Jim took a swig of beer, shrugging his shoulders. "So?"

"You left early," I prodded. "You said you weren't feeling well. Sinus headache. Remember?"

"Not really. So what does it matter now? It's October."

"June fifteenth was the night Brad Avery was murdered."

Jim stared at me. He put his beer down. "What are you trying to say, Kate?"

"Galigani asked me what we were doing that night. You left the party early. You *said* you weren't feeling well. I'm wondering where you went."

I tried to ignore the queasiness in my stomach.

"I came home." He said it slowly, enunciating every syllable as though I were a two-year-old.

"That's just the thing, Jim. I remember calling home that night. You didn't pick up."

He took a slow sip of his beer. He smiled widely, then laughed. Was it a nervous laugh?

"Come on, honey. Cut me some slack. I was probably asleep." He reached out to touch my shoulder.

I sighed. He wrapped his arms around me. I inhaled his familiar scent, a mixture of wind and trees. The nervousness in my stomach dissipated a bit.

He squeezed my shoulders. "You're getting too wrapped up in this Brad Avery stuff. You're letting it make you a little goofy, honey."

I stiffened and pulled away from him. "What do you mean?"

"Christ, Kate, you're starting to hallucinate. Intruders in the house? Asking me where I was on the night some guy I don't even know was killed."

"George knew him."

Jim frowned. "What are you saying? I haven't seen George for months. What? You think I secretly met up with him and helped him murder someone?"

"No. I don't think that." I shook my head and let out a sigh. "Do you think George . . . Do you think he *could* kill someone?"

Jim raised his shoulders. "I don't know." He voice softened and his shoulders dropped. "He's impulsive, irresponsible, and has a temper. Do I think George is a cold-blooded murderer? No. Do I think he could have killed someone under certain circumstances?"

He let his question hang in the air. Both of us nodded to each other, knowing the answer was a definite yes.

After a moment I asked, "Why would that investigator ask where we were that night?"

"Kate, they ask questions. That's what they do. He probably asks everyone the same questions. Why did you even talk to the guy?"

Images of Michelle's body on the floor flooded my mind. I willed myself not to cry. "I found Michelle dead. I wanted to help."

Jim stroked my hand. "Honey, I know having a baby is stressful. It's stressful for me. I can't fathom how it is for you, much less with all this other stuff going on. But you can't let your imagination run away with you. Focus on recuperating. You'll have to be back at work in a couple of weeks."

I sat dumbfounded as he cleared the plates from the table. "What if I don't want to go back to work?"

Jim's eyes clouded. "We all have to do things we don't want to do. I wish we could afford for you to stay home. What do you want me to say, Kate? You know the cost of living in San Francisco. You want to live anyplace else besides California? Montana or Nebraska?"

I shook my head and took a deep breath, fighting the overwhelming urge to cry again.

"We talked about this before? Remember?" Jim asked.

"I didn't know I'd feel this way."

"What way?"

"She needs me, Jim. She's so tiny. She needs me. I knew that. I knew she would, of course. I just didn't know I'd need her." I sighed again. "Do you know how much Galigani gets paid?"

"No, and I don't care. Whatever it is, I'm sure he's worth it. I'm sure he has plenty of *experience* doing whatever he's doing."

"He talks to people all day. I have plenty of experience talking, too."

Jim scrunched up his face. "The point is, Kate, he has a client."

CHAPTER ELEVEN

The Third Week—Grasping

I had a fitful night, tossing and turning during the short time Laurie was asleep. When I awoke, Jim had already left for work.

It was time to acquaint myself with the dreaded breast pump.

After carefully reading the instructions twice and not understanding anything, I decided on the trial-and-error method.

I plugged the pump in and hooked up all the tubes and components the best I could. It didn't hurt as much as I thought it would, but it didn't yield that much milk either. I looked at the pitiful three ounces that I'd pumped. An ounce and a half from each breast. How was that ever supposed to sustain Laurie?

Maybe I had hooked it up wrong.

I grabbed my notebook and stretched out across the bed.

To Do:

1. Lose weight, when can I start exercising?

2. Call work—YUK!

3. Plan alternate career! Can I work from home?

4. Where is George? Does he live at the apartment on Haight?

5. E-mail Paula about alibi for June fifteenth—just in case.

6. Research postpartum paranoia online.

7. Get a haircut.

I logged on to the computer to e-mail Paula. I attached photos of Laurie, asked her how to use the breast pump, caught her up on all the drama around Michelle and George, and finally requested an alibi for June fifteenth. After that, I researched "postpartum paranoia." Every single reference was accompanied by the words "delusion," "hallucination," and "psychosis."

Good grief! Psychosis?

Was I psychotic? Delusional? Wait a minute, no one had broken into my house last night, that much was true, but I *had* found a dead body.

The ringing phone interrupted me from further analysis. I hurried to reach it before Laurie awoke.

"Is this Kate Connolly?" asked a soft female voice with a Russian accent.

"Yes."

"You called me yesterday. I didn't hire an investigator."

"Mrs. Avery?" I asked.

"Svetlana."

"Oh. Sorry. I was trying to reach Gloria Avery," I said.

"Gloria?" her voice sounded alarmed.

"Yes. Do you know her?"

"My mother . . . well, er, mother-in-law," Svetlana said.

The first wife.

"Gloria hired an investigator?" Svetlana asked.

"I think so. That's what this guy said."

Svetlana let out a breath. "Ohh . . ." Silence filled the line. Finally she asked, "Can we meet?"

I clicked Laurie's car seat into the base in the backseat and took off toward Chestnut Street, the metro hip part of San Francisco.

Nothing like an outing to avoid further self-analysis.

I was meeting Svetlana at a teahouse. I had never been to one before and was mildly curious about it, although not as curious as I was about Svetlana.

What could she want to meet me about?

I found parking in a much too small space in front of the teahouse. My bumper hit both cars front and back as I crammed my Cavalier in.

Love taps. Hope the owners aren't in sight.

At least I'd be able to watch my car from inside the tea shop and make sure no one broke into it.

I grabbed Laurie's little bucket car seat and stared into her face. Still sleeping.

Had she even moved?

I gently shook her. She woke up and began to wail.

Great, wake a sleeping baby!

I glanced at my watch. I had been so nervous about being late that I was early. Time to kill, I might as well nurse Laurie in the comfort of my Cavalier.

I settled my feet on her diaper bag, which was squashed in between the baby carrier and a first aid kit.

Maybe the car wasn't so comfortable.

Where had all this gear come from? The infant car seat

took up two-thirds of the backseat and the rest was occupied with rattles, blankets, and stuffed dolls.

I had to clear out my car.

Another item to add to my to-do list.

I watched a tall, elegant woman make her way to the front door of the teahouse. She had straight black hair and was dressed in brown slacks with a russet-colored shawl wrapped around her shoulders. Could that be Svetlana? I finished nursing Laurie and swaddled her tight. She needed a diaper change. There was no room to do it in the car, so the ladies' restroom in the teahouse would have to do.

I nestled her back into the removable car seat and picked up the entire bucket. This bucket was starting to be a real pain. It had seemed so light when we purchased it, testing it against all the other models. But now it seemed to weigh a ton.

Thank God I had parked close.

I stepped inside the teahouse and into another century. Beautiful lace curtains covered the windows, and the pink walls were decorated with fine china from around the world.

I wondered if my postpartum butt would fit on any of the delicate chairs.

The lone customer was the lady I had seen walk in. She eyed me curiously.

"Svetlana?" I asked.

She stood. "Kate? I didn't know you had a baby!"

"Yes." I hobbled over to her, trying to tread lightly. My pelvic bones hadn't stopped hurting since the outing from the other day, and the bruise on the back of my leg didn't help matters.

She pulled out a tiny chair for me. I dropped my bag onto the floor and settled Laurie's bucket beside my chair.

"How old is she?"

"Three weeks."

Svetlana gasped. "In Russia, we never take such small baby out."

More reprimands? What, indeed, was I doing out of the house? Laurie ogled up at Svetlana.

"This is why I love America," she continued. "Baby girl will learn fast."

My guilt was assuaged for the moment. What would I be doing at home anyway? Sleeping? Laurie kicked off her blanket. Ha! Not likely. I yawned as I pulled the blanket up over her again.

"Where's the restroom?"

Svetlana pointed to the back. I removed Laurie from her car seat and picked up her diaper bag. Everything now, even using the restroom, was an ordeal.

As I entered the restroom, I realized that I wouldn't be able to change Laurie. There was no diaper stand, only a small Victorian sink and a retro toilet. I wouldn't even be able to use the toilet myself, since I couldn't very well put Laurie on the floor.

I returned to the table and grabbed the Godforsaken car seat bucket. I packed Laurie into it and made my way back to the restroom.

I changed Laurie's diaper in the bucket seat. Then Laurie watched from her little bucket cocoon as I relieved myself in the Victorian toilet.

Would life be any easier if I returned to the corporate world?

Laurie, as if reading my thoughts, let out a little cry in protest.

I held my finger out to her, which she grasped tightly. "Easier maybe, but not nearly as much fun, peanut."

Svetlana ordered us green tea, cucumber sandwiches, and raspberry cookies. The cucumber sandwiches arrived looking a little lackluster. Svetlana gobbled one up. I joined her.

How could I lose any weight if I ate even the unappetizing stuff?

The teacups were tiny, like having a shot of tea. I had to refill my cup after one sip.

"You were married to Brad?" I asked.

Svetlana nodded, washing down another sandwich with tea. "Three years. We had a lot of trouble. He met Michelle and . . ." She made a gesture with her hands, placing her index fingers together then pulling them apart to demonstrate a split.

Brad had left Svetlana for Michelle? How's that for motive?

"How did you two meet?"

"In school. I study baking. Brad cooking."

The restaurant, of course.

"We drink tea after class." She gestured around. "This was our favorite place. Our old school is around the corner."

"Do you know what happened to Brad?" I asked.

Her eyes searched mine, giving me the feeling she was trying to gauge what I knew. "Police find him in the bay, right?"

I nodded.

"How do you know Brad?" she asked.

"I didn't know him. Michelle was an old friend from high school."

Svetlana looked deflated. "Oh. Michelle," she said, then crammed a cookie into her mouth.

Oops, wrong subject to bring up.

"Why did you want to meet with me?" I asked, trying to get her mind off the woman who had stolen her husband.

Svetlana snapped to attention. "Did Gloria's investigator ask about me?"

"No. Why would he? We don't even know each other."

"Gloria doesn't like me. I wonder if she hire inspector to deport me back to Russia."

"I imagine she hired him to help the police find out what happened to Brad."

Svetlana's lips twitched. "Gloria doesn't like me," she repeated. "I open new business six months ago. I can't go back to Russia now. I have new beginning here."

I nodded. "When was the last time you saw Brad?"

"My birthday. June ninth. Why?"

"You kept in touch?"

She studied Laurie. "We had a baby, Brad and me. We stay in touch."

A child had lost her father. With the hormones in my system, I couldn't control the emotions that flooded me. I grabbed at a napkin and dabbed my eyes, trying to fan myself at the same time.

"Was he going through anything unusual the last time you saw him?"

She frowned. "Unusual?"

"Anything strange. You know, anything out of the ordinary going on in his life?"

She shrugged, keeping her eyes on the floor. "He told me he wanted to leave Michelle. He was in love with someone else."

Nice pattern. Jerk.

"Yes. Michelle told me he was having an affair, that he left her on June fifteenth. The night the police think he was murdered."

Svetlana nodded. Her composure had shifted; her shoulders drooped a little and she seemed withdrawn.

Could Brad and Svetlana have rekindled their love affair?

"Do you know who Brad was in love with?" I asked.

She covered her eyes for moment. "No. Someone from restaurant, I think. Brad always there. Had to be someone from there."

I took a stab in the dark. "Do you know George Connolly?"

Svetlana's face was blank. "Your husband?"

"No. My husband's brother. I think he works at El Paraiso."

She shook her head. "No. I don't know anyone from there. Except the manager, Rich. He was the best man at our wedding."

Ah. Mr. Creepy.

Remembering him caused my hair to stand on end.

"So, you know Rich pretty well?"

Svetlana adjusted her shawl. "He was a friend of Brad's. They were friends for long time, but he's not reliable. When you need a friend, you cannot depend on Rich." She looked down at her hands. "The police call my house to know where I was June fifteenth. I was home. Alone. I don't go out much anymore. Not since . . ." She studied her nails.

I drank another shot of tea and waited in silence. After a moment she said, "My baby drowned. Three years ago."

Every mother's nightmare. My heart tightened and I suddenly felt panicky. Tears flooded my eyes. "Oh my God! I'm so sorry to hear that!"

I grabbed another napkin to wipe my eyes. Svetlana was crying freely, not making any noise, just letting the tears, blackened by mascara, fall down her face.

I pulled Laurie's car seat closer to me and glanced down at her sleeping angel face.

"Brad always blamed me . . . now the police come to ask questions, and Gloria has an investigator. Baby dead, Brad dead. Gloria think only person can be responsible is Svetlana. But I never hurt my baby, or Brad."

"Why would Brad blame you?"

"I took Penny to the park. There is a big lake . . . they had little boats to rent. I thought she'd have fun . . ." Her eyes glazed over. "I was buying popcorn. Penny by my side. She was two. They don't listen. I told her to stay by my side. Then a stranger talking to me, someone spilled a soda, someone yelling . . . When I turn around, Penny gone. She fall in the lake. I can't swim, but I jump in. People help us, but it was too late. I was in hospital for long time." She pointed to her temple. "Depression. Brad blamed me. Gloria blamed me. I blamed me, too. But doctors say it wasn't my fault."

I put my hand on hers. She held my hand a moment, then said, "I tell you, Kate. I didn't hurt Brad, but I'm not sorry he's dead."

We sat in awkward silence. The waitress swung our way. "Anything else, ladies?"

Svetlana looked at me and asked, "Kate?"

Before I could I answer, the waitress said, "I'll leave the dessert menu. Give it a look and let me know."

Svetlana squinted at the menu, then held it farther away. She pulled her handbag off the back of the chair and rummaged through it. She sighed.

"What's wrong?" I asked.

"I don't have my glasses."

I read the dessert menu out loud. Each cake, pie, and pastry was paired with a recommended wine.

"Oooh, who can resist the 'chocolate trio'?" I raised my eyebrows at Svetlana. "A sampling of three chocolate desserts: the chocolate mousse, an orange chocolate pâté in a filo coconut crust, and warm chocolate bread pudding."

Svetlana listened and smiled. "Sounds good. But no. I will have wine. And you?"

No fun eating chocolate by yourself.

"Nothing for me."

Svetlana waved down the waitress and ordered a chardonnay.

My heart quickened.

Relax, Kate. Everybody drinks wine. It doesn't mean a thing.

I poured myself another shot of tea. "Svetlana, can you tell me where you were yesterday morning?"

Her face registered surprise. "Yesterday? I stay home. Sometimes I still . . . it's not good. I know. But sometimes I still feel depression."

"Did you talk to anyone? Can anyone verify you were home?" Now I was starting to sound like Galigani.

Hmmm.

Svetlana shook her head. "When I get depression, I get a migraine, too. So I don't talk to anyone, just try to sleep. Why?"

"I found Michelle Avery dead yesterday."

Svetlana inhaled a deep sharp breath, then closed her eyes and pressed her hands to her temples. "Oh, no!" she gasped, leaning forward in her chair as the waitress placed the chardonnay in front of her.

Svetlana pushed the wine aside. "Migraine coming on."

"Is there something I can do for you?" I asked.

"No. No. Thank you. Must go. Very sorry, Kate." She dug into her purse and pulled money out. When she placed it on the table, her face contorted in pain.

"Don't worry about that," I said.

She waved off my concern about the bill. She kissed her fingers and wiggled them at Laurie, then disappeared through the side door.

I sat in silence, starting at Svetlana's wine. She hadn't known about Michelle? I leaned forward and peeked at Laurie. Still snoozing. The wine beckoned me. Oh well, a small sip wouldn't hurt. I sipped the wine and scribbled *"Missing glasses, drinks chardonnay, but was surprised about Michelle . . . ?"* onto a napkin.

Hmmm.

I'd need to remember to pack my notebook if I was going to launch a new career as a PI.

I settled Laurie into the car and drove home to meet Mom. She was going to watch Laurie this afternoon while I went to the Haight.

To do what? Ring doorbells, looking for George?

What was I thinking? Just because Galigani got paid two hundred an hour didn't mean I was going to. After all, Jim was right. Galigani had a paying client. I was just being nosy.

Still the idea of being in business for myself was incredible. It would mean I wouldn't have to return to my office in three weeks.

After settling Laurie in with Mom, I searched out my notepad and took off. I easily located the apartment house from the day before, but parking was a challenge. I finally found a spot about half an hour later and ended up walking six long blocks to the apartment house.

The smell of incense wafted from the little stores that populated Haight Street. I was asked for money at least four times by homeless people. Each time I passed a transient, I studied his face. None even remotely looked like George. Could he really be on the street?

I stopped to stretch my legs. I had forgotten to take Motrin before I left the house and was hoping that stretching would alleviate some of the now familiar achiness in my hips and legs.

Why hadn't anyone warned me about this soreness? I'd heard, "Your life will never be the same after the baby," but no one said, "You'll never be able to walk again."

I finally made it to the apartment doorstep and examined the call box.

Third floor, third apartment: 303 seemed to make sense. The label next to 303 read JENNIFER MILLER.

My shoulder slumped.

What had I hoped for? George's name to be firmly affixed? Hey, I could still get lucky. Maybe this was George's girlfriend.

Or Brad's mystery lady?

Galigani had wanted something from Jennifer.

What now? Ring the bell and ask her what exactly?

What the hell. God hates a coward.

I pressed my thumb into the buzzer. The door beeped and opened. I had been let in without any questions.

Why would I be buzzed in and not Galigani?

I made my way to the third floor and was surprised to find the door to 303 propped open.

A woman wearing a flowing printed dress stood beside the door. She had long blond hair twisted into a braid. Two mangy cats, one gray the other black, caressed her bare feet and legs.

She didn't seem George's type.

Or Brad's either, for that matter.

George always seemed to go for small ethnic women. And Brad? This woman was nothing like Michelle or Svetlana, both of whom were tall and thin, with dark hair and classical beauty. This lady was a stereotypical hippie, a free spirit.

My heart sank.

"Hi, what can I do you for ya?" she asked.

"Sorry to disturb you. I'm Kate Connolly. I'm looking for George Connolly."

She looked past me, down the hallway. "Maybe you better come in."

She prepared tea while I made myself comfortable in the living room. Well, as comfortable as I could since there was no furniture to sit on, only a few cushions. I sat cross-legged on one, then pulled my freshly packed notebook from my bag. The cats perched themselves on the other cushions. The gray cat studied me, while the black one groomed itself.

A bicycle was propped up in a corner. I supposed she biked everywhere. Good for the environment. Good for Jennifer.

I thought back to how the six-block walk had wiped me out. Before getting pregnant, I ran three miles daily. Now I wouldn't be able to run to save my life. I'd have to start up an exercise routine again soon, try and work off the baby weight.

Jennifer returned holding two chipped mugs. She passed me one that said NO WAR on it. Then with her free hand, she picked up the gray cat and sat on the cushion, placing the cat in her lap. The black cat got up and climbed onto Jennifer's lap on its own.

"You know George?" I asked.

She sipped tea from her mug, which had a butterfly on it. "Yeah. We used to work together at a restaurant downtown."

"El Paraiso?"

She nodded. "You know it?"

So that's why Galigani had wanted to talk to her. She had worked at El Paraiso.

Her boss had been murdered. He probably needed to talk to all the employees.

Did that include George?

I brought the mug to my lips.

Hold on a second. Brad and Michelle were both dead. This lady could be a murderer. Certainly it couldn't be a good idea to ingest something she had prepared for me. I scribbled a note in my notebook: *Next time interviewing suspect bring own water.*

"I was at El Paraiso the other day. Looking for George," I said, placing the mug on the floor beside me.

"He owe you money or something?"

"No, no. Nothing like that. It's just . . . well, my husband and I haven't seen him in a long time. Do you know where I can find him?" I asked.

"I only see him now and then. Not regular anymore, since I stopped working at El Paraiso."

"When did you stop working there?"

A strand of blond hair had worked its way free from her braid. She tucked it behind an ear. "End of May."

"Do you know what George does there?"

She looked at me for a second, slowly placing her tea-cup down. "Are you with the police?"

This was the second time someone had asked me about being in law enforcement. What could George be doing?

I plucked stray cat fur off my pants. "I heard George did delivery but I called to order something the other night and was told they don't deliver."

Jennifer smirked.

"Do you know if he still works there?" I asked.

She nodded. "I heard he's still there."

"From who?"

She crossed her arms in front of her. "I'm pretty good friends with the manager, Rich."

Him again?

"Did you know the owner, Brad Avery?"

Her eyes clouded over. "Sure. Course."

"You know he was killed?"

"Yeah, Rich told me. Awful, huh. Somebody shot him!" She closed her eyes and shook her head. "What kind of world are we living in?" She tsked.

"I know." I tsked along with her.

"Rich told me Brad was killed in June. His body must have been weighed down somehow all this time in the bay." Jennifer shuddered. "It's terrible."

"It's a shame," I agreed.

I leaned in close, trying a girlfriend to girlfriend, very confidential, tactic. I used my best stage whisper. "I think Brad was having a tough time with his marriage." Jennifer eyes grew wide. I waved off her shock. "You probably already knew that."

She circled the top of her mug with her finger. "What do you mean?"

"I was friends with his wife. He was leaving her for another woman."

She looked around uncomfortably.

"He left her on June fifteenth, the same day he was murdered," I continued.

Jennifer sipped her tea. "I was with my boyfriend, Winter, on June fifteenth."

"How do you remember that?" I asked.

"Easy. I was with him every night in June, July, and August. Our first night apart was Labor Day."

"Can you think of anyone who would want to kill Brad?" I pressed.

She tapped her teacup, shrugging. "I don't know. What about his wife? You said he left her. Or the ex? He'd been married before and I don't think it ended well."

She seemed to know a lot about him.

"What do you know about the ex?" I asked.

"Svetlana?" Her eyes darted around the room. "Not much. She's cool."

"Were you close to Brad?"

She retreated slightly. "He was my boss. People gossip about the boss is all."

"Anyone gossip about who he was seeing?"

She flushed. "People gossip about everything. You're friends with the wife. I'm sure you know."

Know what?

I shook my head. "Michelle didn't know who he was seeing."

She pressed her lips together for a moment. "Well, let's keep it that way," she spat.

"That won't be hard. She's dead."

Jennifer gasped. "Oh my God!" She covered her mouth with a ring-ladened hand, shaking her head back and forth in denial. "What happened?"

"I don't know. I found her dead in her house yesterday."

She rose and crossed to a bureau, opened a drawer, and pulled out a bong. "Want a hit?"

"No. No. I'll pass."

She frowned. "It's just a little weed, no big deal."

"I just had a baby. I'm nursing," I explained, mentally kicking myself. Why did I have to defend myself and my choices to this woman I barely knew?

"Suit yourself," she said.

"Were you with Winter yesterday morning?"

"Winter? No. I was working. I work down the street at Heavenly Haight. I open the store every morning at eight A.M."

"Where was your boyfriend yesterday?"

"What?"

I was fishing now, but I pressed on. "Out of curiosity, where was Winter?"

Jennifer looked down a moment. She took her time preparing the bong. "Winter and I broke up. I thought he was pretty cool at first, but it wasn't working out. I don't know where he was yesterday."

"Do you have his phone number?"

"You want to talk to him?" she asked, shocked.

"My friend is dead. I'd like to talk to anyone who could help."

Begrudgingly she gave me Winter's full name and phone number.

Something didn't ring true. I wanted to check her story with Winter, but first I had to go home. It was time to feed Laurie. My breasts were starting to hurt. I worried about mastitis, although I wasn't entirely sure what it was. Could it be related to plugged milk ducts? I didn't know what that was either. Whatever they were, neither sounded good, and I knew I didn't want them.

CHAPTER TWELVE

The Third Week—Ah

I steered the Chevy home, and nearly had a heart attack when I saw Galigani's Honda parked across the street.

Was he staking out my house?

Don't get paranoid, Kate.

I pulled into the garage and ran upstairs. Mother was watching the Spanish language station. Laurie was asleep in the bassinet.

"What are you doing?" I asked Mom.

"I'm trying to learn Spanish."

"Why?" I glanced at the screen. *El Gordo y La Flaca* was on.

"Because Hank asked me to go with him on a cruise to the Mexican Riviera."

I strained to look out the window at Galigani's car.

"Did anyone call or ring the bell or anything?"

"No. So, is it okay with you, dear?"

"What?"

"I'll only be gone a week. But I wanted to make sure I clear any vacation plans with you first. Because of Laurie.

Who'll watch her when you need to go shopping? What did you get anyway?" She searched the floor for shopping bags.

"Oh. Nothing. Nothing fit."

Mother mistook my distraction as disappointment. "Don't worry, dear, it's only been a few weeks. You'll get your figure back in no time."

"Mom, I need to go downstairs a minute, okay?"

She stared after me as I closed the front door behind me and ran down the steps.

Was Galigani having trouble with his car again?

As I approached, I noticed he was slumped over the steering wheel. I felt faint.

Oh, sweet Jesus. Not again.

I knocked on his window. He didn't move. I couldn't tell if he was breathing or not. He looked pretty lifeless.

Had someone killed Galigani in front of my house?

I ran back inside the house, ignoring the excruciating pain that shot through my hips and pelvic bones. I grabbed the phone and dialed 9-1-1.

Mom noticed the alarm on my face. "What it is, dear?"

"I don't know." *Please don't be dead,* I prayed. "There's a man parked outside and he's slumped over the steering wheel."

Mother rushed to the window. "Do you know him?"

I shrugged my shoulders noncommittally, not wanting to lie again, but not wanting to tell the truth either. How many white lies can a person tell before it catches up to her? Before she becomes a liar?

"Is he a neighbor?" Mom persisted, squinting through the front window, trying to get a good look into the Honda.

I ignored Mom and told the 9-1-1 operator what I knew.

The operated asked, "Does it appear that a crime has

been committed? Does the victim have a gunshot wound or anything?"

"Not that I can tell. He's doubled over the steering wheel."

"Does he respond when you knock on the window?"

"No."

"Do you know CPR?"

"Yes."

"All right, ma'am, I'm calling the EMTs. They'll be there shortly. In the meantime, you can try to gain access to the car and attempt CPR."

Maybe I could break a window?

Well, at least I knew there was no one lurking in the car.

I searched my front room for a heavy object.

Nothing.

I ran to the closet and fumbled around inside. The best I could do was grab a broom. I sprinted down the steps.

Please don't be dead, don't be dead, don't be dead, I chanted as I made my way toward Galigani's car.

Mom watched from the window as I swung the broom over my head.

Wait. I hadn't even tried the doors. I let the broom drop to the ground and tried the driver's door.

The door opened. I could hear sirens approaching. I pulled Galigani away from the steering wheel. His body was wet and hot. Blood?

I shook him and called his name, trying to get a better look at him and any injuries he might have. As I pulled him toward the open door and light, he tumbled onto the cement, taking me with him. The sirens grew louder. Suddenly, I was looking straight into the grill of a rapidly approaching fire truck.

Please God, don't let me die this way.

I tried to push Galigani's huge mass off me. He

weighed a ton, but I had a tiny infant to live for. I heaved against him with all my might. My forgotten ab muscles were screaming out, as if to say: "Sure! You don't work us for nine months and now you want action?"

Tires screeched and ground into the cement.

My heart was in my throat. The truck had stopped inches from me.

I took as deep a breath as I could, with Galigani on top of me.

I tried again to push him off me. I could see boots approaching. Two pairs.

The men in the boots rolled Galigani off me. I gasped for air. One gave Galigani CPR. The other bent over me. I tried to get up. He restrained my shoulders with his hands.

"Lie still, ma'am," he said, hovering over me. His breath smelled like mint. His brown eyes searched my face.

"I'm fine."

"Even so, just give me a minute." He wrapped his fingers under my head and gave me a gentle head massage. "Just looking for any abnormalities."

"I've often thought my head should be examined for abnormalities."

He smiled. "From the fall. You don't seem to have any."

I refrained from telling him where I'd landed, lest he want to check my ass for any abnormalities. He helped me to my feet. I glanced over at Galigani. No blood. His shirt was soaked through with sweat. What could have happened?

Another car approached.

A police cruiser.

Inspector McNearny lurched out of the car and approached the firefighter who'd been helping me. They discussed something in hushed tones. The other firefighter continued to give Galigani CPR.

I stepped forward to see how Galigani was progressing and hell, I'll admit it, to try and eavesdrop on McNearny. My foot kicked something on the ground.

Galigani's notebook!

Without taking my eyes off McNearny, I quickly scooped it up and slipped it into my back pocket.

After a moment, McNearny broke away and approached me.

"What a *coincidence*," I said in my best sarcastic tone.

"No coincidence, Mrs. Connolly. I already told you I don't believe in those. I requested the dispatch office alert me regarding any calls from your residence, especially after your 9-1-1 fiasco the other night. You remember, your husband broke into his own house."

Jerk.

"How nice. I feel much safer now." I smiled my best smart-ass smile.

He indicated the abandoned broom, which now lay near the front tires of Galigani's Honda. "What happened? Did you sweep him to death?"

"I found his car parked here. He was slumped over the steering wheel. The broom was to assist me with the rescue attempt."

McNearny glared at me. "How?"

"I thought I might have to break a window to get him out of the car."

"Do you know him? Is he your *friend*, too?"

I bit my lip. I felt a lie bubbling up. What good would it do? When had I become a liar anyway?

"He's a PI. His name's Galigani."

"He's *my* friend," McNearny said, his eyes settling onto mine. The animosity between us seemed to dissipate.

An ambulance arrived. The firefighters put Galigani onto a stretcher.

"Is he alive?" I asked.

"Barely," one paramedic responded.

We watched the ambulance screech off, sirens screaming.

"Former cop," McNearny said. "He was my first partner when I joined the force fourteen years ago. I need to follow them to the hospital. Try and stay out of trouble."

As soon as Mom left, I lay down on the couch and snuggled Laurie, her little breaths warming my arm. I rubbed her tummy and she made a soft "ah" sound.

My thoughts drifted to Galigani. Was this an attempt at murder? Would he survive? I felt chilled and scared. I double-checked the locks on the doors and windows and returned to my position on the couch, bringing along a throw blanket.

Then I picked up his notebook and devoured it.

- *Brad Avery, recovered pier 23 on Sept 19. Body decomposed, coroner puts date of death on or around June 15. Cause of death, bullet wound to the head. 9mm Luger. Survived by G. Avery (mother), S. Avery (ex-wife), and M. Avery (wife).*

- *Last seen by M. Avery June 15. On the record, reported fight with B. Avery, due to extramarital affair. Unable to locate party who'd been having an affair with B. Avery.*

- *G. Connolly bags recovered on Sept 19 at pier 23. Last known address—1482 Rivera (March 9), evicted by Sheriff for wielding chainsaw at property owner Roger Connolly. Unable to locate G. Connolly. Connection to B. Avery?*

- *M. Avery found dead on October 3, by K. Connolly (high school friend). Appears to have alibi for June 15. No apparent motive.*

• *M. Avery survived by KelliAnn Dupree (half sister)
last known address—1878 Haight Street, Apt 304.
Cause of death, overdose of diazepam in combination with alcohol. Suicide?*

• *Interview scheduled October 8: Kiku Ajari 1:00 pm.*

Tucked in the back of his notebook was a list of possible gun manufacturers that matched the rifling on the
9mm luger bullet recovered. I examined the list. The only
manufacturers I had heard of were Berretta and Smith and
Wesson. I'd need to ask Jim about it. Growing up with a
father from Montana who'd introduced Jim to hunting, he
understood more about guns than I did.

I reread Galigani's notes. George had threatened Uncle
Roger. With a chainsaw no less! That's why Roger had
finally kicked him out. It was also probably the reason he
hadn't come to Jim and me. If George had become violent
with Roger, then certainly killing Brad would be in the
realm of possibility.

What about Michelle? Suicide? Not likely. She confided to me she had been scared, worried that whoever
killed Brad might come after her. Why would she tell me
that if it wasn't true? Unless she killed Brad and said it to
cover her guilt. Then ended up killing herself because the
guilt was too great? Could she have accidentally overdosed? Maybe KelliAnn could shed light on this.

I reflected on KelliAnn's address. She lived in the
building on Haight Street I'd first followed Galigani to. I
thought he'd gone to see Jennifer in Apartment 303, but I
was wrong. He had been going there to see KelliAnn. Was
it a coincidence that hippie chick Jennifer had worked at
El Paraiso?

Laurie stirred next to me, stretching her arms over her
head like a kitten. I nuzzled her and she settled back to
sleep.

My thoughts returned to Michelle. If she had been poisoned, could Galigani have been poisoned, too? Had someone tried to kill him right in front of my house?

Who was Kiku?

The interview was in a couple days. Could I go in Galigani's place?

CHAPTER THIRTEEN

The Fourth Week—Exploring

When I awoke the next morning, the space next to me was cold and empty. I could hear water running in the shower. I peered over at Laurie in her bassinet. She was asleep for the moment.

I slipped out of bed and grabbed the phone. I dialed San Francisco General Hospital and inquired about Galigani. They told me that after he'd been stabilized, they'd transferred him to California Pacific Hospital.

They wouldn't tell me anything more about his condition, since I wasn't family.

I had to take Laurie to her one-month wellness appointment today. The pediatrician's office was right next to California Pacific.

Perfect.

I'd stop by and see how Galigani was progressing.

I pulled my notebook out and wrote my to-do list for the day.

To-Do List:

1. Take Laurie to her one-month wellness appointment.

2. Visit Galigani in the hospital, find out what happened to him.

3. Find George.

4. Interview Kiku (bring own water!).

5. Call Winter Henderson re: hippie chick alibi.

6. Read the parenting book from library.

7. Find the parenting book from the library.

8. Oh yeah, diet, exercise, clean car, be good mom/wife, cook, clean, and all that jazz.

I sat and sat in the waiting room. I really liked Laurie's pediatrician, Dr. Clement, but I'd never waited so long for any doctor. Every visit to this office, I had waited at least forty-five minutes. Laurie had already been to the doctor three times in the first month. Twice the first week and once the second week.

At our first appointment, when Laurie was two days old, I had cried because she was losing weight. Dr. Clement told me that it was perfectly normal, but maternal hormones don't listen to any doctor's logic and tears had been shed.

Was Dr. Clement worth the wait?

I watched two children with running noses coo over Laurie.

How does one extract one's baby from runny-nosed little children without seeming rude? I guess you can't help it if you seem rude. After all, this is your *newborn*.

I pulled Laurie's car seat bucket out of reach of the

children. One scowled at me and screamed "Mama!" at the top of her lungs. Her mother glanced up from the fashion magazine in her lap, mumbled something, then continued to read.

Both children found solace in the fish tank in the corner.

As I looked at my watch for the millionth time, Laurie's name was called.

I followed the nurse down a short hallway and into a freezing examination room. "Go ahead and undress her. Everything except the diaper," she instructed.

"It's an icebox in here."

"It'll only be for a second," she snapped.

Maybe I should consider another doctor?

Dr. Clement flew into the room. She was short and stocky with huge hands. I'd liked her from the beginning, thinking she'd never drop a baby with such secure-looking hands.

She stretched Laurie out on the examination table and put little pencil marks at her head and feet, then scooped her into what looked like a fish scale. After balancing all the doo-dads on the scale, she wrapped a tape measure around Laurie's head. She announced that Laurie was in the twenty-fifth percentile. Meaning that Laurie was "petite but perfectly healthy."

Apparently, out of 100 babies Laurie's age, 75 babies were bigger than she was. The doctor explained that Laurie was in proportion and gaining weight nicely, so not to worry. Easier said than done.

Dr. Clement was about to disappear, but then with her hand on the doorknob she turned and asked, "How's tummy time going?"

"Tummy time?"

"I told you at the hospital that you have to put her on her tummy for at least an hour every day."

Who remembers anything that happened a month ago?

"She's not even awake for a full hour," I said desperately.

"You have to do it in ten-minute increments. Ten minutes here, ten minutes there, it adds up." She wagged a finger at me. "Remember, tummy time is going to give Laurie the skills she needs for rolling over, sitting, and crawling."

I suddenly felt anxious. I was blowing it for Laurie! Could she already be behind at only four weeks old?

I nodded at Dr. Clement, who nodded back at me as she strode out the door.

I looked at my watch. All of two minutes had passed, most of it spent lecturing me. If she spent only two minutes with each patient, what in the world had she been doing when I'd been sitting in the waiting room for forty-five minutes?

Before Laurie was born, I spent a good deal of time interviewing pediatricians. I had liked Dr. Clement the best. She had taken her time during the process and had patiently explained the first steps I'd take with Laurie. Now I wondered if all the time I'd spent in her waiting room, she'd been recruiting new patients instead of tending to existing ones.

At least we didn't have to come back for another month. It would be nice to have a month off from doctor's visits. Except, of course, for my own. I still had to schedule that one. I knew I was avoiding it because I didn't want to go back to work. I pulled out my to-do list and added "tummy time" and the ob-gyn appointment.

From the pediatrician's office, I headed across the street to the hospital. I hated bringing Laurie into the hospital but rationalized that it wasn't much different from Dr. Clement's office.

I asked about Galigani at the front desk and was directed to the cardiology department.

Cardiology?

Not poisoned!

No one had tried to murder Galigani. Relief washed over me. Definitely reassuring, especially if I was going to consider poking my nose around some more in Brad's affairs.

When Laurie and I arrived at his room, he was propped up in bed, connected to several flashing beeping monitors at his chest, oxygen tubes in his nose, and a remote in his hand. What is it with men and remotes? He was watching *Fear Factor*.

Ah. Daytime TV.

"What, no *Days of our Lives*?" I asked, gently tapping on the room door.

Galigani's face lit up. "Come in."

He put the TV on *mute*! I tried not to be offended. After all, if I wasn't captivating enough, even during labor, for my own husband, I couldn't expect a perfect stranger to turn the TV off.

I shuffled Laurie's bucket onto a chair.

"Let me see her," Galigani said.

I tilted the bucket up to show off a sleeping Laurie, who managed to pry one blue eye open and peer at Galigani.

"Adorable. Thank you. Makes me feel better to see such a sweet face." He paused, taking inventory of the monitors around him. "Had a heart attack. They said the person who dialed 9-1-1 saved my life." His eyes shone. "I think a 'thank-you' is in order."

Laurie cooed and kicked as if to say, "You're welcome."

"They're not going to release me quite yet. I have to have open heart surgery. Bypass. Not out of the woods yet."

"Is there anyone I can call for you?"

"I'm on my own."

Where was his family?

I nodded. "When's the surgery?"

"Scheduled for tomorrow."

I patted his hand in reassurance. "You're going to be fine." I dug out Galigani's notebook from the ever-present diaper bag and placed it on his nightstand. "This belongs to you. It fell out of your car yesterday."

His eyes lingered on the notebook. "Doc says I need to slow down. No more tracking down murderers."

"You're dropping the case?"

"Yep. Got to. Doctor's orders."

"Is there someone in your office who'll take over?"

His mustache twisted up. "I work alone. Partners aren't what they're cracked up to be."

McNearny had been his partner. What had happened between them?

"I went by your house yesterday to tell you I'd found your brother-in-law."

"You did!"

Galigani laughed. "Don't sound so surprised, okay? I've been doing this a long time."

"Sorry. How is he? Where is he?"

"Alive and kicking. I found him at Pier 23. Claims he was with Michelle Avery on the night Brad was killed."

"Yeah. She told me the same thing."

Now it was Galigani's turn to be surprised. "Really?" He wagged a finger at me. "You didn't say anything to the police about that."

I smiled. "How do you know what I said and didn't say to the police?"

His eyes twinkled at me. "Been doing this a long time."

Laurie fussed. I moved the car seat to the floor and seated myself on the chair, then rocked the bucket with my foot. The rocking assuaged Laurie. She began exploring her hands as though she'd never seen them before. "I didn't say anything about George because . . ." I took a deep breath.

How could I explain the impulse to protect George?

"Let me guess." Galigani said. "Your husband and his brother don't really get along. George is a problem for the family, probably has been his entire adult life. Hasn't ever held a real job, was on the streets for a while. Has a history of threatening people, although he's never really taken any action on it. Probably asks for a lot of favors, borrows a lot of money, never repays anything, burns a lot of bridges. Stop me if I'm getting any of this wrong."

"You know all this because you've been doing this a long time?"

"That and I ran a background check. Anyway, you and your husband didn't say anything to the police because deep down he still loves his brother, and you, of course, love your husband and everyone is in denial that he could be a murderer."

The small room seemed to close in on me, and what I'd intended as a question came out as a statement. "You think George killed Brad."

"Not really. I don't have a motive. Do you?"

I shook my head helplessly. "No."

"My money's on the girl. The supposed affair."

"You think Michelle lied about that?"

"No. I've had several people tell me it's true, but no one's coughing up any names."

"What about Kiku, who's she?"

Galigani's eyes flashed surprised, then amusement. "Why, Mrs. Connolly, don't you know?"

I shrugged. "The supposed other woman?"

Galigani blinked up at me. "Maybe you should go talk to her."

"Why would I—"

Galigani interrupted me by clearing his throat. I stared

at him, silent. He tugged at his blanket. "I haven't got around to telling Gloria Avery that I'm dropping the case."

I continued to watch him, not daring to speak. He pressed the palms of his hands together and studied me.

After a moment I squeaked, "I can tell her."

Galigani nodded his head slowly and smiled.

As Laurie and I drove to the Sea Cliff, one of the wealthiest neighborhoods in San Francisco, I daydreamed of Mrs. Avery hiring me as Galigani's replacement. It could be my first official case. I could launch my own business, not have to return to my corporate nightmare, work from home, and be with Laurie.

I fantasized becoming so successful that I could be Mrs. Avery's neighbor.

Then reality/insecurity hit me. Would I really be able to get her to pay me for being nosy? If I could get answers that perhaps the police couldn't, that would be worth something to her, wouldn't it? And how *exactly* was I going to do that?

I pulled up to the huge house. It was gorgeous, with spiraling towers, Spanish steps, and a manicured front lawn. I rang the bell, enjoying the view of the Golden Gate Bridge as I waited for Mrs. Avery to open the door. Instead, a small Hispanic woman in a maid's uniform appeared.

"Hello, I'm Kate Connolly. Mr. Galigani sent me. Is Mrs. Avery in?"

"*Ay, la Señora Avery, sí, sí.*" She motioned me inside. "*Que bonita,*" she said, gesturing to Laurie.

"*Gracias.*" It was pretty much the only Spanish I remembered from my high school classes.

The maid ushered me from the entrance hall to the sitting room, made bright by three tall front windows from which I could see across the bay to the Marin Headlands.

She disappeared through French doors down the main entry hall, muttering "*Un momento.*"

I took the time to look around—high ceilings and a marble fireplace complemented by delicate ornamental plasterwork. The room was finished with Stickley furniture. Jim and I had stumbled into a high-end furniture shop a few months ago when decorating the nursery and had drooled over the Stickley pieces, only to gag at the price tags in the ten-thousand-dollar range.

Thank God I had dress pants on, even if they didn't button all the way.

Laurie fussed in her car seat. I contemplated taking her out but then I imagined her spitting up on the furniture. I swayed back and forth with the bucket instead.

Prominently displayed on the wall was a photograph of an elegant older couple.

Brad's parents?

On a side table was a wedding photo of Brad and Michelle. Beside that, a photo of Brad holding a little girl who looked to be about two years old.

Could that be Penny, the little girl who had drowned?

"Ms. Connolly?" Mrs. Avery asked from the doorway.

I turned quickly. Mrs. Avery was tall, at least six feet. She was thin and wore a canary yellow suit that paled her complexion. Her gray hair was fixed in a tight bun, her cheeks drawn. She crossed the room in two strides and extended a slender hand.

I gripped her cold fingers. "How do you do?"

"Not well, dear, as you can imagine. My only son is dead. Murdered!" Her eyes shifted off my face and caught sight of the car seat and a tiny Laurie blinking up at us. Mrs. Avery's face softened. "Oh, my dear. Congratulations! A new mommy . . ." Her voice cracked and her face contorted as she pulled out a handkerchief.

My heart felt heavy as I imagined myself in Mrs. Avery's canary-colored shoes. If anything bad happened to Laurie . . . my breath caught. I fought tears, but with the hormones racing through my body, I wasn't able to hold them back.

"Not you, too." Mrs. Avery dabbed at her eyes. "All we need now is for the little one to start." She guided me to the couch.

The maid appeared in the doorway with a tray full of tea and small butter cookies. She set the tray on the coffee table and left.

"Help yourself, dear." Mrs. Avery circled the car seat. "May I hold her? I haven't held a tiny baby, since . . ."

I waited for her to continue, but she paused and looked at me pleadingly.

"Of course you can hold her." I pulled a pink and green striped burp cloth out of the diaper bag at my feet and handed it to Mrs. Avery, then unbuckled Laurie from the car seat.

Laurie extended her arms over her head in a cat stretch. I scooped her up and made sure she was dry before passing her to Mrs. Avery. The last thing I needed was for Laurie to *leak* all over Mrs. Avery's expensive suit.

"She smells so sweet." Mrs. Avery breathed Laurie in. "I haven't held a baby since Penny." She sighed, then walked over to the mantel and pointed at the family portrait I had been looking at. "Here she is. Penny drowned five years ago."

My throat constricted. I fought back more tears. "I know."

Mrs. Avery looked surprised. "You do?"

"Svetlana told me."

Mrs. Avery looked solemn. "Marta said you were here on behalf of Mr. Galigani."

"Yes. I'm afraid he's had a heart attack. He's in the hospital. He's scheduled for open heart surgery tomorrow."

Mrs. Avery's forehead creased. "Poor man. What hospital?"

"California Pacific."

She rose, walked to the edge of the room, and called for Marta. When Marta appeared, Mrs. Avery requested flowers be sent to Galigani.

I felt a flash of guilt as I remembered the thank-you cards I had forgotten to write.

Well, in all fairness, I didn't have a "Marta" to delegate to, but still. Our friends and coworkers had found time to send me and Laurie stuff. I had to make the time to thank them.

I pulled out my notebook and jotted down: "*Stop being rude.*"

Mrs. Avery seated herself across from me in a green and gold upholstered occasional chair. Her face had relaxed a bit. She seemed to enjoy holding Laurie. She motioned to the notebook in my lap. "Are you Mr. Galigani's assistant?"

Why would she think I was his assistant and not his replacement? Did I look that unqualified?

I wavered a second, then astonished myself by saying, "I'm an investigator myself, ma'am."

Mrs. Avery nodded vaguely, tickling Laurie under the chin, causing her to warble and drool.

Emboldened by Mrs. Avery's nonreaction, I pressed, "Mr. Galigani won't be able to finish the investigation."

"I need to find out what happened to Bradley. And now, of course, Michelle. The police are absolutely worthless. They pointed the finger at Michelle almost immediately. Now they tried to tell me that perhaps she killed Brad and then herself." She shook her head sadly. "That scenario doesn't make any sense to me."

"What do *you* think happened to Brad?"

"Hasn't Mr. Galigani filled you in?"

Oh, shit.

"I've been on another case."

Not exactly a lie. I had been looking for George.

She pressed her lips together in thought and seemed to accept my response. "I believed, well, I should say, I still believe Michelle's story. She visited me on June sixteenth, the day after Bradley left her. She told me he'd left her for another woman. She was very upset. Michelle and I were close. Her own mother had passed. She relied on me. And Bradley, I must say, he always had a problem with women. Like his father. One woman wasn't enough for him. Always needed to find . . ." Her eyes flickered about the room. "Never mind. The point of the matter is, I thought Bradley was off with another woman. In Costa Rica or Bora Bora or another of his preferred locations. After all, he left Svetlana like that, told her he was in love with someone else—Michelle. Bradley and Michelle were in Bali for three months." She let out a cynical laugh that jarred Laurie, sleeping in her arms. "But the other woman never thinks that there will be *another* woman. She believes him when he says that she's the one. The special one."

Laurie opened her eyes slightly. Mrs. Avery rocked and shushed her back to sleep.

"Do you know who she was?"

"The other woman? I have no idea. Bradley never spoke to me about his affairs."

"Do you know who would want to hurt him?"

A tear welled in her eye. "My dear, I don't know what to think. I just want to know what happened to him. I want whoever killed Bradley and Michelle brought to justice."

"Can you tell me anything about El Paraiso?" I asked.

Mrs. Avery's eyes narrowed. "I told my son not to get involved. Imagine opening up a restaurant in one of the most competitive cities in the nation. Do you know the failure rate of restaurants here in San Francisco?"

I shook my head but Mrs. Avery proceeded with her rant, ignoring me entirely. "He always gave in too easily to Rich. He was Bradley's best friend. Have you spoken with him yet? El Paraiso was his dream, you know, but Rich never had two pennies to rub together. So Bradley, with my help, of course, funded the restaurant and we made Rich the assistant manager."

Laurie began to squirm in Mrs. Avery's arms.

"Well, dear, why don't we get the paperwork out?" Mrs. Avery said.

"Paperwork?"

"I assume you have a contract for me to sign."

I hated appearing unprepared, but I shook my head as the words "I'll prepare one for you" tumbled out of my mouth.

Mrs. Avery raised an eyebrow. "Very well. Leave me your card."

Oh God! I was going to lose my first client before I even landed her.

"My card. Yes . . . uh . . . I came straight from the hospital . . ."

Mrs. Avery stood and handed Laurie to me. "I understand. Marta will provide you with my card. In the meantime, I'll presume the same terms as with Galigani."

I headed home for lunch, my head spinning. Mrs. Avery wanted to hire me. I'd done it. My first client. Now I had to zip home, draw up a contract, feed and change Laurie, and make dinner.

When would I sleep?

I had been hoping for a nap with Laurie this afternoon, but now, on the verge of my new career, that seemed indulgent, if not impossible.

I glanced at my to-do list. "Find George" stood out like a beacon. Galigani had found him. Why couldn't I?

Pier 23, where his bags had been found, was not exactly on my way home, but one glance in the rearview mirror told me Laurie was sacked out. I'd drive by the pier and take a peek. The rest of the to-do list could wait until tomorrow.

I stopped at a red light in front of the pier. The water that had been so blue outside Mrs. Avery's doorstep now appeared gray. Of course, Mrs. Avery had a clear view of the ocean; this water was in the bay. The bay always looked gray to me.

The pier seemed quiet. A few barrels against a restaurant wall and a homeless woman camped out with a blanket. Two joggers ran by. Then a hooded figure carrying a black bag made his way up the hill. I watched as he walked toward the pier. Something about his gait was familiar.

The car behind me blasted its horn. The light had changed.

I pulled my car forward, trying to keep one eye on the road and the other on the man, who'd stopped in front of a lamppost. His back was to me.

Could it be George?

I strained to see him, but was forced to pick up speed through the intersection.

Damn.

Probably nothing, but I wanted to make a U-turn and get a closer look. I changed lanes. A huge NO U-TURN sign stared down at me.

I'd need to change lanes again and go around the block. It took me nearly ten minutes in traffic to do that. I thought for sure by the time I circled around, the man would be gone.

I was finally in the right lane and able to drive directly past the lamppost. The man was still there. He had pulled off his hood and was straightening his hair.

Hair that looked distinctly familiar.

Hair that was just like Laurie's.

A heavy pit formed in my stomach. I watched as he fumbled inside the bag for a cigarette. He lit it, then looked around impatiently while tapping his foot against the lamppost.

I slowed, rolled down my window, and called to him. "George!"

At the same time, a gold hard-top Mercedes cut into my lane, maneuvering around my car. The driver, a whirl of red hair, shouted something.

I guess I was going too slow for some city people.

George never even looked in my direction. He dropped the black bag and took off running. Why was he running from me?

I watched him in my rearview mirror as he ran in the opposite direction my car was headed. He turned into an alley.

The only way in there was by foot. Laurie was sleeping in the back. There was no way I'd leave her in the car or take her into the alley.

Nice, Kate, you make a great PI. You lose your suspect as soon as you find him.

• CHAPTER FOURTEEN •

The Fourth Week—Recognition

Safe at home, I typed up a contract based on a template I found online and laid it out for Jim to review. Then I did a bit of research on PI licensing. Turned out I was highly unqualified for the job.

I needed to have three years or 6,000 hours of compensated experience in investigative work, or a law or police science degree plus 4,000 hours of experience.

Of course I had zero hours of experience and a bachelor's in theater arts.

The requirements went on to state that the experience needed to be certified by the employer, who could be a sworn law enforcement officer, a military police officer, or a licensed PI.

Great! So launching a business as a PI was going to be more complicated than I'd thought. It wasn't just landing the client, you had to be licensed! Although, I rationalized, Mrs. Avery hadn't actually asked me for a license. Could I do this without one?

Why can't things ever be easy?

Laurie began to fuss. Was it her mealtime already?

The month had flown by in three-hour increments. From one feeding to the next.

I brought Laurie over to our favorite section on the couch and began to nurse her. By now, I had the area all set up: telephone, remote control, an extra pillow, and a big glass of water, all accessible on the side table.

I drank my water and reflected on Galigani. How did he normally get his cases? How regular was the work? Could I land enough clients to justify quitting my job? I visualized calling my office and saying I'd launched a successful private investigation firm during my leave.

The idea seemed so far-fetched, I didn't know whether to laugh or cry.

After burping Laurie, I placed her facedown on her play mat, affectionately termed the "baby gym." She let out an enormous wail. I picked her up, soothed her, and tried again. She cried even harder than the first time. I picked her up.

Tummy time was for the birds. No wonder the manufacturers called it a gym. For a baby, holding your head up is a workout.

Now I knew why we hadn't done much of it in the last month. I immediately felt guilty.

Just because it's hard doesn't mean it's not worth the effort.

I placed her on her tummy again, leaning over her to sing and try to soothe her. She was crying so loudly, I didn't hear Jim come in. I jumped when I saw wingtips under my nose.

"Hi, honey, why are you torturing the baby?"

"It's good for her."

He smiled as he knelt down next to us. "Crying is good for her?"

"Tummy time."

He rescued Laurie. She curled into his shoulder like a little bug, legs protectively drawn up.

"I saw George today," I said.

Jim's eyebrows rose. "Where?"

"At the pier where they found his bags." I crossed my legs under me and leaned back on my hands.

Jim sat back on his heels and squinted at me. "So he's alive, not decomposing at the bottom of the bay?"

I reached out and gently pushed on his knee. "Why do you talk like that? We knew it wasn't him."

"I have a hard time keeping up with the drama that's George." Jim sighed. "What did he have to say for himself?"

"I didn't get a chance to talk to him. When I called his name, he dropped his bag and ran."

Jim scowled. "Why would he do that?"

I shrugged. "I have no idea. What do you think he's doing down there? And why leave his bag?"

"Well, he's always been scattered. Did he just run off and leave it or what?"

"No! I called his name and he dropped the bag like it was on fire."

Jim and I studied each other in silence. Finally he said, "I don't know, Kate, if I stopped and tried to answer every George question I had . . . what can I say, the guy's a piece of work." He absently stroked Laurie's back. "What you were doing at the pier?"

"Looking for him." I wiggled my eyebrows up and down. "I'm replacing Galigani as the private investigator for Mrs. Avery."

Jim stopped rubbing Laurie's back and stared at me. "What?"

"I have the contract ready for your review."

Jim shook his head. "You don't have any experience or training! I don't want you running around and getting yourself into any danger."

"You don't think I can take care of myself?"

"That's not what I mean. Investigators like Galigani have training on how to handle different situations, you know, defuse anger and—"

"Look, I'm not gonna get myself in any potentially volatile situations. I promise. I'm not an idiot."

Jim looked dubious.

"Are you going to support me?"

He reached out and wrapped his free arm around me. "Honey, I always support you."

The following morning Jim and I agreed to stake out the pier together. I knew he was getting increasingly concerned about my safety, not to mention the fact that we were both alarmed at George's potential involvement in the crimes.

Jim called in sick and we arranged for Mom to watch Laurie. I left her with instructions on how to prepare a bottle for Laurie with the measly three ounces I had managed to pump so far.

So much for building a supply of milk up before my return to work.

When Jim and I arrived at the pier, we parked a little ways down the street, which gave us an unencumbered view of all the activity. There were joggers every couple minutes, a few bike riders, and the occasional skateboarder. The homeless woman from the day before was absent.

I sat on the passenger side of the Chevy, and Jim drummed on the steering wheel. After about an hour, I unwrapped one of the ham and cheese sandwiches I had packed.

"Want one?"

Jim shook his head. "We just had breakfast."

"That was at least an hour ago." I bit into the sandwich.

He nudged me with his elbow and pointed to a hooded figure carrying a black duffel bag. "I think that's him."

Jim jumped out of the car and started running toward George. I struggled to put down my sandwich and also get out. Jim was way ahead of me.

When George saw Jim approaching, he stretched out his hand. "Buddy!"

"Cut the crap," Jim said, walking straight up to George.

Jim stood a good four inches taller than George. George had a wiry frame compared to his brother's solid stature.

"What's up?" George asked, unruffled as I finally caught up with them. He nodded at me. "Hey, Kate."

"Glad to see you're functioning," Jim said.

George's head twitched to the side. "Not doing as good as you, man, but who can compare to you?"

"Last I heard you were on the streets," Jim said, disgusted.

"Yeah?" George yanked the hood off and ran his fingers over his hair. "Well, not anymore. Like you care."

Jim's shoulders inched up a degree. "Same old George. Nobody cares about you, huh, buddy?"

George's eyes flashed anger. "That's right."

Jim squinted. "What are you doing here anyway? This your new hangout? What's in the bag?"

George tightened his grip on the duffel. "What's it to you?"

Jim stepped forward, shortening the distance between them. "Who's Brad Avery to you? Why is he dead?"

"You knew Brad?" George said through an oily little smile.

"I know he washed up dead right before Kate went into labor."

George glanced at me, surprised. "You had a baby?"

"I know your bags were on this pier, right where his body was recovered. The same bags that are at my house right now, because no one could find you." Jim continued, "I know I was worried sick, thinking it was you who washed up that night. You shithead!"

"Oh!" George covered his heart with one hand, his voice full of sarcasm. "My big brother was worried about me? You have your own family now. What do you care about me?"

"I know, always the victim," Jim fired back.

"If you care so much, where were you six months ago when I needed a hand?"

"You mean a handout?" Jim said.

George rolled up his sleeves. "You've never done nothing for me!" he yelled into Jim's face.

Jim loosened the top buttons of his shirt, then turned toward me and said in the most serious voice I'd ever heard him use, "Kate, can you go to the car now, please?"

"This is ridiculous!" I said. "Are you two really going to fight?"

They both stared at me, waiting for me to walk away.

"No fighting," I said. "We're in this together."

George ignored me and turned toward Jim. "Did you know Brad was killed with one of Dad's guns? One that you inherited? Since you inherited everything!"

Jim's face flushed. "I never inherited jack!"

I felt my blood pressure skyrocket. "How do you know about the gun, George?" I demanded.

Jim's hands flew to George's neck, knocking him off balance and to the ground. Jim jumped on top of him, never releasing his grip.

Just then a police cruiser appeared. Two police officers exploded out of the car and charged toward us. By the time they reached us, George had thrown a punch squarely at Jim's chest. Jim had stopped strangling George long enough to punch him in the face.

One officer brushed me aside and pulled Jim off George.

The other officer pulled George to his feet. "Are you all right, sir? Do you need any medical assistance?"

George shook his head, wiping blood from his nose. Jim continued to yell at George, even though the officer was restraining him.

"Wait! Wait!" I yelled to the officer holding Jim. "They're brothers!"

The other officer asked George, "Would you like to press charges, sir?"

"You bet your ass I would," George said.

"Charges?" I said. "They were both fighting!"

"He tried to strangle me," George said. "And look at my face!"

The officer holding Jim proceeded to handcuff him.

"Would you like to follow us to the station, sir?" the other officer asked George.

"The station?" I repeated.

The officer holding Jim hustled him toward the patrol car. I ran after them in time for the cop to slam the door between us.

"I'll follow you to the station, okay, honey?" I yelled to Jim through the closed window.

Jim nodded as the cruiser engine started up. He raised his shackled hands and pointed at me through the window, indicating for me to look down.

I glanced at my shirt. It was soaked.

Blood?

Nope. My milk had leaked all over me.

Great, just great.

At the station, Jim was processed, George had yet to show up, and I sat on a hard orange chair trying to cover up my breasts by crossing my arms.

I had searched my car for a jacket, but had found nothing except baby paraphernalia. My trunk always has extra junk in it, but after it had been broken into, Jim had cleaned it out for me.

I called home in a panic, imagining Laurie starving to death.

Mom said Laurie was sleeping peacefully and hadn't noticed my absence in the least. I tried to ignore my feelings of rejection. When I told Mom that Jim and I had found George, she surprised me by saying, "He's here."

"What?"

"George is here. He said Jim told him you had some of his things."

Holy cow! Not home alone with my newborn and my mom.

Although George had always been kind to my mom and me, recent events made me nervous about him being at my house now.

"I'll be right there," I said to Mom.

I spoke with the arresting officer about releasing Jim, given the fact that George had obviously changed his mind about pressing charges.

"I can't release your husband yet, ma'am."

"Why not? No one's pressing any charges against him."

"He broke the law, ma'am. I have specific instructions not to release him just yet."

"Instructions? From whom?"

"My commanding officer, ma'am."

"Let me talk to him."

"*Her*, ma'am, and she's not available at the moment."

I buried my face in my hands. "Look, isn't there someone I can talk to about—"

"Ma'am, your husband's case will be reviewed by the DA within seventy-two hours, or he may be released on his own recognizance earlier, but not right now. That's all I can tell you."

Seventy-two hours!

"Can I speak with my husband?"

The officer gave me a tight-lipped smile. "It's probably best if you go home. He'll be able to call you later."

I pulled into the garage and heard Laurie wailing. I ran up the stairs and saw Mom and George hovering over the bassinet in the living room.

I picked up Laurie and examined her while glaring at George. Mother and George looked at me curiously. How could I explain to them that I had been afraid that George might hurt Laurie?

"She's hungry," Mom said.

I evaluated George. He absently rubbed his eye, where a bruise was starting to form.

Laurie wailed at me. George slumped onto the couch looking exhausted. Since he appeared nonthreatening at the moment and Mom seemed unafraid, I decided I'd better feed Laurie.

"Give me a minute," I said, over my shoulder, as I walked down the hallway.

Mom and George continued their small talk.

I tried to eavesdrop on Mom and George as I breastfed, but I couldn't hear much. Our house was old San Francisco construction, made with three-by-six wood beams instead of two-by-fours. The result was great sound-proofing.

I finished nursing Laurie, burped her, then set her down in the bassinet to sleep.

When I emerged, Mom said good-bye and left.

George and I sat in silence for a moment.

"You want ice for your face?" I asked.

"Nah, I think I'll be okay. Where's Jim?"

"Still at the station. They haven't released him yet."

George looked surprised. "I thought if I didn't press charges, they'd release him right away."

The weight of leaving Jim alone at the station was starting to get to me. I suddenly felt ridiculously tired and in over my head, but if I wanted answers, now was my opportunity to grill George. "Why did you change your mind about pressing charges?"

He shrugged. "I was so pissed off I wanted to get back at him, but by the time I got to the car—"

"You realized how much you love your brother and decided not to, right?"

George smiled. "Yeah. That's right."

I exhaled loudly, letting my impatience show. "Come on, George, be straight with me. You're avoiding the cops."

"I'm not avoiding them . . . I . . ." We stared at each other; George closed his eyes in defeat. "I know they've been asking around for me."

"So why not talk to them? Tell them what you know."

George stood up and shrugged. "I don't know anything! You got my bags?"

I remained seated. "Yeah. I do."

He tapped his foot impatiently. "'Kay, where are they? You want me to get them? You stay on the couch. You look tired."

Part of me wanted George to get the bags and leave. The part that was afraid and wanted nothing more to do with any of this. But the other part, the stubborn part of me that can't ever shut up, said, "Did you break into our cars, trying to get your bags?"

George flinched as if I'd hit him. "What? No. I didn't even know you had them until today."

"Someone did. Both our cars were broken into after I picked up your bags from the ME's office. Once outside Michelle's house, the other outside El Paraiso."

George's eyes darted around the room.

"Do you work at El Paraiso?" I asked.

George nodded.

"What do you do there?" I pressed, wondering how far I could push him.

He looked momentarily confused. I had almost gotten his guard down. "Oh, you know . . ." He waved his hands around, trying to distract me.

"Is it legal?"

"What?" George stared at me, his mouth agape.

I matched his stare. At this point all the runaround was making me angry, and with Laurie tucked away safely in the back bedroom, I felt brave enough to challenge him a bit.

"Whatever they have you do. Is it legal?"

"God, Kate, what are you asking me? I mean, I do . . . I do restaurant stuff."

"Like what? Bus tables?" I probed.

"Yeah, like that."

"George, I was there. I know you don't bus the tables. None of the staff even know you exist."

He paced around the room. "Sure they do. Like who? Who did you talk to?"

"What were you doing on the pier today, George?"

"Pfft, you know," He waved his hand around and gave me his famous, charming smile, trying to disarm me. "Hanging out."

"I don't buy that, George. Your bags were found there a few weeks ago when they recovered Brad. I saw you there yesterday."

"You were there yesterday?"

"Yeah. I called your name. You took off running. And you left your bag there!"

He shook his head back and forth. "Sorry. I thought I saw . . . I thought you were someone else."

"Who?"

He shrugged. "I thought I was being followed."

"Why would you be followed? And why did you leave your bag? How'd you get it back?"

"It's not important."

"How come you've been so hard to get ahold of?" I pressed.

"What do you mean?"

"When the police found your bags, they called here. We didn't know where to find you. What's up with all the secrets?"

"No secrets."

"Where are you staying? Do you have a phone number or anything?"

"Yeah," He pulled out a piece of paper from his pocket and jotted something down, then handed it to me. "Here's my cell phone."

"We tried this number before. No service."

"Temporary thing. I threw some money at it last week, so it should be fine now."

"What about the murder weapon?"

"What about it?" George asked.

"How did you know Brad was killed with one of your dad's guns?" I asked.

"I don't really know that. All I know is that it was the same *type* of gun."

"How?" I pressed.

"I talked to an investigator, a PI. He said he was hired by Brad's mother. To look into things. He told me Brad was killed by a nine-millimeter. Dad had a nine-millimeter Smith and Wesson."

"Okay, so how did one of your dad's guns, or one like it, come to kill Brad?"

I was treading on thin ice here. I knew George was jealous about Jim's relationship with their dad. George had always thought that we had bought our home with inheritance money.

The truth was, we had worked hard and saved for a long time. George hated that scenario because it involved working.

Everything their father had owned, including hunting rifles or guns, had remained at Uncle Roger's, where George had lived for a long time. As far as I knew, Jim hadn't even seen those guns since he was seventeen years old.

George looked trapped. He appeared to be having a conversation in his head about whether or not to come clean with me. He settled on saying, "I had the gun."

"What?"

"When my uncle kicked me out, I took the gun. I was on the streets for a while. You don't know what that's like. I had to find a place to crash every night. I needed it with me, you know, just in case."

Our eyes locked. George studied me a moment, debating whether or not to continue. I waved my hand, indicating that he should spit it out.

He did a nervous little jig. "When I met Brad, he was putting together El Paraiso. You should have seen it when we started. The place was a dump. He hired me, as casual labor, you know, to paint and stuff. He let me crash in the basement."

"What happened to the gun?"

"I don't know. I always kept it with me. In my bag. Only sometimes I left my bags in the basement at El Paraiso, where I slept. No one messed with my stuff. No one really wants to go near a homeless guy's bag."

George paused before continuing.

"Well, I got a place now. I'm not sleeping at El Paraiso anymore, but then I was, you know, in June. Anyway, near as I can tell, someone must have taken my gun and killed Brad. I noticed it missing sometime in July. I was going through my stuff. I didn't think anything about it, except that it sucked to be ripped off. I didn't think anybody had been killed with it."

"Jesus Christ, George! Did you report it?"

"Report it to who?"

"To the police!"

"Are you kidding? The gun was never registered to me. Besides, the police aren't sympathetic to homeless people. I'm only telling you because . . ." He collapsed onto the couch next to me. "I don't know why I'm telling you."

"I'm sorry. Tell me. Go ahead and tell me. I won't lecture you."

George nodded. "When I heard they found Brad dead, I tried to remember, you know, remember anything unusual about that night. But hell, it was months ago. The only thing I really recall is that Michelle was upset when I brought over the cash. We talked for a while. She told me Brad had left her. We drank some, but that was pretty much it."

"What cash?"

"Uh . . . you know, deposits from the . . . the restaurant."

"Doesn't the manager usually handle the cash?"

George scratched his head. "What?"

"Most restaurant managers make a night deposit at the bank, right? Why were you bringing the money to Michelle's house?"

George jiggled his knee up and down so quickly it shook the couch. For a second I thought we were having an earthquake. He stood. "I've really got to run."

I jumped up. "C'mon, George, were you having an affair with Michelle?"

"No. Of course not."

"What about Monday?" I pressed. "The morning Michelle was killed."

George looked around the room. "Can you get my bags?"

"Do you know who would want to kill Brad *and* Michelle? Who could have taken your gun? Who knew you had a gun?"

"I don't know, Kate, geez. And I don't want to know. Don't tell anyone what I told you . . . the less you know about this, the better. I don't want you to be involved."

"I'm already involved!" I exploded. "And you're up to your ears in 'involved,' George. What were your bags doing at the pier?"

"I forgot them there, is all. Stupid. Anyway, I'm taking care of everything. I went to see someone today who can help me."

"An attorney?"

"No, no. Never mind. I've got to get back to the shop."

"What shop?"

George's eyes flicked back and forth. "I mean . . . you know, the restaurant, El Paraiso." He glanced at his watch. "I've really got to run, Kate. Jim will probably be home soon and he'll be frosted."

After he left, I collapsed onto the couch, suddenly realizing how drained I was. I closed my eyes for what seemed a second, okay maybe five seconds, before Laurie let out a howl.

I took a deep breath, pried one eye open, and went to pick her up from her bassinet. She immediately nestled into me and quieted down.

I stared into her lovely face and tried to quell all the voices in my head. I sat and inhaled her scent and studied the curve of her cheek.

When would Jim be released? Were they really going to present a case to the DA? Should Jim have called me by now?

I decided I needed food to fuel my worry. I put on the baby carrier and shifted Laurie into it so I could rummage through our refrigerator. When was the last time I had gone grocery shopping? I spotted a container of leftovers and greedily pulled it out. One whiff and I could safely say there was nothing edible remaining in it. I dumped the container and continued to rummage. I found an apple.

I moved from the fridge to the freezer.

Jackpot.

I'd stockpiled frozen meals that had been on sale. I threw a chicken cordon bleu pasta dish into the microwave.

After eating the chicken, I threw in a Southwestern-style cheese enchilada dish and topped it off with the apple for dessert. Oh, well, at least the apple was healthy.

The phone rang, interrupting my calorie counting.

Jim's voice filled the line. "Honey?"

"Jim! Are you on your way home?"

"I'm still in jail."

The frozen meals turned to stone in my stomach. "For how long?"

"I don't know. The officer in charge isn't very chatty. They told me I had one phone call. Can you call an attorney?"

"How can they hold you? George said he isn't going to press any charges."

"They're charging me with assault with a deadly weapon. At first they told me they were releasing me, but then they came back and said I had one phone call. I'm really sorry, Kate. I hate putting you through this."

"Assault with a deadly weapon! What weapon?"

"It doesn't have to be a gun or anything, it can be your hands. The cop says he saw me strangling George. I need you to call me an attorney."

"Who should I call?"

"I don't know. Start with the phone book."

"All right. Don't worry, honey. I'm on it."

"I shouldn't have let George get to me like that. I should have kept my cool. Whatever George says or does, you and Laurie are my family. I can't do anything to jeopardize you guys, like blow my top and land up in jail. I'm a father now."

I heard noises in the background. It sounded like someone was rushing Jim off the phone.

"Gotta go, honey," he said, hanging up.

I broke down in tears. It felt like something was tightening around my heart. I went to Laurie's bassinet and picked her up. Smelling her sweet scent dried my eyes. I had to be strong for her. Fix things for her. Bring her daddy home.

I dialed Galigani's hospital room. He had to know a good criminal defense attorney.

If someone had told me just a few short weeks ago that I'd be searching out an attorney for my husband, I'd have told him or her they were crazy. Now I hoped I wasn't the crazy one.

Galigani's phone rang and rang.

He'd had the open heart surgery this morning. The nurse who took my message told me he had gotten through it fine and was still in the intensive care unit. They expected to upgrade his condition in the morning.

I settled Laurie into the baby carrier and hopped online, hoping to find an attorney. I did a local search and pulled some profiles. There were several attorneys with nearby addresses. One had his picture on his website. He appeared to be in his late fifties and was smoking a pipe in the photograph. Something about the picture made him look capable.

The pipe maybe?

I glanced at my watch, almost 6 P.M.

Please be working late tonight, Mr. Crane.

I punched his phone number into my cordless.

"Charles Crane here. How can I help you?" the voice crackled.

I filled him in as best I could, asking him to meet him at the police station. He told me to relax, said it sounded like Jim could be released with a few phone calls.

I waited for Mr. Crane to call me back. I paced. I played with Laurie. I did laundry and even dusted. Boy, had things around the house been neglected!

I fed and bathed Laurie. I did everything I could to keep myself busy.

Finally, I lay down on the bed and stared at the phone, willing it to ring.

It didn't.

It was 9 P.M. I was exhausted. I put Laurie into the bassinet. She fell sound asleep. No fuss at all. Of course. Since I couldn't sleep, she'd find a way to peacefully sleep through the night. Where was the justice in the world?

I got online and caught up with e-mail. There was a message from Paula in my in-box:

> *Girl! What do you mean Michelle Dupree was murdered? And her husband, too? I can't leave you alone for a minute without you getting yourself all caught up in a drama! I miss you. I haven't heard from the Galigani guy, but don't worry. If I do, I'll tell him both you and Jim were at my place until all hours of the night. Just like in high school with our all-night parties! Can't believe Michelle is gone.*
>
> *I loved the picture of Laurie. She looks exactly like Jim, doesn't she? I hope we'll be coming home soon. David is getting all sorts of flak from his firm, and I really want to be home to start my own business. Be an entrepreneurial mommy! Oh that and the baby is due soon! Ha! Not that soon—four months—but who's counting?*
>
> *Love, love, love you guys! Write soon.*

She had attached instructions on how to use the breast pump. Well, instructions was a relative term; it was a hand-sketched cartoon which she had scanned. The drawing showed me with boobs the size of basketballs attached to a monster machine. I responded to her e-mail and updated her on the additional hysteria in my life, including Jim's incarceration, George's visit, and my very first client.

The phone rang.

I leapt for it.

"Mrs. Connolly?" I heard a little puff in the background.

His pipe. Crane.

"I've been in touch with the police. I'm afraid they're not going to release your husband tonight."

"Why?"

"There's an unresolved homicide they're looking into."

"I know. Brad, and there's also Michelle Avery, but what does that have to do with Jim?"

"Well, yes, there's those. But I meant another one. Svetlana Avery."

My postpartum belly fell to the floor.

CHAPTER FIFTEEN

The Fifth Week—
Head Held High

I tossed and turned the entire night. I kept reaching out across the bed for Jim, only to be jarred awake by the coldness of the empty sheets. Of course, since I was awake, Laurie was asleep. I checked her breathing a few times and found the rhythm of the rise and fall of her chest soothing.

Svetlana murdered? Mr. Crane had told me she had been shot, killed by a 9mm luger bullet. Ballistics had determined that the bullet had been fired from the same gun that had killed Brad.

Same gun.

George's gun. Or one like it. But what were the odds of that? It had to be George's gun.

Had to be the gun registered to Jim's father. How could we prove that Jim had never had possession of the gun?

I didn't want to think of Jim's lack of an alibi for June fifteenth. I didn't want to think about the police possibly moving forward with a trial against Jim. I didn't want to think about my bed being empty, trying to raise Laurie on my own.

I thought, instead, of fighting like hell to get the love of my life out of jail. Fighting like hell to find the real murderer. *Keep your mind on what you want, Kate, and off what you don't want,* I reminded myself.

I needed to find the murderer. I needed to get Jim off the hook and to launch my new career. I had no option.

At 4 A.M. I fed Laurie. She immediately went back to sleep. I got up and made coffee. I reviewed my to-do list from the day before and modified it.

To-Do List:

1. Free Jim.

2. Interview Kiku (bring own water!).

3. Call Winter Henderson re: hippie chick alibi.

4. Find Brad and/or Michelle's and/or Svetlana's killer.

5. Tummy time!!! (in progress).

6. Make OB appointment.

7. Stop being rude.

It took me a while to understand my *Stop being rude* entry. Then I finally remembered the thank-you cards.

What the hell. It was four-thirty in the morning; may as well start somewhere. I completed the thank-you cards and fell into an exhausted sleep. Laurie woke me at 7 A.M. with hungry cries and I figured then was as good a time as any to begin my day.

Laurie and I waited in a stark white room to see Jim. There was a rectangular table in the center with four chairs around it and an all-too-familiar two-way mirror hanging from the wall. Jim appeared, escorted by a deputy sheriff. Jim was dressed in an orange jumpsuit, which immediately brought me to tears.

His face broke into a sad smile. "You don't think it's my color?" He embraced Laurie and me. "It's so good to see you guys. I had an awful night."

"Me, too. Couldn't sleep."

The deputy sheriff retreated out of the room, presumably to watch us through the mirror, giving us a false sense of privacy.

Jim absently brushed my hair off my face. "You look exhausted. Did you talk to my attorney?"

"He called me last night. He's meeting us here at nine."

Jim pulled a chair out for me. "So you heard about Svetlana Avery?"

I nodded, sitting. "What do you think happened?"

Jim sat next to me and rested his hand on my thigh. "All I could gather is that she was shot."

"She must have known something. When I told her about Michelle's death, she nearly passed out. She told me she had a migraine coming on. It seemed odd to me at the time, but maybe she was afraid."

Jim looked surprised. "When did you even meet with her?"

"The other day. She called the house."

"Why did she call us?"

"Well, actually, I called her, but never mind that."

Jim looked unconvinced. "You think she knew who killed Brad and Michelle?"

"Why else would she end up dead?"

Jim reached for my hand. "You can't investigate anymore, Kate. I can't stand the thought of anything happening to you."

"I have to. You're in jail."

"Leave it to the pros, honey. This Crane guy will figure it out. He sounded pretty confident last night when I spoke with him."

As if on cue, the door to the meeting room opened and Charles Crane appeared, escorted by the same deputy. The deputy waited for Mr. Crane to settle his briefcase onto the table and nod before closing the door.

Mr. Crane had a sweater wrapped around his shoulders and an unlit pipe between his teeth. He looked like his photo. He was small in stature with silver highlights in his dark hair.

He introduced himself as he took a seat across from us. "Not to sound insensitive, Mr. Connolly, but do we need to have our conversation in private?" Crane glanced in my direction.

"Anything you want to discuss with me, you can do so in front of my wife."

Mr. Crane nodded, clearing his throat. "As you're aware, you've been charged with assault with a deadly weapon, for fighting with your brother. The victim, George Connolly, is unavailable. Or, in other words, has not stepped forward to press charges. Therefore, if the case is to be presented to the DA, it will most likely be deemed 'insufficient grounds for arrest' and the case will be dropped."

I rocked Laurie back and forth in my arms, trying to dissipate my nervousness. "So, they're going to let Jim go?"

"Under other circumstances he would have already been released, but homicide left a request for inquiry under the name 'Connolly'," Crane said.

Jim exhaled. "When the cops booked me, they saw my last name and had to hold me so that McNearny could talk to me, right?"

Crane blinked his affirmation.

"You talked to McNearny?" I asked. "What did he want to know?"

Jim shrugged. "About George. When I'd seen him last,

where he was staying and what he was doing, who he was friends with. All that kind of stuff."

Crane tapped his unlit pipe. "Once the police have you in custody, they like to hold you as long as legally possible. Make you nervous, hope anything you've conveniently *forgotten* about your brother might be remembered."

Jim rubbed at his bloodshot eyes. "I really don't know anything—"

"I do. Well, a little." I filled them in on my conversation with George the previous day, including the cell phone number he'd given me.

"This may help," Crane said. "If we can bring George in, it will take the pressure off your husband. The police don't consider Jim a serious suspect, they're just trying to squeeze information out of him."

"That's a relief," I said.

"But there's bad news, too." Crane continued. "I'm told they want to have you participate in a lineup this afternoon, Mr. Connolly. They say they have an eyewitness who saw a man leaving Svetlana's apartment yesterday afternoon."

"That's not a problem. I can do the lineup. I never even met the woman and I was nowhere near her apartment. Well, actually, I can't say that. What I *can* say is that I don't even know where she lives. I was with Kate all morning at Pier 23."

"Unfortunately, we don't have a choice in the lineup. You have to do it. I wish you didn't. You don't know how many times people mistake someone's identity."

I sighed and pressed my head into Jim's shoulder. He squeezed my hand. "Everything is going to be fine, honey."

We looked at Crane for reassurance. He grimaced. "Is there much of a resemblance between you and your brother?"

* * *

I left the station feeling agitated and distressed. I needed to stay busy in order to keep myself from turning into a nervous wreck about Jim's situation.

First thing, I dialed Jim's office and told them he was still too sick to go into work. Next, I decided I should see the woman, Kiku, who had the appointment with Galigani. Her apartment was near San Francisco State University. Parking would be a unique challenge.

As I circled around her building, I reflected on the lineup.

Jim and George did look alike; they had the same coloring and handsome features. But Jim was almost a full head taller than George. I prayed that would account for something. Then again we didn't know anything about the description of the man leaving Svetlana's place. It could have been anybody. Maybe it wasn't George, after all.

I found parking close by and silently thanked the parking gods or goddesses, then threw in a prayer for Jim for good measure.

I rang the bell. A heavily pregnant woman wrapped in a red kimono answered the door. She was all of about four feet tall. Okay, maybe five feet, but barely that. The baby extended from her abdomen as though she had slipped a basketball under her kimono. Her pregnant belly was much more pronounced than mine had ever been, even when I was nine months along.

Maybe she'd have a boy. Could the old wives' tale be true, about boys extending outward and girls curling around?

"Hi, sorry to disturb you. Are you Kiku?"

She nodded, resting her hands on her belly.

"I'm Kate Connolly. Did you have an appointment with Investigator Galigani today?"

"Yes," Kiku said with a heavy Japanese accent.

"Unfortunately, he's in the hospital. Open heart surgery."

Kiku's face creased with the appropriate amount of concern one usually displays when hearing about someone else's misfortune.

Should I go so far as to say Galigani sent me?

Before I could decide, Kiku opened the door and motioned Laurie and me inside.

Her apartment was small. We entered straight into the living room. I could see into the tiny kitchen. There was a door to the left, which I assumed led to the bedroom. The place was sparsely decorated in soft feminine tones, and I could tell by the couch and the paintings that she had expensive taste.

She motioned me toward the sofa. I sat down, placing Laurie's bucket next to me.

Maybe it hadn't been a good idea to bring Laurie along. But this woman was pregnant. She couldn't be a murderer, right?

Kiku admired Laurie. "Beautiful baby girl. Big blue eyes!"

"Yours will be beautiful, too. When are you due?"

"Soon. Soon."

We smiled at each other as Kiku reached out and stroked Laurie's little foot. "Tell me, was labor difficult?"

It seemed odd that for nine months all I had thought about was Laurie's arrival and the upcoming labor. Stressing out about how I would handle everything. And yet now, one month later, I had hardly given labor a second thought.

I looked at Kiku's pregnant belly. "Don't worry about it. It's really not that bad, not like you're imagining. But I had the epidural, so I guess some people would say that's cheating."

After opting for pain relief during labor, I justified my choice by comparing the epidural with modern transportation. If someone said to me, "Women have been having babies without any pain medication since the beginning of time," my response was, "Yeah? And they also walked everywhere, because they didn't have a car. Now we have cars and pain medication. So, guess what? I had the epidural and we drove to the hospital." People didn't bring up the epidural after that.

"Tea?" she asked.

"Sure."

Kiku waddled to the kitchen. I dug out my notebook from Laurie's diaper bag and reviewed my notes.

The note "*next time interviewing suspect bring own water*" stared me in the face.

Oops.

I'd forgotten to pack water. Writing things down didn't help if I didn't read them in time. When was my memory going to come back?

I glanced around the living room. Kiku appeared to be living alone.

Could she have been Brad's other woman? She was short, whereas Michelle and Svetlana were both tall. Kiku was definitely in their league where looks were concerned. Her dark hair shone brightly and her complexion was flawless. Svetlana and Kiku were both immigrants. Maybe Brad had a weakness for . . . what? Accents?

A baby on the way?

Could it be Brad's?

If he'd been expecting a child with Kiku, it would give him a strong motive to leave Michelle. Galigani suspected his murderer was the other woman, but could five-foot Kiku have killed him? Shot him, maybe. But ditch his body in the bay? How? Could she have had the strength? And why? Lover's tiff?

And with Brad dead, what motive would she have had for murdering Michelle and Svetlana?

Although the women were not dumped, only Brad. Did this mean two murderers?

Kiku reappeared with a tray of green tea and ginger snaps.

"How long have you been in the country?" I asked.

"Two years." She propped her legs on the chair across from me, her movement constricted by her large belly. "Hard to stay on my feet."

"I know."

My feet had swelled so much during my pregnancy that I'd had to purchase size eight shoes, an entire size larger than usual, and never mind the style. They were shoes that not even my grandmother would have worn, but boy, were they comfy.

I watched Kiku delicately sip her tea.

I was so thirsty.

A pregnant woman wouldn't poison a new mom, would she?

I remembered Michelle sprawled across her living room floor.

Forget the tea.

"Do you know why Galigani wanted to meet with you?"

She nodded. "Meet about Brad."

She didn't look brokenhearted. This couldn't be the "other woman," unless she was acting. Maybe she was secretly falling apart.

I played with my teacup, hoping she wouldn't notice that I wasn't actually drinking anything. "How did you know Brad?"

"He hired me," she replied.

"You work at El Paraiso?"

She sipped her tea. "No. Not now. Before."

"How long did you work there?"

She tilted her head in thought. "Two months."

"Why did you leave?"

"My English is not so good. Too hard to work in a restaurant. People talking, talking, talking all the time. I go to beauty school now." She smiled shyly and covered her mouth as she giggled.

"Your English is fine," I said.

"Much better now. I study."

I glanced at the fine paintings covering her apartment walls. Where was a beauty school student getting all this money? "Are you working?"

"No. Not now. Later. After baby. Now I study. Beauty and English!" She giggled again.

I self-consciously ran my hand through my tangled curls. "I need to get a haircut."

"No problem. You come back. I can cut for you."

I laughed. "Sure. Why not?" I paused. "Kiku, did you know Brad was killed?" Her expression was oddly blank as she nodded. "He was killed on June fifteenth. I'm investigating his murder."

How could I politely ask if Brad was the father of her baby?

I mumbled, "Do you know who would want to kill Brad?"

Kiku's eyes grew wide. "No," she whispered.

I glanced at Laurie, still in her car seat bucket. She was examining a toy I'd attached to the strap. I felt at a loss. Obviously, Galigani had wanted me to meet Kiku, but why? I didn't know what questions to ask or what to do. I felt foolish. This kind, pregnant woman couldn't have shot Brad. What was I doing here? I stood in frustration, ready to leave. My movement caught Laurie's eye and she began to cry.

Kiku jumped up in distress. "Oh little girl! Little baby!"

I laughed, remembering the panic of the first few days when Laurie's cry would set off all sort of alarms inside me. "She's okay. Don't worry." I freed Laurie from the bucket to find her jumper soaked through. "She needs a diaper change. May I use your bathroom?"

Kiku indicated I should walk through the bedroom. I grabbed Laurie's diaper bag and headed toward the bathroom. Kiku's face still reflected a certain amount of terror. Oh well, she'd get used to life with an infant.

Inside the bathroom, I pulled out a clean jumper for Laurie and quickly went through the diaper routine. I turned her onto her tummy on the diaper pad and washed my hands in the sink. Laurie was now able to hold up her head and at least not have a fit when placed on her tummy. I studied my reflection in the medicine chest. I looked tired and frazzled. On impulse, I opened the medicine chest. A prescription for Valium stared me in the face.

I gagged. From my research online I knew the drug Michelle had died from, diazepam, was the generic form of Valium. Kiku had a prescription for Valium. The label showed a fifty count of five-milligram tablets. I rattled the bottle, then opened it. Ten pills remained. The date on the prescription was November of last year. Before Kiku's pregnancy. Before Michelle's death.

Laurie complained from her position on the floor. I gathered her and all the diaper paraphernalia. When I opened the door to the bathroom, Kiku was waiting for me.

"Everything okay?" she asked nervously.

I gave her an exhausted nod and followed her back to the living room.

While I settled Laurie into her car seat, I asked, "Kiku, do you recall where you were on June fifteenth?"

She tilted her head thoughtfully to the side. "I think June fifteenth Horoaki graduate." She opened a drawer from a side table and pulled out a photograph of a handsome smiling young man.

Was he the father?

I made a note in my notebook and smiled at Kiku. "Oh! Who's Horoaki? He's so cute!"

"My brother."

"Where did he graduate from? San Francisco State?"

"No. Dental school, UCSF."

Her alibi could easily be checked out.

"Ah! Good career ahead of him. Thank you for the tea." I swung Laurie's diaper bag onto my shoulder. "One more thing. Where were you Monday, October first?"

Kiku smiled. "Monday? Shopping. Why?"

"Brad's wife, Michelle, died on Monday. I was hoping maybe you knew something about it. Had seen or heard something . . ."

She frowned, her delicate forehead creasing in the middle. "I didn't know Brad's wife . . ."

I picked up Laurie's bucket and headed to the front door. "How about yesterday morning?"

Kiku looked confused. "Yesterday more shopping. Why?"

I smiled. "Of course. You have to get all the baby goodies ready before D-day."

I glanced around the apartment. It didn't look like she had purchased all that much, but she could have been window-shopping, too.

Kiku pressed her hands against her belly. "What was yesterday?"

"Svetlana Avery, Brad's ex-wife, was killed."

Kiku gasped, her complexion paling. She covered her mouth with her hand. "Poor people. Everyone killed?"

"Did you know Svetlana?"

Kiku shook her head furiously back and forth.

I closed my eyes and sighed. Something wasn't right. She had Valium, along with another million people in the world. Did it make her a killer? She claimed she didn't know Michelle or Svetlana. What did Galigani know that I was too stupid or inexperienced to figure out on my own?

"Thanks for your time, Kiku. If you think of anything that can help me with my investigation, will you call me?"

Kiku wrote down the number I rattled off. I'd have to

add another item to my never-ending to-do list—print business cards!

I waved to her as I stepped out. "Good luck with the birth. You'll have fun with your new baby. You'll love being a mom."

I checked my voice mail as soon as I reached the car. There was a message from Crane; he'd tried the number I'd given him for George and got a "temporarily out of service" message. I threw my cell phone to the floor on the passenger side and screamed out my frustration, startling Laurie enough to make her cry, too. Great!

"Sorry, petunia," I mumbled.

Laurie continued to fuss. I put the car in drive and pulled out. The motion soon settled her down.

I aimlessly headed to Pier 23. No George in sight. Okay, Plan B.

I glanced at my watch as I parked in front of El Paraiso. Not quite lunchtime.

I pulled the baby carrier out of my trunk and put it on, then picked Laurie up out of the car seat and adjusted her inside the carrier. She immediately nestled herself between my breasts and fell asleep.

I walked into the restaurant. It was the lull before the noontime rush. The hostess with stud piercings on her face was sorting menus at her podium. She glanced unenthusiastically at me.

"Hi. Is George Connolly working today?"

She frowned and fingered the stud through her eyebrow. "George Connolly? We don't have anyone here by that name."

"Okay. How about the manager, Rich Hanlen?"

"Oh. He's not in yet. He usually comes in around noon. If it's important, he's probably across the street." She lifted her chin in the general direction of the window.

I looked through glass and saw a bar. "Café du Sur?" I asked.

She'd already gone back to sorting the menus.

I crossed the street and pulled open the door of Café du Sur. It took a moment for my eyes to adjust to the dim interior. A country song was playing on an old-fashioned jukebox against the wall. The bar was practically deserted, except for the bartender, Rich, and two older men playing dice. They all looked up at me as I came in.

Perfect. If I could talk to Rich here, I wouldn't have to suffer through another conversation in his dark office, especially with Laurie in tow. There was no way I wanted to risk that again, although I felt Laurie was much safer now nestled next to me in the baby carrier rather than in the stroller.

The bartender moved down the bar toward me. Rich stood and picked up his drink, as a slow look of recognition crossed his face. I couldn't very well say he was happy to see me.

I managed a weak hello and a wave. He broke away from the other men and met me in the middle of the bar, along with the bartender.

I felt like an idiot. What kind of mother would take a four-week-old baby into a bar?

Rich placed his empty glass on the counter and said, "I'll have another and whatever the lady would like."

The bartender nodded and turned to me. "Ma'am?"

I'd have to get used to the "ma'am" thing quickly. It seemed to be happening far too often these days. On the bright side, I could have something to drink here without worrying that the bartender would poison me.

"How about an orange juice?"

The bartender poured my juice and prepared an Irish coffee for Rich in silence. I watched with longing as the bartender piled the whipped cream onto the coffee, but resisted the urge to change my order.

After we were served, the bartender retreated to the end of the bar where the older men were sitting, out of earshot, although still safely in sight.

"What can I do for you?" Rich asked, placing a twenty on the bar to cover our drinks.

"I'm really in a bind. I need to know where George is. I saw him yesterday, he told me he works at El Paraiso, but your hostess says he doesn't."

Rich played with his glass. "Oh, she doesn't know him. If you're looking for him, why not try his old lady? I mean, the baby's due anytime, so he won't be far."

I felt my heart thumping in my throat. I tried to swallow it down and act casual. My shock must have shown.

He raised an eyebrow. "You didn't know you were going to be an auntie? Gal by the name of Kiku. She's very nice. I'm sure you'll all be one happy, cozy family." He stirred the cream into his coffee and took a self-satisfied sip.

I fought the childish impulse to smash his face into the cream.

Kiku was with George?

"May I ask where you were yesterday morning, say between the hours of nine and noon?"

He frowned. "Here at the bar. Why?"

"Svetlana Avery was found murdered yesterday morning. Shot."

His face paled. "Holy shit."

"A witness saw a man leaving her house. Any idea who that could have been?"

Rich paused, then took a long drink and shook his head. "Nope. I knew her when she was with Brad. Good-looking chick, I'm sure there was no shortage of men in her life."

"What about Monday, more or less around the same time, nine to noon?"

He studied me a moment. "Monday was when Michelle was killed. Are you trying to pin these murders on me?"

"Not at all. Can you tell me where you were?"

Rich swung on the barstool and called, "Hey, Burt, can you come here a sec?"

The bartender sauntered over. "Another?"

"No," Rich said. "Can you tell the lady where I was on Monday from nine to noon?"

Burt smiled, then turned to me. "Rich was here, sweetheart, sitting right there on that barstool, having a couple of Irish coffees."

"How 'bout yesterday?" Rich pushed.

"Same."

"Thanks, Burt," Rich said.

Burt nodded, then retreated back to his corner.

I drank my juice and decided on a different tactic. "Rich, I need your help." I softened my voice. "I've been hired by Brad's mother to find out what happened to him."

His shoulder rose as he inhaled, then dropped a degree as he let out an audible sigh. "I already told you I don't know what happened."

"Who was he sleeping with?"

"Back to that? You're relentless, aren't you?" He studied first my face, then tried my breast, which due to the baby carrier was pushed to the side and conveniently located for his perusal.

I shifted on the barstool. "You won't find the answer there."

He laughed, a curiously embarrassed laugh. And I thought he was beyond social mores.

"Sorry . . . I . . . yeah, you were asking about Brad. Chicks always ask about Brad. All my life they've asked about him, and now, even when he's dead and gone, they're still asking."

"You hardly seem like you'd play second fiddle to him."

"You mean I look okay? That's what you mean. But chicks like money and Brad had tons of it. Not that I'm hurting now either, but, you know, the Averys are loaded."

"Are you close to Gloria Avery?"

"What do you mean?"

"She seemed very fond of you," I lied.

He looked pleasantly surprised. "Old Glo? I always thought she had a soft spot for me."

"You've known her a long time?"

He polished off his drink and pushed the empty glass away from him. "Well, sure. Brad and I met in high school."

"You went to the same school?"

"Are you kidding me? Brad went to Trinity. You know how expensive that school is? I went to good ole Lincoln High. We met at a Holy Rosary dance in '93."

"I went to Holy Rosary."

He looked me over, his eyes narrowed and his brow furrowed.

I couldn't read the look. Was it disdain?

He said, "Right. I forgot you knew Michelle in high school."

How did Rich know Michelle and I had gone to high school together?

"Yeah, but Brad didn't go to any dance with Michelle. I don't think they knew each other then."

Rich tried to hide his smirk in his drink. "Nah, it wasn't Michelle."

"Who'd he go with?"

He shrugged his shoulders. "It was a long time ago. I barely remember the name of my date, much less his." He stood, smoothing down his leather jacket. "I gotta get to the restaurant."

"Who was your date?"

"What?"

"At the dance, when you met Rich, who was your date?"

"Carol something."

He waved at the bartender and slipped out the front door. I pulled out my notebook. What had the interview yielded me?

Nothing.

Well, at least I knew where to look for George and that he was expecting a baby. What now? I reviewed my to-do list, checking things off and adding a few.

To-Do List:

1. Free Jim.

2. Find Brad and/or Michelle's killer.

3. ✓ ~~Interview Kiku (bring own water!)~~.

4. ✓ ~~Tummy Time~~.

5. Call Winter Henderson re: hippie chick alibi.

6. Make OB appointment.

7. ✓ ~~Stop being rude (a.k.a. write thank-you cards)~~.

8. Check out Horoaki graduation date from UCSF.

9. Print business cards.

10. Find George AGAIN.

CHAPTER SIXTEEN

The Fifth Week—
The Need to Suck

On my way home I dialed first Jim's cell phone—no answer—then Mr. Crane's. No answer. I left a somewhat irrational message for Mr. Crane with Kiku and George's address.

By the time Laurie and I got home, we were both exhausted and hungry.

I called Jim's name as soon as I opened the garage door.

No Jim.

In frustration, I threw Laurie's diaper bag across the room.

The witness couldn't have identified him, right?

I melted onto the sofa with Laurie. She howled in my face.

"I know, pumpkin pie. You're hungry."

After all her needs were met, she continued to wail. I fought the urge to join her. "What is it now, jelly bean?" I gazed into her lovely eyes. No tears. Her wail was more of a complaint than a cry.

I found a pacifier I had been given at the hospital and placed it in Laurie's mouth. She stopped crying.

Ah. Peace and quiet.

The pacifier soothed her overwhelming need to suckle, without getting additional nutrition. Nonnutritive sucking, that's what Laurie's pediatrician had called it.

I set Laurie on the floor in her baby gym. She studied the hanging cow, monkey, and chicken.

Now what would I do about food for myself? I needed to eat to keep my mind from spiraling off the deep end about Jim. Stopping at the grocery store had never even crossed my mind. I made a mental note to add it to my to-do list.

I rummaged through our phone book drawer looking for the menu of the Chinese restaurant down the street. Before Laurie was born, Jim and I used to eat there at least once a week. Since Laurie was born, we hadn't eaten there at all. My mouth watered, thinking about their sweet-and-sour prawns.

I found an old receipt from the restaurant that was covered with what appeared to be soy sauce.

Gross.

I would have to clean out this drawer.

Another thing to add to my never-ending to-do list.

I moved on to our map drawer and found nothing helpful except a nail file, clippers, and a bottle of hand moisturizer. What were these items doing in our map drawer?

Time to get organized, Kate. Plus, I needed to do my nails.

Where was the menu for Dragon House?

I wandered through the house. I stopped in the kitchen. On the refrigerator staring at me from under a cookie magnet was the pink menu.

Sometimes I could miss my own nose.

How would I ever solve a triple homicide if I was so

oblivious? Had I missed clues that had been right in front of me?

I dialed Dragon House and ordered chow mein, pot stickers, and sweet-and-sour prawns.

"Anything else?" the clerk asked.

I ignored the pang of guilt as I added Peking-style spareribs to the order. I reasoned that Jim should be home at any minute and would be starving. Besides, I needed the extra five-hundred calories a day for Laurie.

After replacing the receiver on the hook, it immediately rang back.

Hopefully, it wasn't the restaurant calling to tell me my credit card hadn't gone through. Or worse yet, the sheriff's department with bad news about Jim. I pushed the thought from my head and reminded myself to stay positive.

"Kate? It's George."

"George! Where are you?"

"Is Jim there?"

"No. He's still—"

"I really need to talk to you about something, Kate."

"That makes two of us."

"I'm on your corner. Can I come up?"

I felt ready to explode at him, but checked my anger. If I blew up at him for causing all this mess, I might not hear what he wanted to tell me.

In a matter of seconds I heard George making his way up my front steps. I scooped Laurie off the floor and opened the door.

George's face broke into a smile when he saw us. "Can I hold her?"

I hesitated momentarily. What was I afraid of? George had never been anything but a gentleman with me.

George noticed my hesitation. "It's cool. I don't have to hold her. But, I mean, I won't drop her or anything."

I laughed. "I know." I handed her off to him and sank into an easy chair. "What's going on?"

"Things are all messed up, Kate. I don't know what to do." He looked at Laurie then back at me. "I met a gal at the restaurant and, well, she's expecting our baby."

I hid my surprise. I had expected to have to beat the information out of him. Why was he suddenly forthcoming?

Something was wrong.

"When is the baby due?" I asked.

"Pretty soon. I'm getting kinda nervous."

"Are you going to marry her?"

George paced the room, bouncing Laurie in his arms. "I don't know, Kate. I like her a lot . . . well, hell . . . I love her. She's great. It's just that, well, you know, she's pushing me to commit . . . and I'm not good at providing and . . . being responsible."

"It's time to step up to the plate. A baby is a big responsibility. You don't want your baby out there without a father." I tried not to think of my own husband currently behind bars. "It'd be like a rowboat with only one little oar in the water. Spinning in circles. Kids need both oars in the water to go places."

George gazed at Laurie. "You're right. I know you're right."

"So, what's the problem?"

"She doesn't know about . . . you know, about my being on the streets. When I saw her at the restaurant . . . Damn, she was so cute. Brad knew I had a crush on her. He helped me clean up and make an impression, you know?"

I nodded. "If you're worried about my saying anything, don't."

George looked relieved. "There's something else, Kate. On Monday, when I was going to Michelle's to make the drop . . ."

"Drop?"

George looked at me sheepishly. "I mean, you know, the money or whatever."

Anger flared inside me, and I jumped up from the easy chair. "Whatever, what? Were you dropping off money at her house? Or something else? Or what?"

George took a step back and said firmly, "Money."

I raised my voice. "Why? Why not deposit it straight into the bank?"

George matched my tone. "I just do what I'm told." We studied each other a moment. He continued, "Anyway, what I wanted to tell you is that I saw someone. I saw who Michelle was with that morning. I'm scared, Kate."

"Who?" I pressed.

"She was with my girlfriend."

I took a deep breath, hoping it would slow my galloping heart. "What?"

"My girlfriend was over there visiting Michelle."

"Kiku?"

Kiku with the access to the Valium. Sweet, pretty, pregnant Kiku.

"You know my girlfriend?"

"What was she doing at Michelle's place?"

"Well, she didn't kill her, if that's what you're asking."

"Why are you scared? What do you think she was doing there? Did you ask her? Did you interrupt them?"

"No. I left. Because, see, that's the thing. I don't know what she was doing there. What could she have been doing at Michelle Avery's place?"

"Have you asked her?"

He stared at the ground. "No."

"Maybe we should talk to her together," I said.

The doorbell sounded. George jumped. "Are you expecting someone?"

I opened the front door, hoping for Jim, but was greeted by the Chinese food delivery guy. I clutched the pink plastic bag and peeked inside. White steaming containers peered back at me. My mouth watered.

I closed the front door and turned to George. "You've got to try this. The best in town."

I popped opened a box, pulled out a pot sticker, and handed it to him.

George sank his teeth into the pot sticker. "Pretty good," he said through a mouthful. "Hot."

I nodded, biting around the corners of my pot sticker, letting most of the heat steam out before popping it into my mouth. "Let's meet up tomorrow, talk to Kiku."

His face fell. "Can't we do it today? I've been avoiding asking her all week."

"I can't today. I'm . . . I'm waiting for Jim to come home."

"Doesn't he normally get home around five? We've got plenty of time."

My stomach flip-flopped.

How much should I tell George?

"Sit down. Let me get us plates."

I made my way to the kitchen and scrambled for a couple of place settings and napkins. Obviously, George didn't know about Svetlana. Where had *he* been yesterday morning?

I returned to the living room to find George staring down at Laurie.

"She sure doesn't cry much."

"Ha. Not while she's being held. Just try to put her down to have lunch."

I scooped generous portions of steaming chow mein onto each plate. George looked around for somewhere to set Laurie. I indicated the bassinet with my fork and proceeded to shovel a sweet-and-sour prawn into my mouth.

George was able to easily extract himself from Laurie. Sitting down to eat, he said, "Babies don't seem so hard. I don't know what everyone makes such a big deal about."

I refrained from letting my eyes roll into the back of my head and continued to devour the food on my plate. I managed to mumble, "Just wait."

We ate in silence for a moment before I asked, "George, before we saw you at the pier yesterday, where were you?"

He eyed me suspiciously as he slurped up a noodle. "Why?"

"Svetlana Avery was found murdered. Same gun that killed Brad."

George's fork clattered onto our hardwood floor. He stood, then sat back down. "Oh my God. How do you know?"

"Jim's still in jail. Homicide has been questioning him about you. They told him about Svetlana. They have a witness who saw a man leaving her apartment."

George's eyes nearly popped out of his skull. He stood. "I gotta go."

I grabbed his arm. "No, you don't! Where do you think you're going? You have to get to the police station! Jim's still in jail because of you!"

He pulled his arm free. "Sorry. Things are really getting screwed up. I gotta go . . . I gotta try and fix . . ." He bolted toward the front door and pulled it open.

"Wait, George! Where were you yesterday? Was it you at Svetlana's? Is that why—"

George bounded down the steps. "I'll call you later. Don't worry about Jim. I'm gonna fix everything."

My heart plummeted to new depths.

Laurie let out a distressed wail as though sensing my panic. I rushed toward the front window.

Where could he be going? I wanted to follow him, grab him by his ear, and drag him to the police station. I should have never settled for talking to him.

Why hadn't I called Mr. Crane after George called me?

I could phone him now, but what good would that do? George was already gone.

I picked Laurie up and nestled her into my shoulder. I paced, willing an idea, any idea, to come into my mind.

Hopelessness and exhaustion bore down on me.

I was fighting back tears when the phone rang. I grabbed the phone, praying it would be Jim.

I was greeted by a far too chipper voice. "Hi, Kate? This is Rachel from Dr. Greene's office. You haven't made your six-week appointment yet and I was calling to see if I could schedule that for you."

I took a breath. "Oh. Yeah. I guess so."

"Is everything all right?"

"Uh . . . yeah," I said, trying to match her cheerfulness.

"How are you feeling, Kate?" Her voice suddenly carried more weight.

"I'm fine," I said, nearly choking on the lump that was rapidly forming in my throat.

"Are you feeling *overwhelmed*?"

What an understatement. One infant, three murders, a jailed husband, and a new career. No. I wasn't *overwhelmed*!

"I guess you can call it that," I managed.

"Do you have the baby blues?" she asked.

"Baby blues?" I repeated.

"You're not . . ." Her voice changed to a whisper. "*Depressed*, are you?"

"No, no, no," I repeated a little too gregariously, jarring Laurie from her sleeping position on my shoulder.

"It's very common, Kate. You don't need to feel ashamed. Should I have one of our specialists call you?"

"No. I'm fine. Really, just fine."

"Let me just make a note here."

"What? A note? A note where?"

"In your file. I'll have someone call you."

"What are you writing in my file? That I'm depressed? Don't write that. I'm not depressed. I'm fine."

"It looks like Clara has an opening this afternoon. She'll call you around three, okay?"

Rachel hung up, leaving me with a dial tone in one ear and Laurie wailing in the other.

A note in my file?

Another thing to live down. Like the *poor* rating Laurie and I had gotten on breastfeeding. Only this felt worse. I was in this one all on my own.

I fell into an exhausted catnap on the sofa, with Laurie cuddled beside me. When the phone rang again, it interrupted a dream I was having about being stuck in the desert, dying of thirst.

I clucked my dry tongue against the roof of my mouth. No wonder. When was the last time I'd had anything to drink?

I stretched for the cordless phone, trying not to disrupt Laurie.

My voice cracked as I squeezed out a greeting.

"What's wrong, darling?" Mom asked.

"Mom! How are you? How's Hank?"

"We're both fine. Now, what's the matter?"

"Nothing. Why?"

"I can tell by your voice."

"I just need to get something to drink."

"No, that's not it. What's wrong?"

I sighed. How could she know? Maternal instinct?

"Nothing." My voice cracked further and tears streamed down my cheeks.

"Are you crying?"

"No," I sobbed.

"I'm coming over."

"I'm fine, Mom," I said into an empty receiver.

* * *

Mom arrived within ten minutes. She wore a huge hat with feathers on it, as though she had just stepped out of an old Errol Flynn movie.

"What's with the hat? Were you fencing?" I asked as Mom quickly diapered Laurie.

"Isn't it fabulous! I got such a deal on it."

"Clearly." I giggled.

Mom ignored me and gathered the lunch remnants from the living room. On her insistence, I collapsed onto the couch while she did the dishes and made us tea.

Over tea, I reluctantly filled her in on my new client, my hopes to launch my own PI business and stay out of corporate America, Jim's arrest, Svetlana's murder, and George's sudden departure.

Mother's eyes remained glued on me as I finished telling her about Rachel's call and the dreaded note in my file.

Mother chuckled.

"Why are you laughing?"

"Darling, you have enough to worry about without fretting over a note in a chart."

"I want you guys to be proud of me."

"I am proud."

"I know *you're* proud of me. I mean, you're my mom. You're proud of me the way I'm proud of Laurie. I mean, all she can really do is lie there, but I'm proud of her because she's mine. I'm sure that's how you feel about me, but I want you and Jim and Laurie to feel proud of me, proud of my accomplishments. And what am I really accomplishing?"

Mom looked at me, perplexed. "Darling, you just had a baby! You're starting your own business. You're accomplishing a lot. You're going to be very successful. You *are* successful."

She leaned across the coffee table and squeezed my hand. "Don't be upset. Honestly, this is just the hormones.

Don't be so mopey. Have some tea, cheer up. Jim will be home any minute."

"How do you know?"

"The police couldn't possibly hold him overnight again. Jim was with you yesterday morning."

"I'm not considered a credible alibi. I don't think so anyway. And even if I was, I won't be now that they put that note in my file."

"You're not depressed, are you?"

Was I?

I did feel a heaviness.

I suppressed a yawn. "I feel like I haven't slept, I mean really slept, since before Laurie was born. And I feel like I won't sleep until I get to the bottom of these murders, either that or until she's eighteen."

Mom smiled and patted my hand. "I'd tell you to sleep right now, but I know you better than that. Go find George. And this time, don't let him get away. Drag him to the police station, even if he's kicking and screaming. I'll watch Laurie."

I tied a bright gold, cranberry, and orange striped scarf around my neck, hoping to give myself a little lift and relieve my washed-out and tired-looking face. The weather was starting to change from balmy Indian summer to chilly fall so I grabbed my leather jacket and put it on. I searched my dresser for car keys. I felt so light, preparing to go out without Laurie, I thought I was forgetting something.

Where were my car keys?

Ah! Diaper bag.

Where was the diaper bag?

I thought back to what seemed like an eternity ago—this morning.

Oh, yes. I had flung the bag across the living room.

It lay curled in a heap by a corner side table. I rummaged through it and located my keys.

Mother eyed me from her position on the couch. "What are you doing?"

"Trying to find my mind. I know it's here somewhere."

Mother smirked. "Give it a few weeks, Kate. You'll feel like yourself in no time."

I shoved the keys into my jacket pocket and fingered a slithering piece of metal. I pulled it out. In my hand was the bracelet I had pocketed a couple weeks ago, outside the medical examiner's office with Michelle.

"What's that?" Mother asked.

I shrugged. "A bracelet. It fell out of one of George's bags."

Laurie woke and wailed, and Mother got up to get her. "I'll see to her. You go on."

I studied the bracelet a moment. Silver with the inscription BERRY on it. The clasp was broken. Could it be Kiku's?

CHAPTER SEVENTEEN

The Fifth Week—Determination

When I arrived at Kiku's, I was surprised to find the door slightly open.

I knocked and called out, "Kiku!"

No answer.

I knocked again and called louder.

A chill ran down my spine. I reached into my pockets, searching for my cell phone.

Shit.

It was still in the diaper bag on my living room floor.

I pushed the front door open and called again. "Kiku!"

Nothing.

I stepped into the apartment.

Goose bumps shot up my arms. I scanned the living room, half expecting to see Kiku lying facedown on the floor. What I saw instead was an abundance of baby paraphernalia. A swing, a bouncy chair, and a shimmering white bassinet filled the small room.

Maybe she'd had her baby shower? That would explain

the apartment door being ajar. Maybe someone was help-ing her carry up the gifts and she'd be back any second.

I surprised myself by feeling left out. Of course. Kiku didn't know I was her baby's aunt. George had probably never told her about his family.

On further thought, she couldn't be bringing in gifts. The stuff that was here was already assembled. If she was bringing things up, she'd probably bring everything up at once, then assemble it later.

Baby gear always comes in a box, with the ridiculous statement: "Easy to assemble." And I don't care what they claim—none of it, ever, could be opened or closed with "just one hand." The boxes are covered in lies.

I walked farther into the apartment. Everything looked normal in the kitchen.

Why was Kiku's door open?

Had someone kidnapped her?

I imagined Kiku tied up hostage style in someone's filthy garage, gagged, her pregnant belly protruding.

I tried to shake the thought from my mind as I made my way into her small bedroom, looking for any kind of distress.

Nothing seemed out of place. The room was impec-cable.

Where could she be?

I peeked into her closet for boogeymen.

No killer hiding there.

The open front door probably meant nothing.

Could she be having the baby?

Oh, God!

I imagined Kiku running out of the apartment, looking for help, leaving the door open. I hoped nothing was wrong.

I glanced down at a jewelry dish that held several small gold rings. All too small, I was sure, for her to wear at the moment.

I glanced down at my own hands. I had yet to replace my wedding ring. I fingered a pretty gold necklace and matching earrings.

Hmmm, all gold.

No silver like the bracelet I'd found.

I ambled over to the bedroom window that overlooked the apartment house gardens. There, I saw Kiku bent over a bed of dahlias.

I pried open the window and called out to her. "Kiku! What are you doing? You shouldn't be gardening!"

Kiku looked up and squinted toward the window. A look of recognition crossed her face. "Only a few flowers," she said with a laugh. "For Baby."

"Yes, but it's not good for you. I don't think so anyway. You shouldn't be on the ground like that."

I don't actually know anything about gardening. Jim is the green thumb in our family. But I certainly didn't like seeing a nine-month-pregnant lady on her knees, weeding!

"It's okay! My mother gardened until I was born."

I was unconvinced. "Oh. Well, all right. But come inside now. It's getting cold."

Kiku struggled to her feet, holding a few cut dahlias in her hand. She disappeared into a doorway and a few minutes later I greeted her at her front door.

"The door was open," I explained. "I was worried about you, so I came in."

"I didn't remember where I left the key, so I leave door open."

I stared at her. Ah, the forgetfulness of pregnancy. I had locked myself out of my car three times and had been warned by AAA road service that I had exceeded the maximum calls. One more call would have cost me at least a hundred and fifty dollars.

"You can't leave the door open, though," I protested.

"Why? Neighbors good people."

"But I walked right in. What if . . . well, what if it wasn't me and . . ." I stopped myself.

What if I was the one in danger? After all, Kiku had been with Michelle that morning and had access to Valium.

Kiku waved a hand in the air, dismissing my objection, and proceeded to the kitchen. I followed her and watched as she placed the dahlias in a bright vase.

Kiku turned and looked at me expectantly. "You come for haircut?"

I laughed. "Ah! No."

"You need a trim."

What was the harm?

"Sure. Yes. Go ahead and trim."

She motioned me to one of the kitchen chairs. "Sit."

From a drawer she pulled out a plastic wrap and whipped it around me. She grabbed a spray bottle and spritzed my hair.

I fingered the bracelet in my pocket. "Kiku, George is my brother-in-law."

Kiku spun me around to face her. "Brother?" she cried happily. "I didn't know. Didn't know you were George's sister."

"Sister-in-law. I'm married to George's brother, Jim."

Kiku selected a pair of scissors from the drawer. "George has brother? I no meet."

"Do you know where George is now?" I asked.

She stood behind me and evaluated my hair. "At work."

I turned around to see her face. "Yeah, but what's he do exactly?"

"He works at restaurant, El Paraiso. That's how we meet. He's a chef."

A chef? Oh brother, she didn't know a thing.

"Kiku, George told me he saw you at Michelle Avery's place the morning she was killed."

She turned me around and proceeded to whack at my

hair. I tried not to shudder at the length of the locks that were falling around me.

I suddenly remembered the play *Sweeney Todd*. Probably questioning someone about her whereabouts on the morning of a murder while she's holding sharp scissors wasn't a smart idea.

"Yes," she said without skipping a beat.

"You told me you didn't know Michelle Avery."

She stopped cutting my hair. I turned toward her. Her eyes were glossy. "No, I mean, I didn't know Michelle dead. George didn't tell me. I went to see her about George's job."

"His job?"

"Yes. I went to restaurant. George no there. I worry, maybe he fired. Baby is coming, we need money."

"What did Michelle tell you?"

Kiku turned me around and proceeded with the haircut. "Michelle said he still worked for her. At restaurant. She said George good worker. But now I'm worried again because she and Brad are dead!"

What about the wine at Michelle's place? Someone had drunk wine with Michelle. Kiku wouldn't have been drinking in her condition, right? So maybe Michelle had had another visitor.

"Did you see anyone else coming or going from Michelle's place?"

Kiku remained silent for a moment. "No."

I wondered about her hesitation. Then I realized she was studying me and my hair.

My breath caught. "Is everything okay?"

"You're beautiful!" She smiled and brandished a mirror in front of me. The cut, while far shorter than I would have ever conceded to under other circumstances, looked stunning. I felt sassy and hip.

"Thank you."

Kiku smiled. "Ten dollars."

I laughed. "You deserve twenty, at least."

I dug into my pockets.

No wallet.

It was in the diaper bag, along with everything else. I pulled out the bracelet.

"Uh . . . Um . . . I forgot my wallet, but I'm good for it. I promise." I handed her the silver bracelet. "This must be yours."

"No."

"It has to be. It fell out of George's bag."

She read the inscription on the bracelet. "What's 'berry'?"

I shrugged. "I thought you'd know."

She studied the bracelet in silence. "Why George have that?" She handed it back to me. "If he has other woman, I . . ." She picked up the discarded hair scissors and snapped them open and closed. "I kill him."

I smiled in spite of myself. "I don't think he's seeing another woman. Maybe someone lost it at the restaurant or something. See, the clasp is broken."

Kiku nodded but remained pensive. After a moment, I put it back into my pocket.

She moved to get a broom. I got up. "Let me do that." As I swept my curls, I said, "Yesterday you told me you didn't know Svetlana Avery. Did you mean you didn't know she was dead?"

She paused for a split second and said, "No. I don't know Svetlana."

Hmmm.

She said she'd been shopping. That could be true with all the baby gear around, but then where had the gear been this morning?

I finished sweeping. "So, looks like you're ready for the baby with all that stuff." I nodded toward the living room. "Where'd you get it?"

Kiku smiled. "Babies R Us."

Great.

If she had shopped at a neighborhood store, I might have been able to check her alibi, but there was no way with a megastore. Everyone's anonymous.

I arrived home exhausted but felt exhilarated when I saw Jim seated on the couch chatting to Mom and holding Laurie.

He stood when he saw me. I rushed over to him and embraced both him and Laurie. "You're home, home, home!" I squeezed him tight, holding on to him and breathing him in.

"I'm so sorry, honey," he said into my hair. "I shouldn't have let George get to me like that. If I had kept my cool, none of that would have happened."

I shushed him. "Don't worry."

He pulled away to look into my face. "I do worry. You're totally stressed out . . . or . . . or depressed."

I glared at Mom, who raised her shoulders and gave me her best I-couldn't-help-it look. "The nurse called a little while ago."

"I'm *not* depressed!"

Jim hugged me. "I know. I know. *Overwhelmed.*" I nodded. He continued, "I hated putting you through that."

"And me," Mom piped in. "You put me through it, too. I worry, too, you know."

Jim smiled down at Mom, who was still seated comfortably on the couch. "Thanks."

Mom waved her hand in a gesture that said it was nothing. As if on cue, Laurie wailed.

Jim patted her. "I know. You, too."

"It's almost six. I think she's hungry," I said.

"I'll second that," Jim said, handing Laurie to me. "It's Friday night. How about I take us all out for pizza?"

Mom winked. "That's a nice idea, hon, but I have a hot date tonight."

"Oh, Mom, can you ask Hank a question about Valium for me?"

Jim and Mom looked at me curiously.

"It's nothing, really. At least I hope not. Ask him how many five-milligram tablets are a lethal dose when combined with wine."

Jim and I decided to celebrate his homecoming with an outing to our favorite Italian pizzeria. It was relatively close to our home, but not walking distance, so we circled endlessly looking for parking.

Finally, Jim pulled to the front of the building. "You and Laurie jump out and I'll find a spot."

I was more than happy to take him up on the offer. My legs were aching from running around all day, and besides, I was famished. I grabbed Laurie and her car seat and entered the restaurant.

Tony, the son of the owner, greeted me. He had been acting as host for as long as Jim and I had been coming here. "Kate! Long time no see. Now I know why. She's beautiful, like her mommy."

Although Tony was in his thirties like me, he looked twenty. He was tall and slim, with dark curly hair and a permanent smile.

"Always the flatterer. I see you haven't changed."

He grinned as he ushered me to a booth. "Where's Jim?" he asked.

"Looking for parking."

He nodded, letting his lips form a thin line. "He may be a while, then. What can I get you to drink."

"I'll have a ginger ale. Oh, and a high chair please."

Tony looked puzzled. "Isn't she too small to sit in a high chair?"

"I know a trick."

He returned with my soda and the high chair. I flipped the highchair over so it was upside down and placed Laurie's bucket car seat securely on top of the legs.

"I've never seen that before," he said.

The restaurant door flew open and a flustered Jim made his way in. Eyeing Tony up and down, he threatened his usual, "I'm going to stop coming here unless you do something about the parking situation."

Tony laughed. "Good to see you, too."

As soon as Tony was out of earshot, I leaned across the table. "Have you noticed he doesn't age?"

"Do you have the hots for him or something?" Jim asked through a smile.

"No. Just for you, because you're so lovable."

"And free."

"Yup. Men with a record really turn me on."

Jim laughed in spite of himself. His face looked drawn and his eyes were bloodshot.

I reached across the table for his hand. "Was it awful?"

"The conditions? No. It was remarkably clean and quiet, actually. But it still sucked being away from you and jelly bean. And stressing over whatever the hell George has gotten himself into."

I squeezed his hand. "So what happened at the lineup?"

"Not much that I could tell. They told me to walk into a room with four other guys. We stood there, turned around, posed. I prayed."

"Did you see the witness?"

Jim shook his head.

I fingered the menu. "After everything that's happened, I was scared, you know, scared that they would actually try to build a case against you or something."

"God, me, too. Crane made it sound like the wrong person is identified more often than not. But even so, he told me the cops probably couldn't hold me even if they did get a match, because it would have been circumstantial evidence, and I guess they need more than that for a homicide arrest."

"Like a smoking gun."

Jim raised his eyebrows and nodded. I filled him in on George's story about the missing gun. Jim's face was grim as he listened.

Tony appeared with an antipasto, compliments of the chef, his father, who peered at us from behind the pizza oven and yelled, "Beautiful baby, it's about time!"

Tony asked, "What will it be tonight, the usual or something else?"

Jim glanced over at me. I nodded. "The usual."

Jim dipped his bread into olive oil. I continued my George story and ended with the impending birth.

"Is he going to marry Kiku?" Jim asked.

"He says he doesn't know yet. And when I went over there to give her this bracelet, she said it wasn't hers." I pulled the silvery metal out of my pocket and showed Jim.

He took the bracelet from me and read it. "Where'd you get this?"

"It fell out of one of George's bags. Do you think he's seeing someone else?"

Jim shrugged his shoulder. "God, honey, with George, who knows?"

He scooped salami into his mouth, looking miserable. He motioned to Tony and ordered a beer. I poured olive oil on my bread plate and dipped the bread in silence. Laurie cooed and ah-gooed from her bucket seat, determined to get our attention.

After a few pulls on his beer, Jim said, "You know I care about George, Kate. But all my life he's always been more trouble than he's worth. It breaks my heart. You gotta know that. Here's the person who's the most genetically similar to me on the planet and ... if he's like that ... I can't be too far—"

"Stop. You know you're nothing like him. Genetically, okay, I get that. But come on, you guys are totally different."

"It didn't feel that way today, sitting in jail and then having to do a lineup. It was the low point of my life."

I scooted out of my side of the booth and slid in next to Jim. He put his arm around me and squeezed my shoulder. "How do we get out of this, honey?"

"Mrs. Avery hired me to find out who killed Brad. I can solve this, Jim."

He smiled. "Leave it to my lovely wife. She'll get us out of the hole by digging deeper."

"I *can* solve this."

"I'm sure you can, what with all the experience you have." He grinned in spite of himself. "You know, I've got to admit it, honey, if you really want something, you keep on insisting until you get it."

"I really don't want to go back to the office." I rubbed his back. "How can filing drawings, managing schedules, and making coffee compare to being with you and Laurie? Plus I *really* want to keep you out of jail."

Jim smirked. "Tell me your best theory."

Just then a piping hot pizza, topped with Gorgonzola, pancetta, and caramelized onions arrived at our table. "I'll whisper it in your ear."

He served me a piece of pizza, placing his hand on my thigh. "This gets better and better." He leaned in close to kiss me. "And by the way, I love your new haircut."

CHAPTER EIGHTEEN

The Sixth Week—
Separation Anxiety

At 7 A.M. Laurie and Jim were both still sacked out from the day before.

I got out of bed. I had only a week and a half left of maternity leave. Ten days. Two hundred and forty hours.

I needed to build up a reserve of milk. I pulled out the cartoon instructions from Paula and did my best to produce a bountiful supply. I yielded three ounces. Ridiculous! How did other women do it?

I grabbed my to-do list:

To-Do List:

1. Find Brad and/or Michelle and/or Svetlana's killer.

2. Speak to Michelle's sister, KelliAnn.

3. ✓ ~~Make OB appointment~~.

4. Mail thank-you cards.

5. Get some sleep.

6. Print business cards.

7. Go grocery shopping.

8. Figure out how to solve this crime and find a way in the world with my own little PI business.

I needed to meet KelliAnn, Michelle's half-sister, give her my condolences, and see if she had an insight into these awful murders.

Since it was Saturday, Jim could babysit. I left him with the precious three ounces of milk and instructions to use formula if Laurie was still hungry. I studied Laurie before I left: her eyebrows were darkening but the hair on her head remained a delicate strawberry blond. I fought the desire to sit and study her all day. How could I miss her already if I hadn't even left?

When I arrived at KelliAnn's place, I rang the bell and was buzzed up.

KelliAnn stood in front of her door. She had beautiful red hair, the kind that is so red it looks almost orange.

Real red hair, not out of a bottle.

She was tall and thin, clad in a clinging purple sweat suit with a silver chain around her neck. From the chain hung an old-fashioned heart-shaped locket.

She was only a few years older than Michelle and me, maybe thirty-five or -six at the most, yet she hadn't aged well, probably due to a combination of her fair skin, smoking, and/or stress. Her face was lined and she seemed a little angry.

Not unusual, I imagined, for someone whose half-sister had been killed a week ago.

"KelliAnn?"

She looked me up and down. "Yes. Can I help you?"

I extended my hand. "Kate Connolly. You probably

don't remember me; I was in Michelle's class at Holy Rosary."

She smiled, showing off astonishingly white teeth. I self-consciously ran my tongue over my own.

How were people getting their teeth so white these days?

"I do remember you." Her face darkened. "You found Michelle, right? Come in."

I entered the spacious apartment, decorated in cream and green. It was fastidiously clean; the hardwood floors shone and every surface seemed to sparkle. I sat on a leather armchair. She hovered over me. "Something to drink?"

I recalled my vow not to consume anything prepared by a suspect. That didn't include the sister of the victim, did it?

Maybe prudence would be best. "No. I'm fine. Thanks."

KelliAnn sat down on her sofa, her ego deflated, as though my declining a beverage had hurt her feelings.

"KelliAnn, I'm so sorry about Michelle. We weren't close, not since high school, but what a tragedy. I—"

"Thank you. It's been really rough. She was the only family I had left. My mom died when I was in high school, and our dad died a few years ago." She played with the locket around her neck. "The police told me Michelle overdosed."

"Combination of diazepam and alcohol."

"Yes." KelliAnn squinted and dropped the locket. "How did you know?"

"I've been hired by Gloria Avery to find out who killed Brad."

KelliAnn paled, stood, then sat. "Gloria? Really? I never got the impression that she cared all that much."

"About Brad?" I asked.

"Either one of them, really. She's ... well, let's just say she's a lot like Michelle's mother was."

I recalled KelliAnn had not gotten along well with Michelle's mother. Their father, a commercial airline pilot, had lived a double life, married to Michelle's mom on one coast and maintaining a long-term affair on the other coast. When KelliAnn's mother passed away, her father took her in and she came to live with Michelle and her mother.

Our high school was small, about three hundred students, so everyone was privy to the drama that Michelle and KelliAnn were going through as they went from strangers to half sisters.

I did my best to sidestep that land mine. "When's the last time you saw Michelle?"

"We talked daily, but I hadn't seen her since last week. Now, I wish I'd made the time. I had no idea she was so down that she'd kill herself."

"You think she killed herself?"

Her brow wrinkled and creased, highlighting the sun damage on her face and causing her to look angry again. "Well, unless she accidentally overdosed. I mean, yeah. She had a tendency toward self-destruction. When Brad left her, she completely fell apart. She was starting to get better and then the police found his body. She just came apart at the seams." She shook her head. "*And* Brad left her for another woman. I don't know if you knew how vain Michelle was, but she was supervain. So imagine the hit to her ego when he told her he was leaving her."

"Do you know who he was seeing?"

She shrugged. "Sure. It's no big secret."

She knew! I could barely contain my excitement. I tried to remember I was supposed to be a professional.

As calmly as I could, I asked, "Who?"

She leaned over and whispered conspiratorially, "My neighbor, Jen."

Hippie chick was the other woman?

"Jennifer Miller?"

KelliAnn looked confused. "You know her?"

Now I felt foolish. I had met Jennifer, but didn't peg her as the other woman. What other clues were under my nose that I was missing?

I shrugged at KelliAnn and tried to hide my inexperience. "Well, I did speak with Jennifer early on in my investigation. I am a PI, you know."

KelliAnn resumed fidgeting with the locket. "Right. Of course. Well, Michelle knew Brad was two-timing her, but I didn't think she knew with whom. And I certainly didn't want to tell her, 'cuz, I'm the one who got Jennifer hired at El Paraiso in the first place."

"You felt responsible that Brad was cheating on Michelle? That's absurd! If he was a big cheat, that has nothing to do with you!"

KelliAnn looked around the room and sighed. "I know, you're right, but . . ." She shrugged and looked despondent. "Brad would come here, well, there, next door, practically every night until . . ."

My breath caught. "Did he come over here on June fifteenth?"

KelliAnn nodded. "He made kind of a scene that night, pounding on her door and yelling. She finally let him inside. He left after a while."

"He left?"

That meant he'd left alive, not like she'd shot him in her apartment and dragged out a body bag.

"Yeah, but so did she, just a little bit after he did."

"Have you told the police?"

A look of misery crossed her face. "I did tell them. But I never told Michelle. I didn't want her to blame me. Now that she's gone, I can't believe I didn't come clean with her."

"Do you think Jennifer killed Brad?"

"I've told the police that a dozen times. Svetlana, too. After Jennifer quit at El Paraiso, she went to work at

Svet's store." She stood and picked up a handbag off a side table. "Well, I was on my way out. Can I walk you downstairs?"

We left the apartment in silence. In front of the building, KelliAnn embraced me. "Thank you for coming by, Kate."

"I'm sorry for your loss," I said into her red hair.

She released me and smiled sadly. "I know." From her purse she pulled out a pair of glasses, held together in the middle with tape, and a key ring. She pointed the key at a gold hard-top Mercedes. "Can I give you a lift anywhere?"

"No. Thanks. I'm not parked far."

She nodded and put on the glasses, which succeeded only in making her look sadder. She walked to the Mercedes, then waved at me as she climbed into the car.

I crossed the street and peered through the windows of Heavenly Haight. Jennifer was helping an older woman pick through colorful scarves.

I sighed.

My tummy rumbled. Hungry again.

A huge McDonald's sign loomed over me. My stomach roared. I never ate fast food, but desperate times called for desperate measures. I needed time to think, and eat. I ducked into the McDonald's and placed an order.

Was I really burning all this food by breastfeeding? Or was this another old wives' tale that would end up biting me in the ass, literally? What good was it to burn an extra five hundred calories a day if I was craving and *consuming* an extra thousand?

Oh well, at least I hadn't supersized. And of course, I'd gotten the diet soda. Why drink the calories when you can eat them?

I dialed Jim from my cell phone and asked about Laurie.

"Honey, I don't know what you think you're missing, but she's sleeping."

"I'm missing her. Her face, her smell, her entire little personage!"

Jim laughed. "Her entire little personage has been asleep since you left."

"Is she breathing?"

"Of course she's breathing."

"When's the last time you checked?"

"Hold on."

I tried not to panic. I bit into my Big Mac and waited. What was taking him so long?

"She's fine."

"You have to check on her, make sure she's okay."

"I am. I do. I mean, she right here. She's fine. Kate, you haven't even been gone an hour."

"I know, all right. It just feels like longer. Feed her when she wakes up and make sure to check her diaper. I'm having lunch right now. I need to make a couple more stops, and then I'll be home. If you need anything, call me on my cell."

Jim laughed.

"What?"

"You're having lunch? It's not even noon yet," Jim said.

"Yeah, but they stop selling breakfast at eleven."

"Where are you?"

I laughed. "You don't want to know." I shoved a french fry into my mouth.

After we hung up, I ate my lunch and mulled over my notebook. I reviewed the entries from the interview with Jennifer. She told me she'd been with her ex-boyfriend, Winter, on June fifteenth. Never said a peep about an affair with Brad or him coming over to see her that night. Well, why would she?

What did I expect? That she'd come right out and tell me she killed him?

What had Galigani said? That guilty people are not usually paranoid. They want you to ask them questions because they think they can fool you. Jennifer had been extremely forthcoming when I'd met her. Offering up an alibi for the night of Brad's murder without my asking. Of course, she hadn't told me about her affair with Brad. Galigani was right, she had fooled me.

I dialed information as I chomped down on my burger, and requested an address for Winter Henderson.

Luck was with me. As it turned out, he lived in the Haight, a few blocks away. I wouldn't have to deal with parking and I could walk off an entire french fry or two.

I polished off the rest of my burger and packed up my notebook. I refilled my diet soda on the way out, reminding myself not to drink anything offered to me by strangers. By the time I arrived at Winter's house, I was winded, but my bones didn't hurt. Progress was progress.

The house was small and square, tucked in between two larger apartment buildings. I rang the bell. A very tall and bearded man answered the door. He had bright boyish eyes that warmed his complexion. I introduced myself and told him I was looking for Winter Henderson.

His face lit up. "That's me."

I told him I was investigating Brad Avery's murder. "I want to ask you a couple questions about the night of June fifteenth."

He twisted his lips to one side of his mouth. "Him again?"

"You've already talked to someone about him?"

He stroked his beard. "The cops. I guess my ex-girlfriend, Jennifer, told them she was with me that night."

"Was she?"

He shrugged. "I don't really know. That was months ago."

I sipped on my soda. "Do you keep a diary, or a calendar or anything?"

"Nope."

So he didn't remember spending every night with the woman for three consecutive months?

We shared an awkward moment in the doorway. He was obviously not going to invite me in. I had to think up more questions fast or the door would be closing in my face shortly. "Did your relationship end amiably?"

His clenched his hands into fists, his arms dangling at his sides. "Not that it's any of your business, but no. No, it didn't."

"I'm sorry to have to ask this. I'm sure you don't like to talk about it, but do you know if she was seeing anyone else?"

His face flushed. "You mean while she was seeing me? I don't know. Who would she have been seeing? No. I don't think so. We broke up because she got this new job at a store near her house and she kind of changed. Sort of became distant and aloof." His voice cracked. "I didn't like that."

"Of course not," I said, "Who would like that?"

He nodded and seemed to relax. "Yeah, right. See, she kind of turned nasty."

Why would she change after leaving El Paraiso? Unless maybe she was under some kind of stress. Of course, if she killed Brad, that could have caused some major stress.

"I really fell for her. I thought we were going to get married." His voice cracked again.

"Sometimes things work out for the best, even though we don't think so at the time."

From inside the house a voice called out, "Winter! Who's there?"

He turned around as though he'd been struck. "No one, Ma. I'm coming." He turned to me. "I gotta go."

"Thanks for your time," I said, retreating down the stairs.

I walked down the street, reflecting on the case. If Jennifer killed Brad, how could she dispose of the body on her own? Maybe Winter had helped her. Perhaps that was why he didn't want to give her an alibi. If he admitted to being with her, he could implicate himself as her accomplice.

What could have happened?

Brad was in love with Jennifer, Jennifer was in love with Winter. Brad was pestering her. Hounding her. Wouldn't leave her alone.

Maybe Jennifer grew afraid her boyfriend, Winter, would find out about the affair? Would that be motive enough to kill Brad?

Jennifer knew George, so maybe she knew about the gun in his bag. She could have taken George's gun and shot Brad and then asked Winter to help her get rid of the body.

But then *why* would Winter help her dispose of Brad's body? That part of my scenario made no sense. I'd have to work on it a bit more.

I sipped my soda as I walked into Heavenly Haight. Incense was burning. The chime rang as I stepped on the floor mat. Jennifer looked up. She glanced at me, but turned her attention back to the customer she was waiting on, who couldn't decide between unscented candles, which her boyfriend liked, or scented candles, which she preferred.

I fingered a collection of handmade earrings as I waited. As soon as the customer left, Jennifer turned her attention to me.

"What's up?" she asked, nervously tugging at her blond curls.

My visit was clearly annoying her. "Can you tell me again where you were on June fifteenth?"

"I was with my boyfriend, Winter. I already told you, and that fat cop, too. I mean, how many times do I need to answer the same stupid questions? I was with Winter."

"Winter's not really sure about that."

Jennifer blinked. "Well, he's just bitter. He's upset because I met his stupid mother and she didn't like me. She didn't think I was good enough for her little boy, so he broke up with me. Can you believe it? He dumped me because his mommy said so! I was this close to getting engaged." She made a gesture with her hands, bringing her fingers together.

I noticed the nail on her index finger was broken, making it the only short nail on either hand.

Could she have broken it in a fight with Michelle or Svetlana?

"What happened to your hand?"

"What?" Jennifer glanced down at her hand.

"Your nail. It's broken."

"My nails break all the time. I don't think I'm getting enough protein. I'm a vegetarian, you know, so I have to eat beans and cheese and those kinds of things, but they're very fattening, so I try to avoid them and my nails get brittle."

She looked at me. I suppose she expected me to encourage her or applaud her choices. Instead, I sipped on my leftover Diet Coke and wondered what her opinion of McDonald's was.

"Yeah, so *you* say you were at Winter's but *he* can't confirm it, so that kind of leaves you without an alibi."

"Well, I was there." She played with one of the silver rings around her thumb. "You can ask the neighbors, or whatever you guys do. I don't know what to tell you. I was there."

Should I mention the Brad sighting at her apartment?

"How about Thursday morning? Since she's your boss, I presume you know Svetlana Avery was murdered."

Jennifer looked genuinely confused. "I was working. Here. Like I always am. I told the cops that, too. Everyone here was shocked when we heard. But we were told to stay open. Business as usual."

"Someone sure had it out for Brad's whole family, huh? First him, then Michelle, now the ex-wife." I eyed her carefully. "With odds like that, I'd hate to be his mistress."

She grimaced. Our eyes locked. Was that fear in her eyes? She slipped past me and locked the store door, pocketing the key.

"What are you doing?" I said, the panic in my voice scaring even me.

Jennifer ignored me and rummaged through a shelf behind the counter.

Blood roared in my ears. I felt dizzy.

What was she getting, a gun?

If I moved now, I could take her. I was taller. I could push her against the wall, grab the gun, and call 9-1-1.

I rushed the counter and shoved hard against her shoulders. She jumped, dropping the object in her hands. A bong.

"Hey! What are you doing?" she demanded.

I stared at the bong. "When you locked me in here, I thought you had a gun. For Christ's sake, I'm investigating three murders!"

Jennifer rubbed at her shoulders. "Sorry. I didn't mean to scare you. I just wanted a little something to take the edge off." She pulled open a drawer. Inside were baggies filled with marijuana.

Who kept that kind of stash in a store?

She selected a bag from the drawer and squatted behind the counter, safely hidden from street view as she lit the bong and inhaled. "Maybe you need a hit, too."

I exhaled and slumped down next to her. "I'll pass. Want to tell me about you and Brad?"

After a moment she nodded. "We were working at the restaurant together and, you know, one thing led to another. We were staying out late, partying . . . He was really cool and everything, but a little uptight. So, not totally my type, but, you know, he was so good lookin'." She opened the baggie and loaded the bong. "Anyway, we were smoking and drinking, and what can I tell you? The sex was really hot, so we just kinda kept at it."

"Were you seeing each other up until his death?"

"Oh, no! It went down kinda rough. Eventually, I had to tell him that he wasn't my type. By then I'd started seeing Winter. We were much more alike, much more compatible. I thought he was my soul mate." She sighed. "I had to tell Brad. He didn't take it too good . . . cuz, you know, I think he liked me a lot."

"Why did Brad come to see you on June fifteenth?"

She played with the lighter in her hand. "To try and get back together."

"You said no?"

"I told him no way in hell. He left really mad. If I had known that I was never gonna see him again, and that Winter was gonna dump me, well, hell, one final final wouldn't have been too bad."

"Do you have any idea who killed Brad, Michelle, and Svetlana?" I asked.

Jennifer took a hit and slowly shook her head. "Wish I did."

CHAPTER NINETEEN

The Sixth Week—Discovery

Monday rolled around sooner than I would have liked. I hated the idea of Jim having to go to work.

"I wish you could take more time off to be with me and the baby. After all, I'm *supposed* to be back to the office next week."

"What are we going to do about day care?" Jim asked.

My throat constricted. Leave my angel with strangers all day? "We won't need day care."

"Honey, we have to be realistic. I mean, even if you solve this homicide for Mrs. Avery, we still need a second income."

"I could get another client."

Jim looked at me, a cross of pity and love on his face.

"You think I'm kidding myself, don't you?" I asked.

He wrapped his arms around me. "I totally believe in you and support you and love you."

"You think I'm kidding myself."

"How about I ask for a raise today?"

I pulled out of his embrace and looked into his eyes. "You certainly deserve one."

"Yeah. I've been landing them new clients left and right. You should have seen the ad campaign I presented last week. Maybe I can squeeze a few more dollars out of them, or hell, even a promotion."

Relief washed over me. Maybe I could stay home after all.

"You better get going then," I said. "You don't want to be late on the day you get promoted."

To-Do List:

1. Find Brad and/or Michelle and Svetlana's killer.

2. ✓ ~~Speak to Michelle's sister, KelliAnn~~.

3. Get some sleep.

4. ✓ ~~E-mail Paula for advice on pump~~.

5. Figure out how to launch this PI business—need license?

6. Research day care for Jelly Bean—just in case.

7. Start diet.

8. Pick up some dental whitener.

9. Find time for manicure/pedicure.

I looked over my list. How could I prioritize that to-do list? Could I really find a killer?

Well, I had found George, hadn't I?

Please don't be one and the same, I prayed, unable to control the nausea that surfaced.

The phone rang, interrupting my thoughts.

"Kate. Nora Collins here. How are you and the baby?"

My boss from corporate hell.

"Fine. Fine. Everyone is good."

"Great. Glad to hear it. Did you get the basket we sent?"

The staff from my office had sent a baby bathing basket. In it was a little yellow ducky robe complete with a bill hood and two feet dangling from the end of it, a couple of rubber duckies, baby shampoo, lotion and soap, and a waterproof bath book.

I hadn't had the time or energy to mail the thank-you cards. What had happened to my manners? I reached for the pen that was near me and re-added "Mail thank-you cards" to my to-do list.

"We got the basket," I said. "Thank you."

"Glad you like it. Sheryl picked out everything. You know how she likes to shop."

Sheryl was Nora's ever faithful and devoted assistant. Everyone in the office knew Nora would be lost without Sheryl.

"Have you thought about your return date?" Nora asked.

I'd thought of little else, except for Laurie and solving this mystery.

What to tell Nora?

I want to launch my own business so I can stay home with my little treasure and my husband is hopefully going to get a raise today, so maybe I won't be coming back. Besides, I'd probably crack in two if I had to leave Laurie, so you don't really want me back.

"I don't have a return date yet. I have to see my doctor first and get a release," I said.

"Of course," Nora said. "I understand."

Did she understand? She didn't have any children, or a spouse for that matter. She had given up everything to climb the corporate ladder.

I tried to put a little cheer into my voice. "Thanks for calling and checking in. Tell everyone I said hello. I'll let you know about my return date after I see my doctor."

We hung up.

I paced.

Return to work? Ugh!

Not that there was anything wrong with my job. It was a good job, and I worked with decent people. I was responsible for the management of the entire architectural office. It was a creative place to work, and things were always busy around me. But I would have to be away from Laurie all day, every day.

I had to find a way to solve this crime. Investigation was much more exciting than my corporate job ever had been. And more important, if I could launch my own business, it would give me freedom and flexibility.

I googled "starting a business" and got busy reading.

Laurie was nestled comfortably in the baby carrier, lunch barely on the table, when I heard the front door slam. Laurie and I peeked into the hallway in time to see Jim let his briefcase fall to the floor with a loud thud.

"What are you doing back so soon?"

He stared at me. "I was fired."

"Fired? I thought everything was going well." I swallowed the lump in my throat. "You said the presentation went great. What about the promotion? The raise?"

"My presentation *was* great. We got the account. I landed my firm a multimillion-dollar account and they canned my ass."

"I don't understand."

"They found out that I got arrested."

"What? How? And what does that have to do with anything? You're not guilty of anything! You were released."

Laurie began to wail, as though she sensed we were upset. Funny how intuitive people are when they start out.

"That cop, McNearny, plays poker every Saturday night with Josh Garner, the top partner at my firm. Turns out McNearny blabs that I was arrested. Josh pulled me into his office this morning and said I'd violated, get this, a moral turpitude clause in my employee contract."

I sat on our couch, stunned. Waves of disbelief washed over me. "I can't believe it! You haven't been convicted of anything!"

"I know. He said it didn't matter, said it was bad for the firm's image."

"Maybe if you talked to another partner. What about Dylan—"

"Screw it! I'm not going to beg for my job. Ungrateful bastards!"

I stared at the mallard print that hung above our fireplace. A bird in flight. I love that picture simply because it's an incredible act of nature. Such a small creature defying nature's biggest law. Gravity.

I mustered the most courage I could. "Honey, we're a team. We're going to figure this thing out. Together!"

Jim's shoulders slumped. "I've never been fired before."

Pain shot through my temples. "You think I should go back to the office?"

His eyes searched out mine. "I don't know what I think. I know how you feel about being home with Laurie."

We sat in silence. I unbundled Laurie from the baby carrier and placed her on the little play mat. She was happy again, and played with a little witch rattle Mom had brought her in preparation for Halloween. Laurie clutched the rattle and studied her hand in surprise, as if wondering how the witch had gotten there.

Jim and I looked at each other. I covered my face and

burst out crying, shaking all over. It seemed every time we took one step forward, we managed to take two back.

He hugged me tight. "Don't cry, honey. We're going to figure it out. We have our savings and I'll have unemployment, for all that's worth. Don't worry, Kate. Please don't cry."

Miraculously, we ended up getting a good night's sleep. Laurie must have tired herself out playing with the little rattle and ended up sleeping for a blessed six hours straight, which all the medical books comically term "sleeping through the night."

In the morning, Jim awoke at his normal time—6 A.M.—in a panic. "Oh! Oh. This is weird, honey, really weird."

"What is?"

"Not having to get up and go to the office."

He turned over in bed and looked straight into my eyes. "I'm sorry, honey. I feel guilty. If I hadn't picked a fight with George—"

"No! You didn't know. How could you know that you would be fired over that? And by the way, George had it coming for getting us involved in all of this in the first place."

Jim smiled. "You're finally starting to see things my way."

"Let's look at the bright side," I said. "At least this will free you up to help me solve the murders."

Jim nodded. We peeked at Laurie, nestled in the bassinet by our bed. She was still sleeping.

I snuggled into Jim. "Let's go back to sleep."

"Yeah." Jim said, putting his arm around me. "I'm depressed. It sucks to be fired."

I hugged him tight. "Oh, honey! Don't worry. Things always work out for the best."

"How can this be for the best, Kate?"

I sighed. "I dunno. I have to say that to keep from getting depressed myself."

Jim fluffed up a pillow and pulled the blanket around himself. "You're right, we should go back to sleep. Maybe it's all a dream."

We dozed until what felt like a decadent hour—7 A.M.! Then our little Laurie alarm went off.

Wailing.

Jim seemed in better spirits after the additional hour of sleep. "Better start looking for another job."

"Don't worry, you'll find something soon. You're the best ad executive I know."

"I'm the only ad executive you know."

"That doesn't matter. You're still the best." I winked at him. He nodded back at me. "If you don't find another job soon," I continued, "I'll go back to work. We can swing it on my salary for a while, until you find something."

I tried to keep the panic out of my voice and my eyes free from tears at the thought of going back to the office. Something must have shown because Jim's lips tightened into a line.

He stared at me, then we both nodded solemnly together, trying to convince each other that we believed everything would work out.

I snuggled with Laurie while I listened to Jim tap on the computer keyboard in the other room.

At 8 A.M. the phone rang. A refined gentleman's voice asked, "Is Mr. Connolly available?"

"May I ask who's calling?"

"This is Dirk Jonson, with Jonson, Mayer, and Ritler."

Could this be a recruiter already?

With Laurie in tow, I walked to Jim's office and handed him the cordless phone. Before I could tell him who was calling, Laurie began to wail in my ear. I took our screaming daughter out of the room and closed the door behind me, ruining any chance of my eavesdropping, but giving Jim an opportunity to hear something other than Laurie's caterwauling.

I put a pot of decaf on and scrambled around the kitchen looking for anything that vaguely resembled breakfast fixings. I made toast.

I added sugar to my cup and revised my to-do list:

To-Do List:

1. Help Jim find a job.

2. Find Brad and/or Michelle and Svetlana's killer.

3. Get more sleep.

4. Figure out how to launch this PI business—How do I get more clients?

5. Research day care for Jelly Bean.

6. Get a manicure and pedicure.

7. Where is that parenting book?

8. Organize house.

9. Mail thank-you cards.

I grabbed the stack of thank-you cards and popped them into the diaper bag. I would mail them today no matter what.

I called Jim for breakfast.

"All we have is toast," I muttered. "I'll shop today."

"I'll go," Jim said, gobbling every crumb on his plate. "Who was that on the phone?"

"The client I landed for Fortena and Associates."

"What was he calling about?"

"They told him I got fired yesterday. He wasn't very

happy about it and wants to meet with me today." Jim raised his eyebrows.

The phone rang again. Mrs. Avery wanted to take me to brunch and get a status report.

The brunch part sounded fabulous, because, of course, I was still hungry, even after two slices of toast. The status part . . . ?

What would I report?

After breakfast, Jim put Laurie into her bassinet and tapped away at the computer. I showered, trying to pull energy and ideas from the water.

Jim's appointment wasn't until the afternoon, which left me plenty of time to meet with Mrs. Avery without having to worry Mom about babysitting.

I fumbled through my closet and found the best clothes I could that would fit. Dressier slacks that I could almost button and a pink silk blouse, which was designed to tie around the waist, camouflaging my sins.

I even had time to apply makeup. I looked at my reflection in the mirror. Wow! Makeup really did make a difference. Especially at age thirty.

I crept into Jim's office. Laurie was sleeping peacefully in the baby carrier with her thumb in her mouth.

"She's discovered her thumb," I said.

"I noticed," Jim replied.

"I hope she won't develop nipple confusion."

Jim laughed. "I doubt it."

"Right," I said, reassured. "The breastfeeding purists will tell you anything to keep you nursing."

I edged Jim away from the computer in order to prepare my report for Mrs. Avery. What could I possibly put in it, when I didn't have a clue who killed Brad? I fell back on my old corporate skills: "If you have nothing of substance to report, at least make it look good. And when all else fails, overwhelm the reader with information."

"When will you be back?" Jim asked, looking over my shoulder as I typed.

"In time for the next feeding, don't worry."

"What do I do if she cries?"

I looked up into Jim's face. His brow was creased in concern.

"You've been alone with her before."

"Once, and you left me with a bottle. When she cried, I gave it to her and she stopped. What do I do this time?"

"There's a bottle in the fridge. I'll leave written instructions again, okay? I won't be gone long."

A look of relief flashed across his face. He leaned over to kiss me.

He asked, "Are you going to invoice Mrs. Avery today?"

"What?"

"Remember, I'm out of work. If you're serious about making this a business, you should present her with an invoice for your time so far. I mean, you never even got a retainer from her, right?"

"What's a retainer?"

"Request at least twenty-five percent of what you think the total cost to solve the crime will be."

"I have no idea what that is."

"Figure it out fast and err on the high side if you need to. It's easier to return an overpayment than try to collect." He leaned over again to kiss me and said, "And, honey, you look really pretty."

I felt warm inside. I hadn't felt really pretty in months, probably nine to be exact.

I drove to the Olympic Club on Country Club Drive. Judging by all the Mercedeses, BMWs, and Bentleys, I

was more than out of place in my six-year-old Chevrolet
Cavalier.

Oh well, Kate, just try not to sideswipe any of them.

The grounds of the country club were beautiful. There
was a view of the manicured golf course from the top of
the driveway. As I pulled up to the valet, I could see a few
morning golfers grabbing their clubs. I'd never gotten into
golfing, although it certainly seemed like the thing to do
nowadays.

Could I land any clients by networking at a golf course?
How do you get into golfing anyway? Does someone need
to show you how? Like a coach or something? Or do you
just get up and swing? How do you even get a reservation
on the course?

Mrs. Avery waved to me from the entrance of the club,
which was landscaped with blooming chrysanthemums.
How did they keep them fresh so late in the season? Mrs.
Avery looked completely in her element, dressed in
striped golf pants with a coordinating polo shirt.

"Kate! Thank you for coming," she said, wrapping a
protective arm through mine.

She steered me toward the restaurant. The ceiling in
the room was so high I got dizzy looking up. The red vel-
vet high-back chairs stood at attention, like British guards,
over the sparkling silver at each table.

Mrs. Avery squeezed my elbow. "Let's get seated, then
you can tell me what you've discovered."

We were escorted by the host, a serious gentleman
dressed in a three-piece suit, to a table in the corner. Mrs.
Avery whispered to me that not long ago women had not
been allowed into the Club.

The Club. La di da.

The host pulled out our chairs and made sure we were
seated comfortably before disappearing. Instantly, an un-
blemished seventeen-year-old boy appeared and handed
us menus. His hair was slicked back in a pompadour style

and he wore a white dress shirt and black slacks. He looked me up and down.

What was he thinking? Was he wondering what *I* was doing in a place like this?

His eyes lingered on me. He blushed.

Oh! He was checking me out!

It had been so long since someone, besides that creep Rich, had looked at me that way, I'd forgotten what it was like. He averted his eyes. I smiled, remembering that Jim had said I looked pretty.

I sucked in my postpartum belly and sat a little straighter. I'd have to do the makeup thing more often.

"The smoked salmon is divine here, Kate," Mrs. Avery said. She turned to the boy. "Two freshly squeezed orange juices, dear."

He nodded and hustled off without even a look back at me. I guess I wasn't *that* impressive.

I studied the menu, deciding on the "French Country" breakfast, a traditional omelet filled with diced potatoes, served with a green seasonal salad and sherry wine vinaigrette. My mouth watered reading the description. Mrs. Avery settled on the smoked salmon, served with squash cake, dill sauce, and a green salad.

What is squash cake?

Judging by the platters wafting by me, no doubt it would look good.

While we waited for our food, I presented my report to Mrs. Avery. A color-printed PowerPoint presentation of all the suspects, wrapped in a bright blue folio.

Mrs. Avery pulled her reading glasses from her purse and reviewed my notes, the pie charts, and graphs. "Wow! This is a very pretty report!"

"Thank you." I beamed.

"What does it mean?"

Indeed. What *did* it mean?

I squinted at her and tried not to lose my nerve.

"Well . . . it means that each person has an equal chance of being the murderer."

She studied me over her reading glasses, her brow wrinkling. "An equal chance?"

"Well, it also shows that everyone had equal opportunity, but not equal motive," I floundered.

She pointed to a pie chart on the report. "So you think Jennifer has the strongest motive?"

"Well, she was the *other* woman. And apparently, Brad visited her on the night he was killed."

Mrs. Avery's eyes filled with tears. "Why kill him?"

I covered her hand with my own. "Mrs. Avery, I know this is difficult."

"I need you to be straight with me, dear. Don't worry about my feelings. I hire someone else for that."

Ouch.

"I think Jennifer may have killed him because he was leaving Michelle."

"Isn't that what she would have wanted?"

"She was in love with someone else. She could have thought Brad's leaving Michelle would interfere with her plans with her boyfriend."

Mrs. Avery whipped the reading glasses off her face, flashing a look of annoyance toward me. "Bradley was so handsome, not to mention wealthy. How could she be in love with someone else?"

"She's kind of a free spirit."

"What? Like a *hippie*?" Mrs. Avery spat the word, her expression sour, as if the word had left a bad taste in her mouth.

Our waiter appeared at our table and placed a covered dish in front of each of us. A busboy assisted him in uncovering our plates simultaneously. Nice. Country club dining at its finest.

We dug into our meals. After a moment she said, "Do you think Jennifer's boyfriend could have done it?" Her voice softened. "After all, my Bradley was thrown into the bay. It had to be someone with some strength."

"I thought about that, too. It's a possibility." I paused. "Mrs. Avery, what can you tell me about Rich Hanlen? As I understand it, he took over the general management of El Paraiso after Brad's disappearance. Went from assistant manager to—"

"No, no, no." Mrs. Avery shook her head. "Rich would never hurt Brad. They were best friends. Best friends." She waved her hand at me, implying I dismiss any bad thoughts about Rich.

I nodded and took a bite of my meal.

So much for trying to put the blame on Mr. Creepy.

Mrs. Avery replaced her glasses and studied my chart a little bit more, then said the inevitable. "This woman, Kiku, is high on your list, too."

I cringed, remembering Kiku's beautiful smile and pregnant belly. I didn't want it to be Kiku.

"I have a witness who can place her at Michelle's home on the day of her death. And I know she has access to the drug that killed Michelle. But when I spoke with Michelle's sister, KelliAnn, she told me suicide was very probable."

Mrs. Avery tapped her manicured nails on the table and frowned. "Is that what she said? I don't believe it. I can't believe it." She pulled her purse onto her lap, returned her glasses, and extracted a lace hankie. "What about Kiku and Bradley's murder?"

"I haven't been able to find that strong a connection between Brad and Kiku."

"What about Svetlana?" Mrs. Avery sniffed and dabbed at her nose with her hankie. "Do you think Bradley and Svetlana were killed by the same person?"

"It's very probable. They were killed by the same gun."

Mrs. Avery snapped to attention. "The same gun? If they were killed by the same person, how do you explain that my poor son was dumped in the bay and Svetlana wasn't?"

"I can only guess that Brad's murder was premeditated, planned, and that Svetlana may have been killed in desperation. Not enough time or opportunity to dispose of her body."

"Do you think this woman, Kiku, is strong enough to discard my Bradley . . ." Her voice gave out, and she shook her head back and forth with her eyes closed.

"No. I don't."

Not unless someone helped her, someone like George.

A tear slipped down Mrs. Avery's face. I bit my tongue, suppressing my newly acquired maternal instinct to comfort her. Mrs. Avery delicately wiped her cheeks with the lace hankie. I swallowed the last of my omelet and sighed.

After leaving the Olympic Club, I made my way directly home. I glanced at my watch. I was a little late, but not by much. Still plenty of time for Jim to get to his meeting with his former client.

He greeted me at the door carrying Laurie and looking frantic. Laurie's red face was howling up at him, her little fists waving about.

"Thank God you're here. She won't stop crying!"

I pulled her into my arms. She immediately stopped.

"Must be nice to be the favorite," Jim said.

"Not the favorite. Just the mommy. You said she only slept when I was gone!"

Jim threw his arms up in despair. "That was last time."

"Did you change her diaper?"

"Yeah."

"Did you feed her?"

"I tried. No go."

"What about the pacifier?"

"She threw it at me!" He collapsed onto his favorite easy chair. "I've tried everything!"

"Did you try the baby carrier?" I pointed to the contraption that was slung on the couch in the exact location I had left it yesterday.

"I don't even know how to put that thing on."

"I showed you how to put it on."

"I don't remember."

"You don't remember or you weren't listening?"

Jim shrugged. "It's hard to think fast under all the pressure."

"Pressure?"

"The crying."

I laughed. "She's a baby."

"I know. A crybaby. Except when Mommy's around."

I showed him for the umpteenth time how to put the baby carrier on. I must admit with the millions of snaps, straps, and hooks, it's not the easiest process in the world to remember, but after you've done it a few times, it becomes second nature.

Jim put the carrier on, picked up Laurie, and snuggled her into it. She instantly laid her head against his heart. Within moments of Jim pacing back and forth, Laurie was asleep.

"Aw," Jim said, "feels nice."

"To hold her?"

"Yeah. When she's quiet."

I filled him in on my brunch at the country club. "And guess what?" Jim watched me expectantly. "I gave her my bill. The retainer, plus all my time so far at two hundred bones an hour. She didn't balk at all."

Jim leaned in and kissed me. "I'm very proud of you, honey." He headed toward our bedroom.

I followed. "I'll be proud when I figure out who did it."

"Oh. Your mom called. Said her new boyfriend, Hank,

told her that if someone's been drinking, then as little as five pills of diaze . . . something or other—"

"Diazepam?"

"Yeah. That's it. Five pills could bump someone off." He placed Laurie in her bassinet and began to select a suit. "Do you know what that means?"

I felt a dull pain at the base of my neck. "Unfortunately, yes. It means Kiku had enough pills to kill Michelle."

Jim pulled on tan slacks and a white dress shirt. "Honey, if you discover who the murderer is and it turns out it's not the person you wanted it to be, you still have an obligation to tell Mrs. Avery."

"But Kiku's going to have a baby, and if she's in jail . . ." I stopped myself short, suddenly emotional.

Jim hugged me. "You can't stress yourself out about that. You have to be realistic. If she's a murderer, then, obviously, she wouldn't be a fit mother."

He released me and studied my face.

"But I really like Kiku. She's so nice. And it may turn out that Michelle committed suicide. Besides, Mrs. Avery only hired me—"

"Kate! You're not that naïve. You have to be honest. With yourself *and* the authorities."

"I know. I know. You're right. I think the murders are linked, but I don't think Kiku had a motive to kill Brad."

"If Michelle *was* murdered, what would have been Kiku's motive?" From the closet, Jim pulled out a gorgeous green tie with burgundy flecks. "This one okay?"

I nodded. "At one point, when I heard George was going over to Michelle's at night and all, I thought they might be having an affair. Maybe Kiku thought the same thing. If she killed Brad, too, then she would have needed—"

Jim tightened his tie. "An accomplice?"

I nodded my agreement.

Jim pulled on a sports coat. "You can't expect a pregnant woman to get rid of a body, can you?"

"I don't want George to be responsible."

Jim gave a sour laugh. "I've been wanting him to be responsible his whole life."

"I meant . . ."

Jim's face softened. "Whoever is responsible for these crimes needs to be held accountable." He checked his hair in the mirror. "Regardless of his or her relationship to us. You need to do what's right, Kate."

I pressed my cheek against his. "You look incredibly sexy," I whispered.

Jim wrapped his hands around my shoulders and pulled me close, kissing me deeply. I kissed him back as I undid his tie.

CHAPTER TWENTY

The Sixth Week—
Muscle Control

The next morning at 5 A.M., I could hear Laurie shifting in her bassinet. I knew she'd be hungry soon.

I poked Jim. "Can you feed Laurie?"

He unglued one eye and looked at me. "How can I do that? I don't have any boobs."

"Mom bought us some formula bottles. They're in the pantry. Can you give her one?"

"I thought you didn't want to give her any formula."

"Please just give her one," I said.

"Yeah, yeah . . . sure," he mumbled. He got up and returned with the formula. "What am I supposed to do with this?"

Laurie had begun to fuss.

"Jim, I'm exhausted. Can you please figure it out?"

Somehow, he managed to grasp that the only thing necessary was to uncap the premade formula and screw the nipple onto the bottle.

He picked Laurie up and placed her between us. She immediately started rooting at me and wailing even louder. As soon as Jim put the bottle in her mouth, she quieted down.

Hmmm? She was drinking the formula! That seemed kind of easy.

Why was I going through the pain and exhaustion of breastfeeding?

Then I remembered all the benefits. The uterus shrinking, immunization for Laurie, vitamins, blah-blah, all the things they had told me at the hospital.

Not to mention the extra five hundred calories a day I was supposedly burning.

I pulled the blankets up, feeling literally drained. I still needed to build up a supply of breast milk for Laurie, for my return to work. If she was drinking formula, this was the perfect opportunity to get up and use the pump.

I wrapped the blanket tighter around myself.

Was I returning to work?

Could I make this PI thing succeed?

I watched Jim feed Laurie. She snuggled into his arms. It was nice to have a little break, even though I was leaking everywhere.

I probably should have nursed her.

Instead, I selfishly pulled the covers over my head and tried to doze off.

Laurie began to cry. I pried an eye open and peeked over. Jim was asleep and had let the bottle fall out of her mouth. He continued to sleep through her cries.

I poked at him. "Jim."

"Hmmm?"

"The baby. Feeding. Remember? Wife sleeping. Taking a break."

"Yeah, sure," he mumbled, sticking the bottle back into Laurie's mouth. She stopped crying long enough for me to get comfortable. Then the wailing began again.

Jim was back asleep. Laurie was rooting around for the bottle.

"Oh, for Christ's sake." I grabbed the bottle and held it for her. Jim snored next to me.

Unbelievable.

There really is no substitute for maternal instinct.

My breasts were swollen and painful. That's what I got for feeding her formula.

At 9 A.M., Jim was snoring and Laurie was still asleep from the formula. If it was helping her sleep, why was I opposed to it? I crawled out of bed and reviewed my to-do list.

To-Do List:

1. Help Jim find a job.

2. Find Brad and/or Michelle and Svetlana's killer.

3. Check in on Galigani.

4. Day care for Jelly Bean??

5. Take more pictures of my little lollypop.

6. Get a photo book for Lemon Drop!

7. Stop missing Laurie so much when I'm away from her.

I got dressed and noticed that my belt was in a notch. I couldn't believe it! "Hey, honey," I called excitedly to Jim, "look at this! I've lost an inch!"

Jim looked at me while rubbing sleep out of his eyes. "You're the incredible shrinking woman."

I had a long way to go before that was true, but at least this was progress.

"All right," I said, prepping Jim. "Laurie should be hungry soon. There's a milk bottle in the fridge for her."

"Where are you going?"

"Over to Michelle's. I need to do a little more investigating."

I hopped into my Chevy and dialed Mrs. Avery. Marta told me Mrs. Avery was "in de Club."

"Do you have a key to Brad's house?"

"Keee?"

What was the word in Spanish? Clef?

No, that was French.

Somewhere in the recess of my mind the word bubbled up.

"*Jave?*"

"*Llave?*" Marta clarified.

"*Sí,*" I replied.

"You water plants today?"

What the hell. "*Sí.*"

"Hokaay, you come pick up."

I let myself into Michelle's and wandered around the house aimlessly. No crime scene tape? Did that mean the police had ruled Michelle's death a suicide?

I moved from room to room and tried to push from my mind the images of her body sprawled out in the dining room. In the kitchen I poured myself a glass of water and sat at the table, feeling an emptiness I hadn't experienced before.

Although we had been out of touch for many years, Michelle had been a good friend in high school. It would have been nice to have the opportunity to reconnect with her.

I ended up in her bedroom, looking through her jewelry box, a simple wooden box with a mother-of-pearl lid.

Could the bracelet I found in George's bag be Michelle's? I recalled her handing it to me in front of the medical examiner's office. Something nagged me. Had she recognized the bracelet? If it was hers, why not keep it? Why give it to me? Unless she *was* having an affair with George and didn't want me to know her things were in his bag?

I ran my fingers across the expensive pieces in the box. Nothing resembled the silver bracelet. I wished I'd thought to show it to KelliAnn, Michelle's half sister. She would have been able to tell me if it had been Michelle's.

So if it wasn't Kiku's and probably not Michelle's, who could that bracelet belong to, and what was George doing with it?

I recalled Jennifer's silver rings. She'd worked at El Paraiso, and she was having an affair with Brad. Could it be her bracelet?

What if it was Jennifer's bracelet and George, not Winter, her boyfriend, who had helped her kill Brad? How or why else would George have her bracelet?

I opened the closet door. It was deep, full of designer clothes, evening gowns, and a zillion of my favorite thing—shoes.

A black satin gown with silver trim caught my eye.

Ooh la la.

What function had Michelle worn this to? I imagined her at the country club with Brad and Mrs. Avery. Maybe a black-tie event, an auction, or a benefit.

I eyed a box from Via Spiga at my feet.

What size did she wear? Would there be any way a cute pair of shoes would ever fit my fat swollen feet?

I kicked the box open. Beautiful size eights stared me in the face. Pre-Laurie they would have been too big. I slipped them on. Perfect fit. I put them back in the box and picked up the next box. I amused myself with a mini-fashion show.

After trying on a few pairs, I noticed a cubbyhole full

of handbags. I pulled out a few Coach purses and saw a shoe box concealed behind them. I extracted the box from its hiding place. It was full of paperwork.

I carefully replaced the purses, then took the box over to the bed and sat down to examine the contents. It looked like business ledgers from El Paraiso. I couldn't read anything on the charts. Well, I could *read* it. I just didn't know what it meant. One report looked like a profit and loss summary. But what did I know? I was a theater major in college. And the closest I got to accounting in my corporate job was ordering pencils and staples.

Jim would know. At least he had a business degree.

Flipping through the reports, I saw one for Heavenly Haight.

My breath caught. Svetlana's store? Even after her marriage to Brad had ended, she'd stayed connected to him and by more than the memory of their daughter. Had they started the store while they were married? Did he still own shares in it? Maybe those shares had gone to Michelle.

I stuffed the reports into what I now lovingly referred to as my "diaper purse," a very far cry from a Coach handbag, and stood. I placed the empty shoe box back into the closet and closed the door.

Without a clue about what to look for next, I decided I'd check out the makeshift office area in the guest bedroom. If memory served, what little I had left, I thought I'd seen at least a desk with a computer and printer. But first a stop in the master bath.

I rummaged through Michelle's medicine chest, looking for Valium. It was practically empty. Maybe the cops had gone through and confiscated everything they could find.

Wait.

If Michelle had an office setup, why would she store paperwork in a shoe box at the bottom of her closet?

She must have been hiding those reports, but why?

Just then I heard a click and a creak.

The front door?

Someone was entering the house.

I froze. Footsteps approached from the hallway. Two voices, a man and a woman. The man's voice was clearly recognizable to me. Rich, the manager of El Paraiso, aka Mr. Creepy.

He had a key to Michelle's house?

"That fucking bitch! She can't screw me like this!" Rich fumed.

"Calm down," the female voice said.

Who was he with? I couldn't place her voice.

"I won't let her screw me over!" Rich said.

Something crashed to the ground. The woman yelped.

"Jennifer is going to sing like a canary. I gotta be sure there's nothing here. Go check her stupid office, will ya?"

Footsteps sounded down the hallway. "I already told you: I checked before and didn't find anything."

"Yeah, well, check again!"

More footsteps in the hallway. Heavier ones. Rich's. Coming right toward me in the master bath.

A drop of sweat stung my eye. I needed to get out of the house. But how?

Footsteps sounded dangerously close. I heard the closet door swing open.

"Look at all these shoes!" Rich said.

He slammed the door shut.

I listened as his footsteps retreated toward the kitchen. I breathed a sigh of relief.

Now's my chance.

I cracked open the bathroom door and peeked out into the bedroom.

Empty.

I leaped toward the window. It wouldn't budge. I pried harder.

Nothing. Painted shut!

Old houses were exasperating. Michelle had done a lot of renovation work, but obviously she hadn't gotten around to replacing the windows in the bedroom.

Could I break the window and get out?

I heard arguing from the living room and a crashing sound. Glass breaking. I thought of Michelle's gorgeous crystal lamps and hoped they weren't the victims.

If Rich and his gal pal were going to start throwing things, maybe they wouldn't notice if I broke a window.

I heard footsteps outside the bedroom and took a nose-dive under Michelle's king-sized bed.

Dust balls were everywhere. I repressed a sneeze by rubbing the tip of my tongue across the roof of my mouth.

Aha! A theater degree was good for something!

How long could I hide underneath the bed? Certainly if they were looking for something, under the bed might be a good place to search.

I heard drawers being pulled open.

Rich mumbled to himself, "Okay, if I were that stupid bitch, where would I put it?"

What a pig.

"Look at this!" the woman called from a different part of the house.

I heard Rich tread out. I peeked out from under the dust ruffle. The room was empty.

I could hear them arguing in the kitchen, but couldn't make out any of the words. I had to find a better hiding place.

I scooted over to the far-right-hand side of the bed and wondered if I could make it back into the master bath before they returned to the bedroom.

What then? Was there a window in the bathroom? I didn't recall seeing one. Could I hide out in the bathtub until they left? I figured the bathroom was my only hope.

I crawled out from underneath the bed and dashed back

to the bathroom, diving into the tub. I pulled the shower curtain closed, trying to keep as quiet as possible.

There was a small window, also painted shut. Even if I could pry it open, it was way too small to squeeze out of.

There were two of them and one of me. I hoped they were unarmed. Were they the killers? Was my life in danger? I immediately thought of Laurie. I couldn't bear the thought of anything happening to me. The thought of leaving her so tiny and vulnerable, without a mommy, almost brought me to tears.

I pulled my diaper purse close and rummaged past the reports to find my cell phone. I grabbed it from the bottom. Thank God I'd remembered to pack it.

I punched in 9-1-1.

Nothing happened.

I'd remember to pack it, but not to charge it.

I heard footsteps again. Tears sprang to my eyes. I was going to die in this half-renovated Victorian. Just like Michelle.

Who only renovates half a house anyway? Why couldn't she have put new windows in the bedroom? It wasn't like she didn't have the money.

I crouched down farther into the bathtub.

The front door squeaked open, then slammed shut.

Were they gone?

Thank God. I crawled out of the bathtub and pulled open the bathroom door.

I had to get out of here fast.

What kind of stupid idea was it to come here anyway? I left the bedroom and entered the hall. I flew past the kitchen toward the entryway and smack into Rich.

I gasped.

He stared at me, his face beet red. "What the hell are you doing here?"

I had to think fast!

"Oh, my God!" I covered my heart with my hand.

"You startled me. I was in the garden, watering." I smiled my most innocent, sincere smile. All those years of improv couldn't go to waste. "What are you doing here?"

The redness in his face was dissipating. He smiled now, too. His flirt smile, honed by years of skirt chasing. "Well, I came over to water, too!"

Right.

Still in character, I squeezed his arm. "Aw! If I had known, I could have saved you the trip."

I delicately sidestepped him, heading toward the front door.

Move, move, now! a voice inside my head ordered.

Rich pushed his shoulder out a bit, just slightly but enough to block my way. "How long you been here?"

I blinked up at him. "Not long. It only took a few minutes to water."

Why didn't I have a gun, dammit? Or mace or something, anything, to protect myself! I hated to have to suck up to this creep.

If I was going to be legit, I'd need the PI license *and* a gun permit.

Rich pushed his hand against the door. He looked me up and down. "You want to get a drink?"

Oh, for God's sake!

I feigned disappointment. "I'd love to, but I have to get back home. To my baby." I enunciated "baby" for good measure.

He nodded. "Right! Hey, listen! I'd appreciate it if you didn't mention my being here to Mrs. A."

It took every ounce of self-control not to break the flirt/airhead character I was in. I smiled, and tilted my head to the side. "No prob."

He let go of the door. "Thanks. I . . . she . . . just gets weird about stuff."

I seized the moment to pull open the door. "Got to

run," I called over my shoulder, wiggling my fingers as I bounced down the steps without looking back.

My heart was racing. Laurie, Jim, and safety were the only things on my mind.

As soon as I was out of sight, I ran toward my Chevy. I glanced over my shoulder. Rich hadn't followed me. I got into the car and started the engine as quickly as I could.

I locked the doors, just in case. An image of Rich running after me, trying to get in through the passenger side window, flashed through my mind. Something like you'd see in the movies. A quick check of my rearview mirror told me he'd already forgotten about me and was probably busy searching the house again.

• CHAPTER TWENTY-ONE •

The Sixth Week—Pushing

When I arrived home, I found Jim wearing my green flannel bathrobe. I laughed "What are you doing?"

Jim flapped his arms up and down in despair. "It's the only thing that would calm her down."

"Wearing my robe?"

"I read it online. I guess the robe has your scent on it. She feels like Mom is holding her when I'm wearing it."

I kissed him. "You are so sweet! Anything for your little girl, huh?"

He nuzzled my neck. "Anything for my girls, big or little. I even vacuumed."

Raising my eyebrows, I said, "Anything?"

Jim winked.

"I need you to look at something." I pulled the reports from the diaper purse and handed them to him. He seated himself on the sofa to read the reports.

The phone interrupted his reading. It was Jim's former client, Dirk Jonson. He wanted a follow-up meeting.

When Jim left for his meeting, I fussed around the

house, carrying and rocking Laurie. I jumped on and off-line, e-mailing Paula and doing research. On a whim, I asked Paula if she recalled any "Carol" from our high school class, since Mr. Creepy had gone to a Holy Rosary dance with someone by that name and met Brad Avery that night.

I wondered about background checks. Galigani said he'd run one on George. Maybe I could run one on Mr. Creepy.

I finally admitted to myself it was time to recruit help on the PI front. I dialed Galigani in the hospital.

"How's your recovery coming along?"

"They're releasing me today. The miracles they work with surgery!" He paused for a moment, then continued, "I got very nice flowers from my *former client* Mrs. Avery."

I swallowed the lump in my throat. "Oh, yeah?"

"Yeah. She enclosed a curious note."

No!

"Curious, how?"

"She thanked me for sending over such a wonderful replacement."

Relief washed over me. "That was nice."

"Nice? I don't remember sending you over there as my replacement."

"You said . . . You told me . . . I went there to tell her you were dropping the case . . ."

"Yeah. That's what I thought."

"But she thought . . . she thought . . . I let her think I was your replacement. That I was a PI because I want to start my own business and set my own hours to be with my daughter and I'm having fun and being challenged and she was ready to hire me, so I—"

"You let her think you were my replacement!"

I steadied myself for his wrath. "Yes."

Galigani burst out laughing.

Instead of relief, I felt annoyed. I let him laugh a moment longer. When he didn't stop, I said, "It's not *that* funny."

He kept laughing.

I played with the antenna on the cordless phone and waited him out. "Are you done?"

"I'll just wipe these tears."

"Ha ha."

"Okay, let me guess, are you calling for a little guidance, a little help?"

"I was calling to see how you were doing." We both chuckled. "I didn't call for a little help. I need a lot of help."

"Ah! Okay, you're talking to an expert. And since you saved my life, I'll give you a ten-minute consult on the house."

"I might need more than that. I'm completely in over my head."

"Why? Jennifer Miller was arrested last night."

Air rushed into my lungs. "Arrested? Jennifer?"

"McNearny had a search warrant, they found the gun that killed Brad and Svetlana. They also found a supply of diazepam, the drug Michelle overdosed on."

"And you know this how?"

He laughed. "McNearny and I were partners a long time. Loose lips."

"But it doesn't make any sense. How could Jennifer get rid of Brad, alone? She couldn't lift him, could she?"

"Oh, I don't know about that. Women can be pretty strong. And you know, 'Hell hath no fury—'"

"Jennifer wasn't scorned. She had scorned Brad."

"Who told you that?"

"Well, Jennifer. She said—"

Galigani snorted. "Never, ever believe what a suspect tells you. If she didn't think twice about shooting someone, you think it's gonna hurt her feelings to lie to you?"

"Right. Right. Of course." I paused. "Did McNearny tell you who the gun was registered to?"

I cringed, waiting for the answer. Galigani was silent.

"No, but I didn't ask either. You want me to find out?"

I played with Laurie in her exercise gym. She could now push herself up onto her arms. I guess tummy time really does work.

I thought about my encounter with Rich. I'd overheard him complain about Jennifer. Something about her squealing? No, singing like a canary. About what? How had he known she'd been arrested?

The front door opened and Jim walked in.

"How'd it go?"

Jim grimaced and walked to the kitchen. He reappeared holding an unopened beer can and tapped it on the side. "I'm not sure. Pretty good, I think. They want me to put together a new ad campaign for them with a proposal for my services as an independent contractor. But it's hard for me to tell if I'm wasting my time. I should probably be looking for a full-time job, instead of—"

"It sounds like a good opportunity."

Jim opened the beer. "You think that because you're such an optimist."

I picked up Laurie and dangled her in front of Jim. "Ask her what she thinks."

Jim laughed, scooping Laurie into his arms. "What do you think, pumpkin pie? You think it's best for Daddy to get a real job with health insurance and benefits and vacation and all the things that provide security for you and Mommy or should Daddy try to land this consulting gig?"

I flopped onto the couch. "So do both. Keeping looking for a job and prepare the proposal for them."

Jim took a swig of beer. "I'm stressed out about not bringing in a paycheck."

The phone rang. I leaned over and grabbed it. Kiku's voice filled the line. "Kate! The baby's on the way! I'm scared and I can't find George!"

Excitement fluttered inside me. "Are you sure?"

Kiku groaned.

"Okay. Yeah. That sounds pretty real. Hang on, okay? Jim and I will be right over."

CHAPTER TWENTY-TWO

Labor Again?

I felt like an old hand at this mommy business. Of course, it's totally different when you're not the one in labor.

"Where could George be?" I asked.

Jim rolled his eyes. "Another birth that the shithead is going to ruin."

We pulled up in front of Kiku's apartment. She was pacing the sidewalk as we doubled parked.

She bent to pick up her overnight bag.

Jim popped out of the car and yelled, "Don't worry about that. I'll get it."

Laurie began to cry. She had settled down when the car was in motion, but now that we had stopped, her howling had started again.

I moved to the backseat. No need to make Kiku sit next to a screaming child before she had to.

Kiku studied Jim. "You look like George."

"He looks like me. I'm older," Jim said through a smile as he picked up her bag and took her arm. "Have you timed the contractions?"

"Fifteen minutes."

"We have time," I said, feeling like a pro.

Kiku settled into the front seat and I rubbed her neck as Jim raced down the street.

We arrived at the hospital and checked Kiku in. They wouldn't let Laurie into the room, so Jim and I decided to take shifts with Kiku.

We tried calling George on his cell phone. No answer.

"Why don't you go home with Laurie and rest for a while?" Jim said.

"Really?" I asked, trying to stretch my neck.

"You look really tired, honey. Besides, George is my brother, so I should be here."

"I'd like to be here, too. Let me see if Mom can watch Laurie."

"Go home and rest, and if Mom can come to the house later, come back in a couple of hours. We'll be here."

I drove Laurie and myself home.

Where could George be? I tried his cell phone again. Still no answer.

As soon as I reached home, I unloaded the bucket car seat and breathed a sigh of relief that Laurie was asleep.

I napped for two hours, then awoke to Laurie's hungry wails.

I selected a fresh Winnie the Pooh sleeper and got Laurie out of her grungy onesie and diaper, but before I could get a clean diaper on, she peed all over the changing table.

Nice.

"See all the fun stuff I'd miss if I had to go to the office every day?" I asked Laurie.

She cooed up at me.

"You're going to have a little cousin soon," I said as I cleaned her off and settled her into the bassinet. After I mopped up her changing table, I went to hunt down some food for myself.

The refrigerator was practically empty again. Who had time for shopping?

I glanced at the clock. Six P.M. No wonder I was hungry. When was the last time I'd eaten? I settled into our "nursing station"—anywhere on the couch, near the phone—and called Mom.

The paperwork I had taken from Michelle's lay discarded on the coffee table. Jim hadn't had time to review it. I picked it up as I left a voice mail for Mom.

The reports didn't look any clearer to me now than they had earlier. I'd take them to Jim at the hospital, along with some dinner.

Thoughts of the taqueria near our house flooded my mind. Maybe I could pick something up on my way back to the hospital. I hoped Kiku had eaten. They don't let you eat once labor has started.

To-Do List:

1. Help Jim find a job.

2. Find George AGAIN.

3. Figure out what Michelle's reports mean.

4. Get more diapers for Sugar Pop. (size 1!!! No longer Newborn!)

5. Return overdue books to the library.

6. Exercise.

7. Stock up on pumped milk.

8. Ask doctor about pelvic pain.

Mom arrived a little after 7 P.M., dressed in a flowered skirt that clashed with the striped shirt she had on. "Darling! Kiku's in labor?"

I nodded, appraising Mom's outfit. "What are you wearing?"

"Festive, isn't it? It's my 'salsa uniform.' Hank and I are taking a class."

"A salsa class? As in dancing?"

"Yes. Preparing for our cruise on the Mexican Riviera."

"Is salsa a requirement?"

Mom winked. "To me it is!"

I drove straight to the taqueria down the street. When I left, Mom and Laurie were watching the Spanish language station, which had made me even hungrier for a burrito.

I ordered a *carne asada* taco for me and a chicken burrito for Jim.

What about poor Kiku? Suppose she hadn't eaten?

I ordered a cheese quesadilla for her, just in case. Maybe I could sneak it past the nurse.

By some miracle of the parking goddess, I was able to park directly outside the hospital.

I tried George's cell phone again.

No answer.

I dialed Kiku's home phone number.

Nothing.

I knew he'd been evading the police, but now that they'd made an arrest, why go into hiding? I tried to ignore the bad feeling creeping into the pit of my stomach. Where was he? How could he miss the birth of his child?

I climbed the hospital front steps and made my way toward the maternity ward, clutching the food bag in my hands. It had taken all my willpower not to tear into the taco, burrito, and quesadilla in the car.

I asked the nurse at the front desk for Kiku's room.

"She's in room twelve. Let me see if she wants any

visitors." The nurse indicated some hard plastic chairs against the wall.

I sat and waited. When the nurse didn't return in five minutes, I tore into my taco. I had salsa and sour cream dripping down my face when I felt a tap on my shoulder.

Jim laughed. "Geez, Katie, did you just get off a life raft?"

"Breastfeeding makes you really hungry," I said, covering my mouth with my hand.

Not even talking was going to stop my chewing.

Jim nodded sympathetically, then looked hopefully into the white bag on the chair next to me. "So does labor."

"Right! Like you'd know. Last time you practically slept through it all."

Jim stared at me. "I did not!"

I laughed as I handed Jim his aluminum-covered dinner. "How's Kiku?"

He tore into the chicken burrito. "Asleep. They gave her the epidural and told her to rest awhile. Any luck finding George?"

I shook my head.

"Typical," Jim muttered through a mouthful of food. "This is good. What else did you get?"

"I got a quesadilla for Kiku."

Jim raised his eyebrows, looking like a puppy asking for a bone.

"You can eat it," I said.

Jim happily gobbled down the quesadilla. "We haven't had Mexican food in a long time."

I smiled, although my mind was on George. "Where could George be?"

Jim grunted. "Who knows? Flake!"

We sat in silence as Jim polished off the rest of my taco.

"You really were hungry, huh?"

Jim ducked his head. "Nerves, I guess."

I leaned in to kiss him. "You've already been through this once, and this time it's not even yours."

He nodded. "You see any vending machines around? I'll buy you a Coke."

I stretched my legs. "I'll go. I think I saw one on the way in."

I wandered through the maternity ward in search of a soda machine. I peered through the window at the newborns. Laurie suddenly seemed so big to me. Her umbilical cord had fallen off long ago, she was holding her own head up, and she definitely didn't need the swaddling. Not to mention she could pee all over her changing table!

My eyes welled with tears. My little girl was growing so fast!

I turned down the hallway toward a Coke sign. Something connected in my mind. The last time I had had a Coke was at Heavenly Haight. Brad and Svetlana had owned that together—that much I'd been able to gather from the reports.

The reports!

With my rush to eat, I'd left the reports at home on the coffee table.

I returned to Jim and handed him the Coke. "Do you think it's strange that Jennifer worked first at El Paraiso, owned by Brad and Michelle, and then later at Heavenly Haight, owned by Brad and Svetlana?"

"Strange? Not really. If Brad liked her, and we know he did, then he probably moved her 'job.' Maybe people at El Paraiso were getting hip to the affair and he wanted her out of there or something."

"All the owners are dead now."

"Not all. Mrs. Avery owns everything now." Jim said.

"You think Rich is also managing Heavenly Haight?"

Jim shrugged. "Don't know. Why?"

"Maybe George is hiding out there."

"Forget about him, honey. What's the use? We can't force him to come to the birth of his child."

"He may not even know she's in labor."

Jim snorted. "Why wasn't he staying close to her, then? Why isn't he picking up his cell phone? I know you like to hope for the best in people, and I don't want to disappoint you, but my brother is a major loser, Kate, with a capital L."

Thoughts of Brad dead in the bay flashed through my mind, followed by the image of Michelle sprawled in her living room.

"What if he's in trouble?"

Jim pivoted on the plastic chair. "What kind of trouble?"

A nurse cruised by us. I stopped her with my hand. "How is Kiku doing?"

"Are you her family?"

Jim nodded.

"Let me get her doctor to speak with you."

Kiku's doctor, a tall Indian man with a very pleasant demeanor, assured us she was all right. He reported that despite all the efforts to assist in Kiku's labor she wasn't dilated past three centimeters. They had scheduled a cesarean for the morning.

We peeked in on Kiku, who was sound asleep.

Ah! The miracle of drugs.

Even though it was half past one in the morning, I convinced Jim to drive past El Paraiso on our way home, thinking that George might be there. All the lights were out. Not a single car in the parking lot.

"Let's get home and look at those reports," Jim said.

"Can we swing by Heavenly Haight first?" I asked.

Jim glanced at me.

"It's on the way," I pleaded.

No lights were on at Heavenly Haight. I asked Jim to get out and bang on the door anyway.

No answer.

Jim shrugged and made his way back to the car. "You want to check out the pier, too?"

"Yes, but it's totally out of our way and I thought you didn't care about finding him."

Jim grimaced. "Of course I care. The bum is my brother, after all."

The trip to the pier didn't get us any closer to finding George. We headed home, only to find Mom sacked out on the couch and Laurie asleep in her bassinet. I shook Mom awake.

She pried her eyes open and looked up at me. "Laurie's been a dear! She's been asleep the entire time!"

Figures. Why did Laurie always sleep when someone else was watching her? Now she'd probably be up the rest of the night.

"Kiku's only dilated to three. There's gonna be a C-section at eight in the morning."

Mom yawned, then stood and stretched. "I'll be back at seven." She gathered her things together. "Oh! A nice man named Galigani called as soon as you left. Said they released Jennifer today." She picked up a Post-it note and read the message. "The DA doesn't have enough evidence to prosecute." Mom looked up from the note. "And he said the gun was registered to William Connolly."

Jim sucked in his breath. "Dad's gun."

I lay down next to Jim, who was studying the reports.

"How can you read right now? I feel like someone threw sand in my eyes."

Jim put his arm around me. "I have to do something to keep my mind off my stupid loser brother. Go to sleep, honey."

I rested my head on his shoulder and tucked my ice-cold feet in between his calves. That's another thing I love about my darling husband—no matter how cold my feet, the man has never ever complained or hesitated in warming them up. He's my own personal heater.

"Anything interesting in those reports?" I asked through a yawn.

"They were making a ton of dough for selling knick-knacks on Haight Street."

"Maybe we should go into retail, too. I could sell Mom's beautiful knit items."

Jim laughed. "Seriously, there's something hinky about these ledgers."

I sat up. "Like what?"

"I don't know, exactly. Something's not right, but I'm too tired to figure it out."

I reached across him and shut off the light. "We'll look at them in the morning."

He kissed me. "Night, honey."

"Night."

There was silence for a minute, long enough for me to see the edge of sleep in my mind. Long enough for my subconscious to ask the question again: *What had Rich been looking for at Michelle's house and who had been with him?* Then Laurie began to cry.

After a fitful few hours of sleep, I awoke again, this time to Laurie's hungry cries. I pulled her into bed with us and fell back asleep while breastfeeding.

Something was nagging at my mind, not letting me rest properly. What was it?

Kiku! The new baby! We were going to miss the birth.

I struggled to open my eyes and look at the clock. Quarter to seven.

I shook Jim. "Wake up, Jim!"

He didn't move.

"Jim, Kiku's going to have the baby soon! Mom will be here in eighteen minutes! Wake up!"

Jim turned and slowly rolled over toward me. My hand shot out to stop him. "Laurie's right behind you."

Jim moaned, then sat up. "We've got to get to the hospital, huh?"

"Yeah. Get up."

Jim's red eyes peered at me. "I'm exhausted."

"Welcome to the club."

"Why don't you stay here? I'll go."

"No way. I want to see the squishy baby."

Jim smiled. "Okay, you go. I'll stay here with our cheesy little one."

"Nope. Get up."

"Thought so." Jim swung his legs over the edge of the bed. "I'll make coffee."

We arrived at the hospital in record time. The nurse would only allow one of us into Kiku's room. We decided that Jim would stay in the waiting room.

I went into the labor and delivery room and, to my astonishment, saw George at her side.

"When did you get here?"

Kiku looked over to see me. "Kate!" she cried happily. "George here for baby!"

"Of course he is," I said, making my voice sound as casual as I could.

The nurse started to prep Kiku for the cesarean. I slipped out into the hallway to wait with Jim.

After about an hour, George appeared, looking haggard. "Healthy baby boy, ten pounds, two ounces. We're going to name him Robert. Momma's doing fine. They're going to move her now."

Ten pounds, two ounces? Good Lord, that was almost twice as big as Laurie had been at birth! Even now at six weeks she was still only about eight pounds.

"Congratulations, Daddy," Jim said, patting his brother on the back.

Tears streamed down my face.

George leaned into Jim and said, "I thought I was going to pass out in there, man."

We laughed. Jim embraced George. When they let go of each other, both of them had tears in their eyes.

"I do love you, buddy. You know that, right?" Jim said.

George nodded. "I know. Me, too."

Kiku and Baby Robert had been moved to a third-floor recovery room with a partial view of the Golden Gate Bridge. We sent Jim to get breakfast for Kiku and me.

Hey, why not? I was always hungry now anyway.

I settled myself on the bed, at Kiku's feet, and cooed at Robert. George couldn't let go of him. Looking at him holding his baby made me miss Laurie. How could I miss her so quickly?

Kiku dozed off.

Now was my chance.

"George, we gotta talk."

George looked up from the baby and bit his lip.

"Where have you been? Are you behind these murders?"

His eyes grew wide. "Come on, Kate. 'Course not."

"I found ledgers showing monkey business at Heavenly Haight and El Paraiso."

George's shoulders drooped. He exhaled and shook his head back and forth. "So, you know then."

Know what?

Without giving it a second thought, I blurted, "I can help you."

George moved toward the corner of the room, away from Kiku. He motioned with his head for me to follow.

"Rich's been looking everywhere for those ledgers. We figured Michelle was keeping records. But we didn't know where."

I wanted to shout, "What does it mean?" but bit my tongue.

"I never wanted to sell dope. But I was on the streets, so in exchange for a place to crash, I sold a little for Brad, you know?"

Cash deposits to Michelle, bags at the pier, secrecy about everything. Now it was starting to make sense.

I kept my voice steady. "After Brad was killed, you worked for Michelle. Now you work for Rich, huh?"

George nodded, misery showing on his face.

"You were selling drugs for Michelle. She denied you were at her place the night Brad was killed because she didn't want the police to make the connection between her and the drugs, right?"

George sighed. "I was over there to drop off the cash from that night. I had no idea anything was going on with Brad. I knew he and Michelle were having problems, but, you know, everyone has problems. I didn't think he'd end up in the bay."

"Is the pier your drug drop?"

George nodded.

"Rich was looking for those reports because they show how the money is being laundered, right?" I asked.

"Through Heavenly Haight," George said.

"So, Svetlana was in on this, too?"

"No!" George said emphatically. "She was clean. I was trying to get her to help."

"It *was* you. At her house. The day she was killed!"

George's eye opened wide. "Well, yeah, but I didn't

kill . . . I was just there for help. I thought I was being followed. I thought she'd know what to do."

"Who was following you?"

"I don't know . . ."

"Jennifer Miller?"

"Who?"

"Jennifer Miller was arrested for Brad's and Svetlana's murders. Michelle's, too."

George looked puzzled. "Jen?"

"Did she know you had a gun?"

"Not that I know of."

"It was your gun, George, the ballistic report confirms it now. Jennifer was released by the DA for insufficient evidence, so whatever you know, you better cough it up right now, because guess who'll be the next person the cops come after."

"It wasn't me."

"Who then? Rich?"

George brought his hands up, covering his ears with them. "Geeze, Kate. Rich didn't kill anybody. Is that what you think?"

I waved my hand in despair, motioning him for a better idea.

George shook his head. "Rich is just a stoner at heart. He didn't want the business to get busted. In fact, we're thinking of getting a medical marijuana license and going legit."

Now I'd heard everything.

George continued, "Rich wouldn't kill anybody."

"Somebody did. Somebody killed them with your gun, George! Who knew you had a gun?" George stared at the floor. "Think. Come on."

George remained despondent.

"Does Rich have a girlfriend?" I asked.

George shook his head. "No. I don't think so."

I glanced at Kiku, who was still asleep. I dug into my

pocket and pulled the bracelet out, using my last-ditch effort to get George to talk. "Whose is this?"

George frowned. "What's that?"

"It fell out of your bag."

Fear flashed across his face as he examined the bracelet. "It's not mine. I've never . . . I've never seen it before."

Jim and I rode home in silence, both of us caught up in our own thoughts. Jim had another meeting scheduled with Dirk Jonson later today and I imagined he was rehearsing it in his head. He also had a couple of interviews scheduled for full-time work. I said a little prayer that Jim would land something soon.

I filled him in on George's activities. He convinced me to give Mrs. Avery an update. Especially since she was now the sole owner of both the restaurant and the shop on Haight.

At the very least she needed to know what was going on. If she wanted to press charges against Rich and George, so be it.

When we got home, we found Mom hovering over Laurie, putting something red and green on her head.

Another cap?

"What are you doing, Mom? What's that?"

"It's her Halloween costume! I needed to try it on before I sew the last of it. Halloween's only a few weeks away, you know."

"What is it?"

Mom could barely contain her excitement. "She's going to be a strawberry! I saw the pattern in a magazine. Isn't it adorable?"

The look on my face must have betrayed me, because Mom pursed her lips. "What did you want her to be? A pumpkin? That's so overdone. You've got to be original, darling."

Mom packed her craft supplies, gave Laurie a final squeeze, and departed. Jim got dressed and left for his appointment. I collapsed onto the bed exhausted and slept with Laurie for about an hour. I dreamt a huge strawberry was chasing me, then the strawberry turned to a wash of red blood. I woke up with a start when the doorbell rang.

I stumbled down the hallway and peered out the peephole.

Jennifer?

Tears were streaming down her face.

Should I open the door? I thought of Laurie in the back of the house. No way.

"What's up?" I asked through the door.

"Kate?"

"Um-hum."

Jennifer looked at the door nervously. "Can you open the door?"

"Uh, I'm not dressed," I lied.

What are you doing on my doorstep, you pothead?

"I'll wait," she said.

"What do you want, Jennifer?"

"I need to talk!"

"About what?"

"I need your help! I was arrested. They think I killed Brad and Michelle and, God, my boss even! I didn't do it, Kate! I need your help. You're a PI, right? I didn't do it!"

Sounded good, but how could I trust her? I'd meet her in public.

"All right. Go to the little café on the corner. I'll be there in a bit," I said.

I looked through the peephole as she wiped her nose on her sleeve and nodded. "Okay, I'll wait for you there," she said.

I watched from the front window as Jennifer made her way down the street. Then I packed the diaper purse and got myself ready. Finally, I placed Laurie into her stroller and took off toward the café.

Jennifer was seated at a booth, sipping a latte. I ordered a green tea and maneuvered the stroller next to the table.

Jennifer peeked in on Laurie, who was studying the hanging doll attached to her stroller.

"Thanks for meeting me," Jennifer whimpered.

I nodded.

"I was framed," Jennifer continued.

Now I had really heard everything.

I took a deep breath to keep my cool. "By whom?"

"Mrs. Avery."

CHAPTER TWENTY-THREE

The Sixth Week—All Wet

I let my jaw drop. "You think Mrs. Avery framed you?"

Jennifer nodded, pressing her thin lips together. "She's had it out for me. No doubt about it. She hated that I was seeing Brad."

"She didn't know you were seeing Brad."

"What do you mean? She saw us together one time at the country club. When Brad went to use the restroom, she warned me to stay away from him or else!"

I shrugged. "She told me she didn't know who he was seeing. Maybe she thought it was a one-time thing at the club."

Jennifer sighed, looking defeated. "Maybe. But she's evil."

"What do you mean?"

"Well, look at the Penny thing." Jennifer must have noticed the confused look on my face because she clarified, "Brad and Svetie's daughter. Svet was convinced that someone Penny knew lured her into the water that day."

Okay, I *thought* I'd heard everything, but now I *knew* I'd heard it all.

"You think Mrs. Avery lured her own granddaughter to her death?"

Laurie gave a little kick in her stroller for attention. I rocked the stroller forward and back to soothe her.

Jennifer flipped her hair. "It sounds bad, I know."

"No offense, but it sounds preposterous. Maybe you've been smoking a little too much of that hippie hay."

Jennifer shook her head. "I don't really smoke all that much."

"Does Rich?"

Her eyes narrowed. "I wouldn't know."

"Don't you run drugs out of Heavenly Haight for him?"

Jennifer's face registered shock. "How . . . how did you know that?"

"Well, I am a PI." I felt momentarily proud of myself. *Maybe I really could do this!*

"Does Mrs. Avery know about the drugs?"

"Who do you think pulls all the strings?" Jennifer asked.

I tried to ignore the sharp pain that burned behind my temples. Mrs. Avery did have an awful lot of money. Could it have come from drug dealing?

I pressed against my temples with my fingers. "What about Svetlana?" I asked. "Was she involved?"

"She knew it was going on, but kinda turned a blind eye. I think she was really depressed after Penny. She tuned a lot of things out."

"Did she know about your affair with Brad?"

"No! God, no! Svetie still wasn't over the fact that he left her for Michelle. She hated Michelle and her sister. And I really liked Svetlana, so why rub her nose in it?"

"What about the gun? The police found the gun in your apartment."

"Yeah, so? It must have been planted there."

"Who has keys to your apartment? Did Brad?"

"No. Just the apartment manager/handyman guy in 101. But he's a worm. I'm sure Mrs. Avery could have bribed him."

I stopped at home only for a moment to pick up the car, then drove straight to Mrs. Avery's. My head was pounding and dread was growing in my stomach. "Please don't let Mrs. Avery be involved," I prayed.

I needed somebody, somehow, to be clean in this whole situation. Even worse, I had a selfish reason for wanting her to be innocent. I wanted to get paid.

I pulled up in front of Mrs. Avery's house. Her Sea Cliff home stood brightly before me. I carefully parked my Chevrolet between a Jaguar and a Cadillac.

I got out of the car and examined my outfit. Jeans and a maroon top. Not bad, but not great either. I searched for my lipstick in the diaper purse.

What had happened to fashionable Kate? I pulled out a pacifier and a tiny headband with a small white hairbrush.

No lipstick! I tried a second pouch and found a rattle and a red lipstick.

It clashed with the maroon top, but I put it on anyway. Lip color has a way of making me feel more presentable. And I knew I'd need to feel as self-assured as possible for this confrontation.

I pulled my shirt down and hiked up the waist of my jeans. Hey, they were fitting a little better. I plucked Laurie's car seat from the Chevy and walked up Mrs. Avery's driveway.

I was out of breath when I arrived. The fatigue of not sleeping well and the case were getting to me.

Huffing and puffing, I climbed the few stairs to her house.

Mrs. Avery's maid, Marta, greeted Laurie and me at door. She ushered us into the sitting room and directed me to a tan chaise lounge with delicate purple and green flowers on it.

After a few minutes, Marta reentered carrying a silver tea service, which she placed on the coffee table in front of me.

Mrs. Avery emerged, dressed in a red power suit. "Kate! Oh! And little Laurie! How are you, dear?"

I pulled the ledgers out from my bag and showed them to her. "I found these at Michelle's house."

Mrs. Avery crossed to a side table and retrieved a pair of reading glasses from the top drawer. She studied the reports a moment, her eyes darting back and forth across the pages. "Rich was hired to look over the affairs of the restaurant and the store. Are you saying he's cheating me, Kate?"

I looked at her, surprised. What if Mrs. Avery was ignorant of the whole drug operation?

"Well, what do you make of these?" she asked.

I hesitated. *Why not go for it?* I thought. "I thought maybe you were involved in an illegal activity, Mrs. Avery."

"Illegal activity? Like what?"

"Like drug dealing," I said, feeling foolish. The woman was in her seventies. What was I accusing her of?

Well, hey, hadn't George said they were looking into going legit with medical marijuana? Maybe Mrs. Avery was involved in that campaign. I imagined her setting up shop at the country club, dealing pot to seniors.

Mrs. Avery made no effort to hide her indignation. "Do you know what you are saying, Mrs. Connolly? I have no such involvement," she said firmly. "And neither did my son."

"Mrs. Avery, I happen to know for a fact that there is a

drug operation functioning under the auspices of the restaurant. You can't deny it."

Mrs. Avery's blue eyes locked on mine. They seemed cold in a way I hadn't noticed before. "I won't have this kind of talk in my house."

"All right, I'll leave," I said, gathering up my things.

"Have you gone to the police?" she asked.

"Not yet," I said.

"Why not?" she challenged.

"I wanted to talk to you first."

Her lips puckered. "Thank you for that. I didn't have any knowledge of this drug business, Kate. In fact, if what you say is true, I'm shutting the businesses down myself. I won't have it. I'm not that type of person. I would have thought you'd have known better by now." She got up from the couch, nearly knocking over the tea service. "I don't deal in drugs. My family doesn't deal in drugs." Her anger was building. Her voice cracked as she tried to restrain herself and she nearly spat out, "My family is very respected in the San Francisco community and the nation at large."

"That may be," I acknowledged. "I may be totally wrong. All I know is that drugs have been going out of El Paraiso and Heavenly Haight and somebody *you* appointed is in charge."

Mrs. Avery froze. She turned on her heel and grabbed the phone from the den. "Well, we're going to call Rich right now and straighten this out. I won't have you thinking I'm some sort of common criminal, bandying about accusations and slandering my family name."

She dialed a number into the cordless phone and spoke quietly into it. "Rich assured me he's on his way," she said.

I sat, defeated, and put my head into my hands. "How long will it take him to get here?"

Mrs. Avery pulled the glasses off her face, then served herself and me tea from the beautiful silver server that Marta had brought in. "He should be here shortly. Fifteen minutes at the most."

I remember the glasses found at Michelle's house.

"Mrs. Avery? How long have you worn reading glasses?" I asked.

"Thirty years now, dear. Why? Are you starting to have to push things further out to read them?"

God. Did I look that old? I had to get some sleep!

I smiled tightly. "No. Not yet."

After about ten minutes of waiting, Rich's car finally screeched onto Mrs. Avery's driveway. A moment later Marta entered and announced Rich's arrival. He came into the room and immediately approached Mrs. Avery, kissing her cheeks. He acknowledged me with a nod and a curt hello.

Mrs. Avery gestured toward the sofa. "Sit, Rich. Thank you for seeing us on such short notice."

Rich smiled. "What can I do for you ladies?"

"I think you have a few things to explain. Show him the paperwork, Kate."

I pushed the reports toward Rich. "Here's a ledger for El Paraiso showing a loss. It's dated July. And here's a ledger for El Paraiso for the same month, showing a profit."

Rich nodded and said, "Hmmm. That's odd." He sucked on his teeth for a moment, then finally asked, "Where did you get these?"

I leveled a glare at him. "I know you're laundering money through the shop on Haight as well."

He shook his head from side to side, putting his ear to one shoulder then the other, and jiggling his legs up and down. He looked at Mrs. Avery. "Uh, what would you like me to say, Gloria?"

Mrs. Avery frowned. "Is it true?"

"That we're dealing drugs out of El Paraiso?"

"Yes," Mrs. Avery said.

He looked from Mrs. Avery to me, then back to Mrs. Avery. "Yes, it true."

Mrs. Avery paled as though she'd seen a ghost. Then as quickly as the color had drained, it returned, turning her face red with fury. "How can you do this? How can you do this to Bradley's memory?"

"Well, Brad was the one who started the whole business, Gloria. I'm surprised you didn't know."

"How would I know such a thing?" Mrs. Avery demanded.

"This city is very competitive in regards to restaurants. I mean, you didn't really think we were turning a profit selling hamburgers and frittatas, did you?"

Mrs. Avery looked stunned. I felt sorry for her. She really had had no idea.

She reached for the phone and dialed 9-1-1.

The Sixth Week—Revelation

When I got home, Jim was searching the Internet for job opportunities. I asked him to give Laurie a bottle while I slept. I napped two hours and woke feeling semirefreshed to a ringing phone. Would I ever wake up feeling that I'd gotten enough sleep ever again in my life?

Jim hovered over me. "Are you awake?"

"Sort of."

"It's Galigani."

I grabbed the phone.

"Congrats, kid. I heard you're responsible for a drug bust."

"Yeah. I'd put my own brother-in-law, a new daddy, behind bars. Yippee."

Galigani tsked. "You are not responsible for other people's actions. Only your own. As for your brother-in-law, he committed a felony. He's old enough to commit the crime, he's old enough to do the time. Which we hope will go a long way toward making him a better father."

"I hope you're right." I worried about Kiku and the

new baby being all alone. I'd have to find a way to help her. After a moment, I said, "What about Jennifer, do you think she really did it?"

"Why not? The cops think so."

"But she was released and now she's pointing to Mrs. Avery."

Galigani guffawed. "Mrs. Avery? Hell, is she reaching or what? Look, Jennifer Miller was released on a technicality. Not enough evidence for the DA to prosecute doesn't mean 'not guilty.' McNearny will keep digging until he finds something the DA likes. As for you, you don't work for the DA, so it doesn't matter what he says. You just need to satisfy your client."

"Something's not right. I just don't know what it is."

"That happens. What I do when I'm stuck is go over all my notes again. Just read everything in your notebook and think. Sometimes the answer is right in front of you, but you can't see the forest for the trees. It helps to get a little rest and not think about anything for a while."

I snorted.

Galigani laughed. "How's the baby?"

That evening I followed Galigani's advice and tuned everything out. Jim and I watched a football game and carved pumpkins. I read every single line I'd written in my notebook and reread Galigani's book for good measure.

Feeling no closer to solving the case, I reviewed my to-do list.

To-Do List:

1. Help Jim find a job.

2. ✓ ~~Find George AGAIN~~.

3. ✓ ~~Figure out what Michelle's reports mean~~.

4. Research day care for Laurie.

5. Prep for return to the office.

6. Stock up on pumped milk.

Depressed about having to return to corporate hell, I logged on to the computer to check e-mail. I found a note from Paula.

Kate! Sounds like you have too much going on to be healthy. Launching a new business sounds good, but girl you just had a baby for crying out loud. I'm going to have to get home soon to knock some sense into you. Either that or join you :)

Oh and about Carol? The only Carol I remember from high school was Carol Reilly, she wasn't friends with Michelle, but was she friends with Michelle's sister? Can't remember, high school was a long time ago and since I'm pregnant I can't even recall what I ate for breakfast.

Baby due in three and half months, not that I'm counting!

Say hi to your mom and Jim. Kisses to the tiny one.

Love, love, love you guys! Write soon.

Inspired by Paula's note, I searched through my garage for an old yearbook. I found the one from our freshman year and flipped through it.

Pictures of Paula and Michelle and me covered the pages.

I located our sophomore yearbook and searched the pages. There was a photo of Michelle and me in the school play. Michelle had inscribed a message in purple handwriting: "Kate, best of luck to you in the theater!"

My junior yearbook was missing. I vaguely recalled lending it to Paula. She'd probably never returned it.

I leafed through our senior book. Pictures of the prom splashed across the page.

I found a picture of Rich. There he was, with Carol Reilly. Whatever happened to her?

Then I saw it. Brad staring back at me. A pretty date on his arm. A familiar bracelet on her wrist.

I dropped the book.

Hmmm? How had her bracelet ended up in George's bag?

I picked up Galigani from his home on Telegraph Hill. He limped to the car.

"Thanks for meeting me on such short notice," I said.

"Hey, I'm not supposed to be out. But who listens to doctors anyway?"

I nodded and steered toward the Haight district. There was no traffic to speak of at this hour of the night. Galigani and I rode in silence. I wondered if he was falling asleep and eyed him suspiciously. He jerked his head up and glared at me.

"What?" He smiled.

"How are you feeling?"

"Fair to middling. Did you see my scar?" He opened his shirt a bit. A fresh scar crossed his entire chest.

"Ouch!"

"Funny thing is, this one doesn't hurt so bad. It's my leg. I've got a scar there that runs down the whole thing. It's where they took the veins out to put into my heart."

I found parking in front of the apartment house. We climbed out of the Chevy. "My legs hurt, too," I complained.

With a pang I remembered my pain relief pills sitting on my kitchen counter.

"Too much running around for just having a baby," Galigani acknowledged.

Who did I think I was?

He patted me on the back. "You're doing great, kid. I knew you were a bulldog from the start."

"Is that supposed to be a compliment?"

"Sure. Bulldogs are persistent and smart."

"They're also short and ugly," I retorted.

Galigani laughed.

"If I was so smart, I would have figured this out a long time ago," I continued.

"Don't be so hard on yourself. You got no experience." He raised his eyebrows at me. "What you need is a mentor."

I held my breath. "You're supposed to be retired."

"Right." Galigani laughed. "We can talk about the future later."

Despite the gravity of the situation facing us, I smiled. "You got your gun?"

Galigani nodded. "Always. So should you. We'll see about getting you a license, training, all that."

He said "we"!

"Although we won't need it tonight," he continued. "She won't try anything with both of us there. Even if we are both crippled."

I laughed as we limped toward the apartment building.

"I don't want to ring the buzzer and alert her prematurely," Galigani said. "Let's wait for someone to leave."

We didn't wait long. A blond man in his early twenties exited the building. Galigani grabbed the door saying, "Ladies first."

We both hobbled up the stairs and took a minibreak outside the apartment to catch our breath.

Galigani asked, "Ready?"

I threw my shoulders back, took a deep breath, and nodded. Galigani banged on the door. The redhead opened it a few moments later. She was wrapped in a robe, her hair enveloped in a towel.

She smiled widely to see me. "Kate Connolly! What can I do you for?"

Galigani flashed his investigator badge. "May we come in? I don't think this is a conversation you want to have in the hallway." He walked past her without waiting for a response. I followed him into the living room.

He circled around the room, then made himself comfortable on the couch. KelliAnn and I remained standing. Galigani eyed an opened box of chocolate chip cookies lying on the coffee table. He picked up one of KelliAnn's magazines and flipped through it casually. "Can you tell us, again, about your whereabouts on the night of June fifteenth?"

She blinked. "What are you talking about? You two need to leave or I'll call the police."

I watched her fidget with the towel on her head.

"We have reason to believe you were at El Paraiso," Galigani said.

KelliAnn rolled her eyes. "Come on. My stupid neighbor killed Brad. The police know all this. They arrested her."

"You were still in love with Brad after all these years," I said. "You took him to the prom. You never got over him."

KelliAnn laughed. "That's absurd!"

Galigani jumped in. "You overhead Brad and Jennifer that night. You knew he was leaving your sister. You heard Jennifer reject him."

"Maybe you thought you'd try a last-ditch effort to get back together with him," I said.

The corners of her mouth twisted downward, creating a half-crazed look on her face. "This is ridiculous! You can't come over here and accuse me of this!"

"I have something of yours, KelliAnn," I taunted. "Something you lost that night at El Paraiso. It must have slipped off your wrist when you reached into George's bag to take the gun you killed Brad with."

Her eyes flashed. She blinked rapidly. "I don't know what you're talking about."

"You broke into both my cars, looking for your bracelet. Michelle saw it fall from George's bags. She told you I had it, right? She suspected you were involved. Is that why you killed her? Because she'd figured it out?"

KelliAnn shook her head frantically, the towel unraveling, her red hair falling to her shoulders. "You're wrong. Michelle killed herself. And Jennifer . . . They found the gun at Jennifer's place."

Galigani tsked. "That would have been easy for you to plant. What with her being your neighbor and all."

"The handyman in 101 must like you a lot, huh, Kelli-Ann?" I winked. "He let you into Jennifer's place, didn't he?"

KelliAnn snarled. "Jennifer is an ungrateful bitch. She was unemployed and pitiful when she moved here. I asked Michelle to hire her, as a favor to me, thinking Jennifer would be a good little spy. I knew Michelle and Brad had a racket going on, but I didn't know what."

Galigani scratched his head. "Your plan backfired. Brad fell for Jennifer."

KelliAnn swung her hair, trying to appear nonchalant. "Please, I didn't care about that."

"You cared about him enough to lure his child into a lake."

KelliAnn took a step back from me, paling. Her expression told me I had hit the nail on the head.

"You didn't think anybody knew about that, did you?" I asked. "Svetlana confided in Jennifer that she thought someone had lured her little girl, Penny, into the lake. The way I figure it is, you ran into Svetlana and Penny, or maybe you were following them like you did George, and when you saw an opportunity, you lured Penny—"

"Or just plain grabbed her and drowned her," Galigani said from the couch.

KelliAnn gasped, then abruptly covered her mouth.

"You must be really sick, lady," Galigani continued. "You couldn't stand the thought of Brad being with anyone else, much less having a child with her. You get rid of the kid, hoping Brad would blame Svetlana for negligence—that's one way to ruin a marriage. But instead of rushing into your arms, Brad finds comfort in your sister."

"You have no proof," KelliAnn said, her eyes flaring.

"George went to Svetlana for help," I said. "He knew you were following him. You didn't find the bracelet in my cars, so maybe you figured I had given it to George. One day at the pier, you cut me off in Michelle's Mercedes. George saw you and ran. When he told Svetlana, she confronted you, is that right? She had it all pieced together. You killed Svetlana, her little girl, her ex-husband, and your own sister."

Galigani stood. "Then you pointed the police toward Jennifer. What better motive? She kills her ex-lover and his wife, then kills her boss. Everyone has a motive to kill their boss."

"The other day you were at Michelle's with Rich."

KelliAnn's eyes grew wide. "How do you know—"

"This what you were looking for?" I pulled out the bracelet from my pocket. She impulsively reached out to grab it. I closed my fist around it and tucked it safely away into my pocket. Now it was my turn to smile. KelliAnn stared at me, her mouth pressing into a thin line.

"I thought Rich might have been looking for the business ledgers I found. But now I get it. He's the one who helped you get rid of Brad's body."

KelliAnn's eyes darted back and forth, landing on the side table next to Galigani. On the table was a heavy lamp and a small jade phone.

Was she thinking of calling for help?

"I overheard Rich say something about a fight," I continued. "You fought with Brad. He didn't want you romantically. You got upset, found George's gun, and killed him. You needed help with the cleanup, right? Rich was willing to help. Why not? With Brad out of the way, he could buffalo Michelle, Svetlana, and Mrs. Avery about the business profits and pocket more money. And you, of course, would keep quiet about all of it. If he turned you in, you'd tell the police about the drug operation. Ruin his game."

Galigani said, "Rich probably hadn't factored in that you'd totally lose control and kill Michelle and Svetlana, too. Who would have been next? Rich? George? Only now they're safe behind bars."

"What I don't understand is how you could kill your own sister," I said.

KelliAnn's face turned as red as her hair. "My sister? Yeah, right. She didn't care about me. My dad's the only one who really loved me," she said. "My mother passed away when I was fourteen. I was sent to live with Dad and that awful woman and Michelle. Michelle always wanted a sister, and I guess, at that age, she didn't realize the implications. She didn't . . ." KelliAnn moved toward the mantel and reflected on a ceramic vase. "I was her father's child and we were only a few years apart. Michelle didn't realize that that meant her father had been living with my mother while he told Michelle and her mother that he was away on business trips. He was really living a double life."

"Rough," Galigani said, sidestepping the coffee table and squaring himself off with KelliAnn.

KelliAnn closed her eyes, lost in the past. "He was a commercial airline pilot. I guess my mom and I were the 'other port' for him. It's okay. I forgave him. I loved him. The bracelet was from him. He engraved it for me, with

BERRY, because of my 'berry berry red hair,' like he used to say. I never took it off." Tears streamed down her face. "He did his best to take care of me, even though it ruined his other marriage and, eventually, his relationship with Michelle."

Galigani surprised me by saying, "The *other* marriage was already ruined before you got there."

"Michelle and her mom never really accepted me. I see that now," KelliAnn said. "At the time I didn't. Something like that is difficult to explain to a fourteen-year-old whose mother has just passed away. Yes, I was the red-headed stepchild, quite literally. They tried to send me to the same school as Michelle. Your school," she spat, eyeing me contemptuously. "It was obvious that I didn't fit in there. And wouldn't. You know how that school was with 'problem' children.'"

"I remember you were there only a short time."

"Yes," KelliAnn said, gripping the ceramic vase. "I was sent to a 'special needs' school." She let out a blood-curdling scream and hurled the vase at Galigani's head.

He ducked and it smashed against the back wall. I dove behind the sofa. KelliAnn continued to scream as she grabbed the lamp next, knocking the phone off the table. I'm sure she would have loved to peg me with it but decided Galigani in the open room was a better bet. She swung the lamp from its cord in a wide circle. Galigani dodged her.

I surfaced from behind the couch long enough to grab the phone.

No dial tone.

The cord had fallen out the back. I jammed the cord in place as KelliAnn closed in on Galigani. "I'm *not* going to an institution!" she screamed. "Never again!"

I watched in horror as KelliAnn swung the lamp again and this time hit Galigani square in the chin. He stumbled back and hit the wall dazed. She changed her grip from the cord to the base of the lamp. I dropped the phone and seized the moment to charge her. She raised the lamp above her head ready to smash Galigani just as I tackled her from behind.

She crumpled beneath me, taking the lamp down with her. It broke in several pieces, leaving KelliAnn with an ugly jagged piece in her hand. She rolled me off her quickly and waved the piece near my face.

Galigani regained himself and grabbed KelliAnn's hair. This pulled her off me long enough for me to retreat to the phone. I dialed 9-1-1.

Even though Galigani had her by the hair, KelliAnn was still swinging and, because she was on the ground, found his weak spot. She was going for his groin but missed and hit his right leg, which was still fresh from surgery. Galigani went down like a rag doll.

The 9-1-1 operator came on the line, although it was difficult to hear because KelliAnn was laughing hysterically. To my terror, she was staring at Galigani's exposed ankle holster.

Adrenaline shot through my body with a force I've never felt before, and with what seemed like supernatural strength, I dove right for KelliAnn.

If she got to Galigani's gun, I was a dead woman.

Laurie's face flashed in my mind and I hardly realized I was screaming and crying as I descended onto KelliAnn, smashing her nose with my elbow.

She recoiled, momentarily dazed, her hands covering her bleeding nose. I fumbled for Galigani's gun but perhaps he mistook me for her, or maybe instinct took over, because he scissored my hand between his ankles.

I drew back, which gave KelliAnn the opportunity to kick me in the ribs. Winded and in excruciating pain, I doubled over.

She took advantage of this and grabbed my head, wrapping her fingers into my hair. This really pissed me off because recently it seemed my hair was falling out left and right.

Postpartum hair loss and this bitch was going to pull out the few remaining strands!

With a fury only a mother can know, I heaved myself up and rammed my hard head into KelliAnn's face. As my head connected with her no doubt broken nose, she yelped and released my hair. I quickly pulled her face into my knee. She moaned and fell to the ground.

The room was finally silent, until I heard the voice through the phone.

I lunged to grab it, only to hear sirens down the street. I put the receiver to my ear.

"Help is on the way, ma'am," the operator said.

I was shaking uncontrollably. "Thanks," I muttered into the phone.

Galigani stirred. He observed KelliAnn lying at his feet. "You did great, kid. Only next time, try to tackle 'em before they hit me."

CHAPTER TWENTY-FIVE

The Sixth Week—Bottom Line

I drove home with mixed emotions. I should have felt elated that I'd finally solved the mystery. At least I could cross that off my to-do list. But I had unresolved feelings.

People were dead, some were behind bars, and others hadn't slept in weeks.

Maybe it was the hormones or being overtired, or the adrenaline leaving my system; whatever the reason, I broke down and cried.

In the morning I woke up more exhausted than ever. I showered and delighted in shaving my legs. Shaving your legs while pregnant not only feels unsafe but is next to impossible. I fussed in the closet and decided on a gray and white striped wool skirt with a very forgiving elastic waist and a cashmere sweater.

When I got to the shoe part, I tried my best not to cry. I stuffed my feet into open-toed heels, only to find that they were so tight they made my feet look like sausages.

Can't anything ever be easy?

From the back of my closet, I pulled out some open-heeled pumps. Definitely sexy, but the problem was, they were higher than what I normally wore. It had been so long since I'd worn heels, I feared I might break my neck in them.

I had a three-hour window until the next feeding. Time to hustle.

I kissed Jim awake.

He raised a sleepy eyebrow. "Are you wearing a skirt?"

"Yeah. I even shaved my legs."

"Oh my God! What's going on that I don't know about?"

"I need you to watch Laurie. I have a very important meeting."

"Lucky guy."

"What makes you think it's with a man?"

"You wouldn't have shaved your legs for a woman. You'd wear jeans."

"Ha ha! I have my six-week postpartum checkup this morning." I winked at him. "But I'm free for lunch."

I made my way to Laurel Heights to Dr. Greene's office. I couldn't believe that the last time I had been there I was nine months pregnant, suffering from high blood pressure, swollen feet, carpal tunnel, and a compressed bladder.

I took the stairs to her second-floor office. I had never done that in all the months I'd come here, because I supposed I was entitled to get fat if I was pregnant. Now I needed the exercise.

As soon as I arrived, I was greeted by Dr. Greene's cordial staff. No waiting, not like at the pediatrician's. I was ushered into an examination room and told that Dr. Greene would be right with me.

I sat on the table fully clothed, not knowing if I needed to undress or not.

When Dr. Greene entered the room, she surprised me by wanting to reminisce about Laurie's birth.

After our brief walk down memory lane, she asked, "How do you feel?"

"Tired all the time."

She nodded. "That's normal."

"My bones hurt."

She laughed. "That's normal, too."

"I can't stand the thought of going back to work."

"My dear, you sound fully recovered."

I drove straight home. When I arrived, I found Jim vacuuming the house.

"You're cleaning again?"

He was standing next to the bassinet, holding the vacuum cleaner in one place. "No. Not really. Just trying to keep Laurie quiet."

"What?"

"She wouldn't stop crying, so I did everything the same as yesterday," Jim shouted over the noise. "The robe, the baby carrier, all of it. None of it worked. The only other thing I did was vacuum. So I figured I'd try it. Sure enough, as soon as I turned it on, she stopped crying."

He flicked the vacuum off. Laurie instantly woke up and howled.

"Oh, my God!"

"I know. She's been like this all morning."

I scooped Laurie up and did a little bouncy dance with her. She continued to cry. Jim flipped on the vacuum, and after a moment Laurie settled into my chest and snoozed.

Jim and I exchanged glances. "If she keeps this up, we'll have the cleanest house in the neighborhood," he said.

I put Laurie down in the bassinet. Out of the corner of my eye, I spotted the cordless phone flashing. It was ringing, only we couldn't hear it with the vacuum cleaner on. I flipped off the vacuum. Laurie wailed.

Jim sighed, then leaned over and grabbed the phone. After a short conversation he hung up and said, "Honey, you look beautiful, but can we do dinner instead of lunch? I just got a job interview."

I spent the rest of the day aimlessly playing with Laurie. Thoughts of calling my boss, Nora, crowded my head. We couldn't afford to wait for Jim to land a job. Even if this interview went well, an offer would likely be weeks away. And we needed an income.

As for my little PI business, it would have to go on hold. Sure Galigani had been impressed, but when would another client come along?

I breathed Laurie in as tears streamed down my face. "I don't want to leave you, little one."

Laurie turned her face into my shoulder. I cuddled her.

Finally, at five to five, I picked up the phone and dialed Nora.

What was the point of putting off the inevitable?

Nora picked up on the first ring.

"Nora, it's Kate."

"Kate? When's the magic day? Tell me it's soon. We're drowning here without you!"

I sighed, imagining my desk piled with paperwork from the last six weeks. "My maternity leave is over tomorrow. How's Monday sound?"

Today was Thursday and I silently thanked God that at least I'd have the weekend.

"Great! We'll see you at eight A.M.," she said, hanging up.

I hung up, annoyed. I had wanted to ask her where

I was supposed to use the breast pump. But the words hadn't come out.

I imagined hauling my breast pump into the ladies' room. Didn't the office have any place private?

I thought about the lone little package in the freezer. Two measly ounces of breast milk. All the brochures on breastfeeding by working moms recommend having about thirty-two ounces on hand before starting work.

I pulled out my breast pump and thought about calling Mrs. Avery.

I knew I needed to talk to her, but I'd been putting it off. I supposed I wanted to stretch out my fantasy of being a private investigator for as long as I could.

As soon as I connected all the tubes, bottles, and breasts, the phone rang. I disconnected everything with a sigh and picked up the phone.

"What's wrong?" Mom said.

"How do you know something is wrong?"

"I can tell by the way you said 'hello.'"

"Mmm."

"What is it?"

Hot tears spilled down my cheeks. "I have to go back to work on Monday and I can't help it, but I feel guilty for having to leave Laurie. I wish I'd never gotten involved with this stupid PI thing. I wasted my whole maternity leave running around, instead of being with her."

"You were with her the entire time."

"I'm stupid. I should have solved the thing much sooner, and then at least I could have slept."

"You're not stupid, honey. Besides, nobody sleeps with a newborn."

"I don't even have enough milk stocked up," I wailed. "I'm a total failure!"

Mom laughed.

"What's so funny?" I demanded.

"Kate, if you're a failure, what about the rest of us?"

"What do you mean?"

"Kate, you accomplish more in a day than most of us do in a week. When you tried to launch your business, you were taking a chance. A murderer is behind bars because of you. Don't feel guilty about having to leave Laurie for a little while each day when you go to the office. She's going to be fine. Lots of mothers work."

"But I want to be with her." Tears slid down my face.

"And you will. Darling, just because you have to go back to the office right now, it doesn't make it permanent. Jim's going to find work soon. And you never know. You might be able to find another client. Building a business takes time. It's like having a baby. You can't have the baby in a month, even if you are really *really* good. It takes nine months. Do you understand?"

"I know you're right, but I can't help feeling sorry for myself. Am I allowed that?" I asked.

"No. You are not allowed to wallow! You have a beautiful, healthy daughter, a husband who loves you, and at least you have a job to go back to. Some people don't have any of that, Kate. Feeling sorry for yourself would be selfish and petty, and I know you're not either of those."

I wiped the tears from my face. "Moms always know best, huh? I love you."

"I know you do, and now that you have a daughter of your own, you know how much I love you."

Laurie let out a wail from the other room. "I gotta go, Mom. The alarm is going off."

I drove up the now-familiar driveway to Mrs. Avery's beautiful house. She surprised me by greeting me in the driveway.

When the car stopped moving, Laurie immediately awoke and began to kick and flail about, protesting. I hopped out of the car, unsnapped the car seat straps, and held her in my arms. She was still fussing as I made my way toward Mrs. Avery. One small pink shoe wiggled off, and I sighed as I looked at it on the ground. Mrs. Avery held her arms open to receive Laurie. I handed her over, and she instantly stopped fussing.

"You have a way with her. She was so excited to see you, she kicked her shoe off," I said, stooping over and picking it up.

Mrs. Avery took the shoe from me and slipped it back onto Laurie's foot.

"We found your son's murderer," I said.

"I know," she said. "Inspector McNearny called me this morning."

"He did?" I asked, surprised. Even though I had put off this moment, I was disappointed not to be the one breaking the news to her. "I'm sorry he beat me to the punch. We had a late night last night."

"Don't apologize! I have closure. Come inside. I rarely drink, although today I think I'm going to have a small glass of champagne. What would you like?"

"I shouldn't have any alcohol. I'm breastfeeding," I added as way of explanation.

"One drink won't hurt." Mrs. Avery tsked. "Besides, we need to have something to toast a job well done. Brad would have wanted that."

She called Marta and requested a bottle of Dom Perignon.

Well, in that case!

As Mrs. Avery poured the champagne, I filled her in on the pertinent details about KelliAnn. We both wept as I told her about Penny.

When we had finished crying, Mrs. Avery pulled out a checkbook.

"You found my son and my granddaughter's killer. I'll always be indebted to you. Please accept this."

She handed me a check for twice the amount due. "Consider it a little bonus for bringing the nasty drug business to my attention. You didn't really think I could have been involved, right?"

"Only for a moment."

I drove home with the bonus check burning a hole in my pocket. I couldn't believe Mrs. Avery had been so generous. It would help pay our mortgage until Jim found a new job.

I waited for Jim to come home, to share the news. I was able to pump out another entire three ounces. Now I had five ounces in the freezer. I was starting to feel proud of myself—only twenty-seven ounces to go to get to the recommended thirty-two-ounce supply. Maybe over the weekend I'd be able to squeeze out a few more ounces, and then at least Jim would be able to give Laurie breast milk the first day I was back at the office.

I looked in my closet, peering desperately at my wardrobe, wondering what I would wear to work on Monday. I tried on a couple of outfits and got even more disheartened. The only things that fit comfortably were my maternity clothes. When was that supposed to change?

This morning, at my six-week appointment, Dr. Greene said I could begin working out again. I knew I needed to schedule gym time and abdominal work, yet I felt so tired all the time. Breastfeeding was taking its toll on me, and I wondered with a pang how long I would be able to do it.

I searched the floor of my closet for my shoes. What a joke. None of those fit either.

Dr. Greene had also said that my bones would go back into place, whatever that meant. Was that really going to happen? Would my size seven Nine West shoes ever fit?

And what would I do in the meantime?

I slipped into the unattractive size eight *wide* flats I'd been forced to wear during my pregnancy. They fit fine, which served only to make me feel awful, bloated, and unattractive.

Laurie was sound asleep, and I wondered if she would enjoy a trip to the mall with me. I heard the front door open. Within seconds, Jim was in the kitchen picking me up in his arms.

"My God! What's going on?"

He kissed my face all over. "I love you, I love you, I love you!"

"I love you, too," I said. "What's going on?" I repeated, then added, "And shhh, you're going to wake the baby."

"She can be awake! We're a family! Go get her, get her, get her," he said excitedly, running his words together so they sounded like "gethergethergether."

"I'm not going to wake a sleeping baby," I said firmly.

Jim laughed. "Come on."

"No, I'm not," I said sternly, trying to hold back my laughter.

"Okay, okay, okay," Jim said, disappointed. "Guess what?" he asked, excited again.

"The interview went well?" I asked hopefully.

"Forget the interview," Jim said.

"What?"

Jim took a deep breath. "Dirk Jonson called me. I got the account!"

My stomach flip-flopped.

"It's big, Kate. The account is big," Jim said, a smile crossing his face. "In fact, it's huge! We're set for at least a year. Look at this." He pulled the contract out of his briefcase.

My eyes nearly popped out of my head. "What does that mean?" I said, indicating the six-figure number on the page.

"That's the amount I'm going to get paid. Me. Not the firm that fired me. But me."

I nearly choked. "You're going to get paid this amount? For what?"

"For doing what I always do. Creating an ad campaign. I've already come up with a lot of it. Check out my proposal."

Jim flipped through the pages of the contract, until he got to some pictures.

"Oh, my God. My husband's a genius!"

Jim laughed. "The genius part was getting fired from my old firm."

"Getting fired turns out to be a good thing?"

"I'll make four times as much as an independent contractor."

"Does this mean I don't have to go to the office on Monday?"

Jim smiled. "That's right, honey," he said, stroking my hair. "That's exactly what it means."

To-Do List:

1. Quit Job.